Magical Mischief

Also by Anna Dale

Whispering to Witches
Dawn Undercover
Spellbound

Magical Mischief

Anna Dale

NEW YORK BERLIN LONDON SYDNEY

First published in Great Britain by Bloomsbury Publishing, Plc. in June 2010
Published in the United States of America in July 2011
by Bloomsbury Books for Young Readers
www.bloomsburykids.com

For information about permission to reproduce selections from this book, write to Permissions, Bloomsbury BFYR, 175 Fifth Avenue, New York, New York 10010

Library of Congress Cataloging-in-Publication Data
Dale, Anna.
Magical mischief / by Anna Dale. — 1st U.S. ed.
p. cm.
Summary: Mr. Hardbattle, aided by his friends Miss Quint and resourceful thirteen-year-old Arthur, seeks a new home for all of the magic that has gone out of control and taken over his bookshop and home.
ISBN 978-1-59990-629-4 (hardcover)
[1. Magic—Fiction. 2. Bookstores—Fiction.] I. Title.
PZ7.D15225Mag 2011 [Fic]—dc22 2010035627

Typeset by Dorchester Typesetting Group, Ltd.
Printed in the U.S.A. by Quad/Graphics, Fairfield, Pennsylvania
2 4 6 8 10 9 7 5 3 1

To my niece, Lily,
with love

Magical Mischief

Chapter One

A Whiff of Magic

"My shop stinks!" said Mr. Hardbattle.

He had first noticed The Smell a few months before but had been too busy to do anything about it. Running a bookshop single-handedly meant that his time was at a premium. Finding the source of a strange new smell had been put at the bottom of his list of things to do, along with dusting and tidying up.

It would not have been a problem if The Smell had been a nice one. If it had smelled of cotton candy or perfume it would have been delightful, but Mr. Hardbattle's smell was of the noxious variety. The Smell had been mild to start, but over the months it had grown more powerful—until Mr. Hardbattle had felt compelled to express his disgust out loud.

To Mr. Hardbattle's nose, The Smell resembled the stench of dung—the kind that you might find in a big heap in a farmyard—and it baffled him how such a smell could get inside his shop, which was miles from the country, in the middle of a town. Equally as puzzling was the fact that none of his customers seemed to be able to detect it. They could, however, smell other unpleasant odors of which he was unaware.

"Eww! Hyacinths!" exclaimed one customer.

"It reeks of vinegar in here," said another. "I'd lay odds that somebody had fish and chips for their supper last night."

"Might I suggest," said a well-spoken lady, pink-cheeked with embarrassment, "that you get someone in to look at your drains?"

Conscious of the need to please his customers, Mr. Hardbattle tried to find the source of all the offensive smells. He looked in vain for horse manure; he poured a newly purchased bottle of vinegar down the sink; he examined all his potted plants but failed to find a hyacinth; he even called out a plumber to inspect his drains. None of these actions had any effect at all. Thinking that the smells must be seeping into his shop from outside, Mr. Hardbattle closed all his windows.

Over the ensuing months, The Smell grew even stronger, forcing Mr. Hardbattle to wear a clothespin on his nose. Realizing that bad smells were not good for business, he introduced other odors into the shop to smother the nasty ones. He bought a gallon of lavender water and sprayed it in every corner, and when it failed to make any difference, he tried perfumed candles and potpourri. Despite his best efforts, however, The Smell remained.

Customers wrinkled their noses and frowned the instant they came through the front door, and the stream of people who had always frequented Mr. Hardbattle's shop dwindled to a trickle.

After The Smell came the hallucinations. They started on a small scale and progressed to the spectacular.

At first, Mr. Hardbattle thought he had had too much sherry when he saw one of the black cat bookends, which sat on a shelf above his desk, twitch its whiskers and yawn. And he rubbed his eyes in astonishment at the sight of a glass marble chasing a spider across *The Times* newspaper that he had left open on his desk. When his wastepaper basket uncoiled itself and went for a slither around the floor, Mr. Hardbattle made an urgent appointment with an optometrist. The optometrist did lots of tests and shone a bright light into his eyes. She could not put her finger on the problem, but she advised that it might be worth replacing his old glasses. Mr. Hardbattle chose a new pair with horn rims and hoped they would do the trick.

Then books began to rearrange themselves. One morning, he came downstairs at nine o'clock to open up and found all the books shelved upside down. On another day, he discovered that the books with similar-colored jackets had grouped themselves together. The rainbow effect of the blue books sitting next to the green books, the yellow books, the red books, and so on might have appealed to Mr. Hardbattle if the whole thing were not so deeply disconcerting. Thinking that he must have sleepwalked in the night and done the rearranging himself, Mr. Hardbattle went to see a doctor. The doctor listened to Mr. Hardbattle's troubles, nodded often, and asked if he was suffering from stress. When Mr. Hardbattle said that yes, he thought so, the doctor prescribed a hot, milky drink before bed.

"And a cookie?" Mr. Hardbattle asked.

"I don't see why not," said the doctor. "I'd recommend a Fig Newton or an animal cracker."

Despite enlisting the help of medical professionals, buying a new pair of glasses, and drinking a cup of cocoa every night before he turned in, strange things continued to happen.

It all got to be too much for Mr. Hardbattle, so he called his auntie Pearl. His aunt was a spirited lady who had made a lot of acquaintances in her ninety-seven years. Mr. Hardbattle was surer than sure that if anyone knew the right person to ask what he should do about his predicament, it was Auntie Pearl.

"Strange events, you say? How thrilling!" said the gung-ho, upper-class voice of Auntie Pearl through the telephone line all the way down from her cottage in the Quantocks. "If I were you, dear boy, I'd give Bertie

Braithwaite a ring. Hold on a second while I find his number . . ."

Bertie Braithwaite's field of interest was the supernatural, and when he heard Mr. Hardbattle's accounts of marbles with minds of their own, restless wastepaper baskets, and yawning bookends, he was able to assure him that his bookshop was not haunted. Eager to be of help, Bertie told Mr. Hardbattle about a salesman in Crewe who advised him to try a retired commander in Nempnett Thrubwell who suggested that he should pay a visit to Mrs. Elizabeth Trinket of Two Bolton Gardens, Brightlingsea.

Mrs. Trinket was not in the phone book, and the strange events in the bookshop seemed too fantastic to put in a letter, so the following day Mr. Hardbattle picked out his best bowtie, closed his shop, and started up the van, which he used for his deliveries. The van was bottle green, and on both sides and the rear doors the name of his bookshop, Hardbattle Books, had been painted at a slant in cream. Mr. Hardbattle took with him a map, a beef and horseradish sandwich, and coffee in a thermos flask and drove his van the hundred and twenty-one miles to Brightlingsea. He knocked on the door of Two Bolton Gardens. Fortunately, Mrs. Trinket was in.

"Magic. That's what's behind it," Mrs. Trinket said, waiting until her guest had lowered himself into one of her armchairs. She had learned from experience that momentous news was best delivered after its recipient had sat down. "It's a classic case," she continued, setting down a tray and pouring two cups of tea. "You've been in the same premises for years, you said. I'll bet it's dark and dingy and has never seen a feather duster."

Amazed by her powers of deduction, Mr. Hardbattle nodded.

Mrs. Trinket slid a teaspoon into the sugar bowl. "They're just the sorts of conditions that magic would thrive in . . ."

"Magic? Fairies and so on? Loose in my shop?" blurted out Mr. Hardbattle, gripping the cushiony arms of the chair. "It's incredible! Why, I had no inkling that magic even existed. Good heavens, madam. You've taken my breath away."

Stunned and bewildered, Mr. Hardbattle took the cup and saucer that were offered to him. His first sip of tea made him splutter. It was as if he had just dipped his tongue in syrup.

"*How* many sugars are in here, dear lady?"

"Six," answered Mrs. Trinket, stirring her own cup of

tea and smiling at him in a motherly way. "Sweet tea is good for shock. Most folks find it hard to swallow."

Mr. Hardbattle murmured, "I'm not surprised," and placed his cup back on the tray.

"Closed minds, that's what most people have," observed Mrs. Trinket, gesturing to her guest that he should try her coconut cake. "Can't entertain the thought that magic might be real and not something you just find in storybooks."

"Could you tell me some more about magic?" Mr. Hardbattle asked. He was a well-read, intelligent fellow, and a few months ago, before the arrival of The Smell, he might have regarded talk of magic as whimsical nonsense. However, Mrs. Trinket's theory was the only one that he had been presented with and, besides, he did not want her to think that he had a closed mind. "How did it come to be in my shop, do you suppose?" he asked. "Could some prankster have put it there?"

Mrs. Trinket set her cup of tea to one side and leaned forward in her chair, lacing her fingers together. "Magic is its own master, Mr. Hardbattle," she explained. "It chooses where it goes, and it gets there by any one of a hundred different ways. It can ride on the wind or attach itself to the sole of a shoe. It's even been known to burrow through the earth . . ."

Mr. Hardbattle's horn-rimmed glasses slid down his nose as a sequence of images flashed through his mind.

First, he pictured magic as a host of downy dandelion seeds, then as globs of chewing gum, and finally his mind conjured up a clump of glistening toadstools, gradually spreading and festering under the floorboards of his shop.

"Magic's very fussy about where it takes up residence," Mrs. Trinket continued. "Everything has to be just so. It arrives in dribs and drabs: a smidgen here, a trace there. But if enough magic turns up, it will form a cluster. You can't see these clusters, and you can't feel them either, but the smell they give off is unsavory, to say the least."

"There's been an outbreak of awful smells in my shop!" Mr. Hardbattle said, spitting out coconut cake crumbs in his excitement. "My customers have inundated me with complaints but, curiously, none of the odors they've smelled has been the same."

"That's magic, all right," said Mrs. Trinket. "It doesn't like to be disturbed, you see, so it gives off a bad smell to keep people away. But humans are all unique. A shockingly awful stink to one is a balmy bouquet to another. Magic gets around that by evoking the smell that each of us hates the most."

"In my case that's horse manure," Mr. Hardbattle told her. Just the mention of it made his insides squirm.

"With me, it's cooked cabbage," Mrs. Trinket said. "My grandmother couldn't abide fresh fish. In her day, of course, the smells weren't so ripe. Magic was found all over, and the more thinly it's spread, the fainter the aroma. Everybody's attic had a sprinkle, but mostly it liked out-of-the-way places: barns, old churches, rambling farmhouses, water towers, and stuffy museums. Places like that are rare these days. They've either been knocked down or done up. Half of them have been made into homes for the ridiculously rich. Dark, dry, secluded places are hard to come by in this day and age. Your bookshop's like a raft in a flood. No wonder magic's taken such a liking to it."

"I should feel privileged, I know," said Mr. Hardbattle worriedly, "but the truth is, it's quite inconvenient." He explained about his recent loss of customers and consequent plummet in sales.

"You could buy a vacuum cleaner. That would do the job. Magic's worst enemy, they are." Mrs. Trinket shot him a piercing look, challenging Mr. Hardbattle to take her advice if he dared.

"Er . . . well, hmm . . . ," he said, unable to look her in the eye. "It seems a little *insensitive*."

Mrs. Trinket relaxed her stare and took a slurp of tea.

"Perhaps I should package it up and send it abroad. It would be smart to relocate my magic somewhere wild and unfrequented . . . like Borneo . . . or Antarctica." Mr. Hardbattle beamed, mildly amazed by his own resourcefulness.

"Heavens, no, that would never do!" said Mrs.

Trinket, so appalled that she spilled tea down the front of her blouse. "You can't go mixing up magic! There are different strains, and they've all got special requirements. English magic is like a house spider. Remember I told you it wants to hide in old buildings that are dimly lit? Well, in Holland, magic likes to be on the move. It clings to the roofs of trains and sneaks inside the saddlebags of bicycles. And Scottish magic's only content when it's somewhere dank and marshy. There's an old Scottish saying: 'Where'er there are midges, there's magic.' Surely, Mr. Hardbattle, you've heard of it?"

"No, I can't say that I have," he replied before heaving a sigh. "What do you suggest that I do, Mrs. Trinket? Put up with the smell? Try to ignore the peculiar happenings?"

"If you really want to get rid of it, flick a feather duster around . . . redecorate," said Mrs. Trinket, her tone a bit crisp. "It will move on if you goad it enough, but *where*? That's the question."

"It seems to me," Mr. Hardbattle said after a few minutes' thought, "that magic has had a raw deal. It can't have been easy for it, pushed from here to there . . . its old stomping grounds taken over . . . people like me viewing it as a nuisance." He shook his balding head despairingly. "I'm at a loss to know what to do."

"Poor dear," said Mrs. Trinket tenderly. "Have more cake."

Chapter Two

Birthday Surprises

Tea at Mrs. Trinket's had proved to be very illuminating. When Mr. Hardbattle returned to the town of Plumford that evening, he knew about every aspect of magic, so he was only slightly unnerved to find his ruler and poker engaged in swordplay on the hearth.

"Careful you fellows don't hurt yourselves" was all he said.

Mrs. Trinket's assertion that magic had recently had a tough time won Mr. Hardbattle over. He began to see himself as the protector of an underdog species (a smelly, invisible, odd one though it was), and he vowed to let the magic settle wherever it pleased and not to interfere with it or threaten it with a dust-removing apparatus. This meant that he was unable to do any housework, which he was secretly pleased about.

Living alongside magic was, at first, a pleasurable thing. Mr. Hardbattle would come down in the morning, armed with a can of air freshener, to find staples playing a skipping game with a piece of string, or books reading themselves, or ducks, escaped from a painting of Lake Tahoe, flying around the room. Sometimes the magic would leave him a handmade gift. On more than one occasion, he discovered an item of headgear made from cobwebs hanging on the hatstand (the ten-gallon hat was his favorite); in his briefcase he chanced upon a rubber-band band, pinging *The Blue Danube* by Strauss; and underneath his desk, in a corral of colored pencils, he came across a flock of bleating origami sheep.

Naturally, his profits took a nosedive. The trickle of customers drained to a drip. Of the small number of people who dared to brave The Smell, most left soon after they had entered the bookshop, spooked by something strange they had seen or heard. The only customers with any staying power were the loners who liked to stop by for a chat, or the devoted bibliophiles who were so absorbed by the books in the shop that they failed to notice anything odd.

Mr. Hardbattle helped to make ends meet by concentrating on the delivery side of his business. He could often be seen behind the wheel of his bottle-green van or carrying boxes in and out of its rear doors. With his modest profits, he treated himself to a moleskin vest (a crimson one) and a spotted mutt with black frilly ears and a plumelike tail, whom he chose to call Scallywag.

He also acquired an elephant, but unlike the vest and the dog, it arrived quite by accident. It was left behind by a small girl, who carried it into the shop in a pink beaded bag, read it a story, and departed without it. The elephant was a he, and Mr. Hardbattle named him Trunk. Trunk was soft, gray, and made in China, and every time the bell over the door jingle-jangled, he got to his bean-filled feet and looked to see if the person who came into the shop was his little owner who had, at last, remembered him.

As more and more magic descended on the tall Victorian building that housed Hardbattle Books, the situation inside became harder to bear. In the ten years since Mr. Hardbattle's visit to Mrs. Trinket's, the magic had evolved from manageable clusters into wayward, roguish clumps. It had wriggled into every crack and crevice, and The Smell had grown so powerful that fainting fits were commonplace among the bookshop's customers.

Far worse than The Smell, in Mr. Hardbattle's opinion, was the magic's erratic behavior, which could vary from mischievous to uncontrollable. Most of the time, the magic was content to play with the curtains, switch things on and off, and bring inanimate objects to life. But every so often it went berserk, and the mess it made on these occasions took hours and sometimes days to clean up. These instances of unruliness were happening more and more frequently, and Mr. Hardbattle soon learned to watch out for the warning signs, which signaled that a chaotic episode was about to begin. If the potted palm on the landing began to shake its leaves, or if the second-to-last step turned to custard, Mr. Hardbattle whistled to Scallywag, snatched up a copy of *The Times*, and took himself off to his toolshed, where he stayed until all of the magical hoo-ha died down.

On the morning of his seventieth birthday, Mr. Hardbattle woke to find that he had spent the entire night in his shed. He had slept in a deck chair with a picnic blanket tucked around him and was dressed in his shirt, trousers, and vest from the day before, all of which were now as creased and rumpled as a tramp's. "Fine place to wake up on your birthday!" he grumbled, feeling inclined to go back to sleep again. However, when he remembered why he had taken refuge in his shed, he sat bolt upright and threw off the blanket.

"Stir your stumps, Scallywag!" Mr. Hardbattle shouted, making a determined effort to get out of the low-slung chair. "If we're going to open by nine o'clock, we'll have to work like Trojans!"

Scallywag had made a cozy nest for herself in a pile of wood shavings. She pricked up her ears but did not budge.

"There's bacon and eggs for breakfast," Mr.

Hardbattle said. "Do you want me to give your share to the cat next door?"

His lively tone and the word "cat" had the desired effect. Scallywag sprang out of her bed, scattering wood shavings everywhere, and sat by her master's ankles while he fumbled with the latch. Once outside, Scallywag made sure that the backyard was cat-free before rejoining her master at the back door of the shop.

Mr. Hardbattle drew the key from his vest pocket and inserted it in the lock.

"Brace yourself, Scally!" Mr. Hardbattle warned, pausing on the step before he opened the door. "Remember the terrible mess the last time the magic went wild? I nearly wore out the bristles on my broom sweeping it up!"

Steeling himself to expect the worst, Mr. Hardbattle turned the door handle and went in. The sight that met his eyes made his jaw drop.

"Well, I'll be!" he declared.

The shop was festooned with decorations. Strung from each corner of the ceiling and from bookshelf to bookshelf all around the shop were long, quivering paper chains. As Mr. Hardbattle walked past each bookshelf, dozens of streamers uncoiled themselves and threw out their ribbons of paper so that his shoulders were covered in a cloak of colors. When the final streamer had unraveled itself, a team of spiders wriggled into action and lowered a crown made from cobwebs on to Mr. Hardbattle's head.

"What's this?" he asked, patting the fragile crown with his fingertips. "My, how kingly!" he said.

The magic had gone to extraordinary lengths to mark Mr. Hardbattle's birthday. Most impressive of all was the banner the magic had suspended from the ceiling. It was made from the pages of the largest world atlas in the shop, and a greeting had been cut into it that read: MANY HAPPY RETURNS.

His uncomfortable night in the toolshed forgotten, Mr. Hardbattle tried to express how grateful he was to the magic for all the trouble it had taken, but he was hampered in his efforts by a sudden attack of awkwardness and a sizable lump in his throat, which made his speech shorter and less fluent than he would have wished. "*Never* expected . . . I'm a lucky chap . . . can't thank you enough . . . very touched," murmured Mr. Hardbattle, dabbing both eyes with his handkerchief.

Scallywag had been unfazed by the dangling paper chains and the drifting ribbons of paper. She was used to the magic's theatrical ways, having lived in the shop for most of her life. Trotting over the streamer-strewn floor to the doormat, she gathered the morning's mail in her mouth and delivered it into her master's hands. Of the four envelopes, three contained birthday cards, which Mr. Hardbattle stood on the mantel. The fourth envelope had a letter inside. The letter had been typed, and it began: DEAR TENANT . . .

Mr. Hardbattle's face clouded over immediately. He stopped reading the letter and removed his birthday crown. It was not the sort of letter that he felt should be read while wearing frivolous attire. Crownless and solemn faced, Mr. Hardbattle sank into a chair by the fireplace. Sensing that her master needed comforting, Scallywag sat down beside him and rested her chin on his knee. For the next few minutes, all was quiet in the bookshop apart from the loud, insistent ticking of the mantel clock.

When he finished reading the letter, Mr. Hardbattle sat stock-still and stared ahead with unseeing eyes. It took a nudge from Scallywag's nose to bring the old man to his senses.

"Bad news, Scallywag," he said to her gloomily. "Our dear landlord, Henry Honeycomb, has died. You remember him, don't you, girl? He was the kind old gentleman who visited from time to time and always made a fuss over you. I've paid rent to Henry Honeycomb for thirty years!"

Feeling choked up, Mr. Hardbattle slipped his handkerchief from his sleeve and blew his nose ferociously. "This letter is from his son, Piers. It's Piers who owns the property now—and he's *not* a chip off the old block, it pains me to learn. Piers is raising the rent by five hundred dollars each month! He says that I've been paying a pittance and that his father was a fool." Mr. Hardbattle sighed and clasped his forehead. "I can't see how we're going to manage. We're living like paupers as it is!"

The arrival of magic in the bookshop had wrecked Mr. Hardbattle's chances of running a highly profitable business. He struggled to find the money to pay the rent each month, and a hike in the payment was nothing short of disastrous. Mr. Hardbattle sat in his chair several minutes longer, trying to think of a way he could raise the extra funds. When he realized that it would soon be time to open the shop, Mr. Hardbattle put Piers Honeycomb's letter in his desk drawer and went upstairs to prepare his birthday breakfast.

By the time he had eaten his fill of bacon and eggs, changed his clothes, and opened his shop, it had started to rain. It rained all morning and Mr. Hardbattle's waning celebratory mood was further eroded. (There is nothing more depressing than rain on your birthday.) Detecting his glum demeanor, the magic attempted to cheer up Mr. Hardbattle. The black cat bookends jumped down from their shelf and wound themselves around his legs, and some leather bookmarks ran on their fringed ends doing somersaults, but their efforts only succeeded in bringing a tired smile to his face, which faded almost as soon as it had appeared.

It turned cold. Mr. Hardbattle put some logs in the

grate and lit a fire. Magic turned the flames green, then purple, then green again.

Outside in the street, umbrellas vied for space. Puddles were stepped over by grown-ups and splashed through by children too young to be at school. Damp pigeons huddled in the eaves of buildings. The sky was dark and overcast.

In the morning, the bookshop had no customers, and Mr. Hardbattle's frame of mind grew more and more despairing. Then, in the afternoon, the bell jingle-jangled. Trunk got up to see who it was and sat down again, disappointed. The customer was a thin student with glasses and a beaky nose. He bought a collection of Edward Thomas's poetry and left.

Then, at a quarter to four, when Mr. Hardbattle's thoughts had once again turned to his financial problems, something of interest happened in the street.

The collision occurred on the stretch of sidewalk right outside the shop. It was a drama worthy of an audience. Magic breathed on the window of the bookshop so that Mr. Hardbattle could see out. Putting her paws on the windowsill, Scallywag joined her master, and the rumpus proved enough of a lure for Trunk to shuffle along his shelf and peer out too.

A boy wearing a rain slicker, his hood tied tightly around his face, and a woman with an umbrella were sprawled on the ground. The spokes of the woman's umbrella protruded at strange angles and her white woolen cap had slipped off her head. In a matter of seconds, passersby had rushed to her aid and pulled the woman to her feet, but the boy jumped up by himself, preferring not to be helped.

On the ground, close by, were two bags in a puddle. The largest of these, a shopping bag, had spilled its contents onto the sidewalk and, one by one, oranges were rolling into the gutter. Next to this bag was a schoolbag with a broken strap, which had leaked some books, a lunch box, and a pencil case. Before the boy and the woman could make a move to recover their gear, the passersby had collected the pair's scattered goods like chickens pecking at grain. Once the Good Samaritans had dispersed, the boy stooped to rescue the last of the oranges from the gutter while the woman tried in vain to close her mangled umbrella. She gave up and looked over at the bookshop, and it was then that Mr. Hardbattle realized who she was.

Her name was Beatrice Quint. She was a spinster, in her forties, and had once occupied the bookshop's comfiest wing chair by the fire for a whole afternoon, during which time she had drunk three cups of tea and told Mr. Hardbattle her life story. So intent had she been on talking that Miss Quint had not noticed any magical shenanigans. Before she left she had bought a paperback romance for two dollars.

"I do believe they're coming in," said Mr. Hardbattle, perking up when he saw Miss Quint and the boy approaching his shop doorway. "Three customers in the same afternoon!" he said brightly to Scallywag. "How about that, eh? Things are looking up!"

Chapter Three

Magical flames

The rain slicker–wearing boy was named Arthur. His full name was Arthur William Goodenough, but his siblings—of which he had five—called him Artie; his friends shortened this to Art; and his schoolteacher chose to refer to him simply as Goodenough (or, more often, *Not* Goodenough, accompanied by a smirk).

On the rainy Wednesday in April that was Mr. Hardbattle's birthday, Arthur had been in a hurry to get to the library.

Plumford Library was where he did his homework every day between the end of school and dinner. With five brothers and sisters at home, a father and mother, two guinea pigs, a salamander, and a cockatiel, it was almost always noisy and crowded and an impossible environment in which to focus on schoolwork. Arthur found studying hard, and without plenty of peace and quiet he could not concentrate. His older brother was brainy, and his older sister was too. Arthur did not like being described as "an average student"—and he absolutely detested being called Not Goodenough by Mr. Beaglehole, his bully of a teacher. Doing well was important to Arthur and that was why he always tried to do his best, even if it meant giving up games of soccer with his friends and hanging out in the library instead of the video arcade.

On Wednesdays the library closed early, so Arthur tended to hurry on this day of the week. On this particular Wednesday, with the rain pelting down, Arthur had hurried all the more. He had lowered his head against the driving rain, droplets running off his hood into his eyes. Miss Quint's approach had not registered with him until it was too late.

Neither blamed the other for the collision. Both had been swift to admit that they had not been looking where they were going. When Miss Quint mentioned that she knew of a place close by where they could dry off and get a hot drink, Arthur agreed to go with her.

The bell above the door jingle-jangled as the two disheveled, dripping-wet people lugged their sodden bags into Mr. Hardbattle's shop. Trunk glanced at them with his black felt eyes.

"Good afternoon," said Miss Quint shakily. Her mascara was smeared, her tights had runs, and there were streaks of dirt on her raincoat. "Do you mind if we sit by your fire for a moment? We've taken a tumble and, as you can see, we're soaked from head to toe. I'm sure you saw the whole thing. It was my fault as much as this boy's. His name's Arthur."

She turned to Arthur and whispered, "Say hello, dear."

"Er . . . hi," said Arthur bashfully, pulling back his hood to reveal a thatch of wavy brown hair that grew almost to his shoulders. His ears poked out either side, like mushrooms pushing through undergrowth.

Miss Quint ventured farther into the shop, leaving a trail of dark spots on the Turkish rug. "I thought I might catch the ten-to-four bus if I hurried," she explained to Mr. Hardbattle, "but the oranges weighed me down." Frowning disappointedly, she poked around in her shopping bag. "All split or bruised," she declared. "I won't be making prize-winning marmalade with these!"

"You make marmalade," said Arthur, astonished, "that wins *prizes*?"

"If everything goes according to plan, I do," Miss Quint told him with a wink. "I'm a member of the Women's Institute. They're holding a cooking contest on Friday. There are prizes for marmalade, jam, pies, cakes . . . all sorts of things."

"Couldn't you cut off the damaged parts?" Arthur asked Miss Quint, taking an orange out of her bag and trying to squeeze it into shape. It seemed very wasteful to write off all the oranges, especially as he and the people in the street had gone to the effort of gathering them up.

"I'll never win a blue ribbon with substandard oranges," Miss Quint told him with a shake of her head. "*I* know what I'll do. I'll make a batch of scones instead. Scones don't have the prestige of marmalade, of course, but such is life. It can't be helped. Scones are quick to make, which is just as well. Mirabel gets moody if I hog the kitchen for too long—and I can see her point, since it is *her* kitchen after all."

Arthur opened his mouth to ask who Mirabel was, but Miss Quint was too fast for him.

"I'm living with a friend at the moment," she said. "I did have my own apartment, but there was an explosion. All my belongings were blown sky-high. A faulty gas pipe, they said it was. Luckily, nobody was in the building that night. Mr. and Mrs. Jones, below, were on vacation in Spain, and Mr. Clark, above, had gone for takeout. It took three fire crews to get the flames under control!"

Arthur gaped at Miss Quint with a mixture of horror and awe. He thought of his own house and his salamander and cockatiel and everything in his bedroom, which he would be brokenhearted to lose. The only comforting thought was that if *his* house exploded, his guinea pigs would be all right because their hutch was on the far side of the yard.

Arthur thought that Miss Quint was extremely brave to talk about the destruction of her home so matter-of-factly. It appeared that Mr. Hardbattle had formed the same opinion because he moved closer to where Miss Quint was standing and held out his hand.

"You told me of your unfortunate mishap the last time you were here," he said, seizing her cold hand in his warm, dry grip. "In January, I think it was. It's Miss Quint, isn't it?"

"That's right!" said Miss Quint, delighted to be remembered. She beamed at Mr. Hardbattle and began to unbutton her raincoat.

"Yes, do get out of those wet things!" Mr. Hardbattle urged, relieving them of their coats, Arthur's scarf, and Miss Quint's woolen cap. He hung them on coat hooks by the door. "Why don't you make yourselves comfortable while I put the kettle on?" he said.

"May I use your bathroom first, if you don't mind?" asked Miss Quint, patting her hair, which was collar-length, auburn, and not looking its best. She plunked her shopping bag in the middle of the floor and, clutching her handbag, disappeared upstairs. Miss Quint had been to the bathroom on her previous visit and knew where it was. (You cannot drink three cups of tea and not need to use your host's facilities.)

Arthur dragged his schoolbag over to a wing chair. Rather than being concerned with warming himself up, he unzipped his bag and began to line up his books on the hearth, resting them on their spines and opening each one.

The young boy's regard for his books gladdened Mr. Hardbattle's heart. The magic, too, was impressed. It stoked the fire and made the flames leap higher. Arthur bowed his head and did not see the poker lurch sideways and plunge its tip three or four times into the heap of ash and blackened logs. The tapering flames burned indigo blue.

"It's Arthur, isn't it?" Mr. Hardbattle said, stooping to look at the boy's collection of literature. "You like to read, I can see that. Well, you've come to the right place."

"I'm not hooked on books, exactly," said Arthur. He glanced up at the old man before delving into his bag once more. The book he lifted out was a small dictionary. With the utmost care he separated its soggy pages. "These are for homework. I've got a test tomorrow, and an essay to finish as well. I was hoping to get some work done in the library. That's why I was rushing and didn't see the lady till she nearly knocked me out with her umbrella."

"Nasty things, umbrellas," Mr. Hardbattle said. He pushed his horn-rimmed glasses up on his nose and knitted his graying brows together. "So, Arthur, what's your essay about? My bookshop isn't as well stocked as a library, but I daresay I can find a book or two on your chosen topic, which might help."

"Thanks," said Arthur. He sat back on his heels and looked around him. "I've never been in here before. Mom always takes us to that bookshop in the center of town—the big one with the coffee shop. She likes their comfy sofas and their discounts. Mom won't buy a book unless it's discounted." Arthur bit his lip, aware that what he had said might have sounded rude.

"Shops like that are a dime a dozen," Mr. Hardbattle said, smiling at the boy's stricken expression. "There are hundreds of bookshops like that all over England—whereas *my* little shop is one of a kind. It's got something that no other bookshop has."

"What's that?" said Arthur, casting his eyes around. "Paper chains? Huge cobwebs? I know . . . a dog!"

Mr. Hardbattle shook his head at Arthur and grinned. "Let's have a look at that essay first, young man. Then we'll have some tea, and *then*, if you haven't figured it out for yourself, I'll tell you."

Miss Quint had spent an inordinately long time in the bathroom. When she emerged from the stairwell, she had neatened her appearance, her face was powdered, and she was wearing a pair of new tights.

"There's a cup of tea for you on the mantel," Mr. Hardbattle said to her, peering out from behind a stack of papers. He was busy reading through Arthur's essay. "This

is good stuff, Arthur," he murmured, "thoug
spelling is . . . how shall I put it? *Unconventio*

Arthur grunted in response. He was sitti
in front of the fire with Scallywag's head in
heat from the flames, the dog's steady breathing, and a stomach full of hot tea were sending him to sleep. The only thing that spoiled the ambience was the smell of anti-lice shampoo. "So, are you going to tell me what's special about your bookshop now?" asked Arthur, his eyelids beginning to droop.

"It's a magic bookshop," Mr. Hardbattle said in an offhand way.

"Magic?" said Arthur drowsily. "What d'you mean by that?"

"How pretty!" said Miss Quint, taking her cup of tea from the mantel. "The flames keep changing color! A state-of-the-art, hi-tech gas fire, I suppose. Was it very expensive? I wonder if I could manage to talk my friend Mirabel into buying one. A fire like that would look breathtaking in her living room."

Miss Quint lifted her cup off its saucer but did not lower her chin to drink. The desire to continue talking was too great.

"I must say, Mr. Hardbattle," she chattered, "I wouldn't have thought you'd be the type to embrace new technology. Upstairs, Arthur, there's a mirror that writes messages. It tells you if your part is crooked or if you've lipstick on your teeth. That fire takes the cake, though. The logs seem almost real, don't they? It's neat the way the flames switch color like that."

Arthur's eyes, which had been closed, suddenly opened wide. "Gosh, they were pink and now they've gone back to orange!" he exclaimed. "But it doesn't look modern to me. It's a real fire, I'm sure." He breathed in through his nose. "I can smell the woodsmoke!"

"Well, I can't," said Miss Quint, sniffing the air and recoiling. "The only thing I can smell is curdled milk."

Mr. Hardbattle crouched down stiffly by the fireplace. He lifted the lid off the log basket and dropped another log into the grate. Turquoise sparks shot up the chimney, making Arthur gasp.

"It's a wood fire all right," Mr. Hardbattle said, "but every so often the flames act unusually. It's the magic that's behind it. It likes to interfere." Mr. Hardbattle gave Arthur's elbow a nudge. "I told you that my bookshop was magic, didn't I, Arthur?"

Tearing his eyes away from the flames, which had turned a resplendent dark red, Arthur stared at Mr. Hardbattle, overwhelmed but still respectful. "Are you some kind of wizard, sir?" he asked with a gulp.

"Good heavens, no!" Mr. Hardbattle chuckled. "I'm just an old man who created the perfect place for magic to thrive, quite by accident."

Miss Quint snickered to herself. "That's nonsense, of

course. Don't believe a word he says, Arthur!" she warned. "He's teasing you." She sat down in a chair and heaved her shopping bag onto her knee, but not before she had glared at Mr. Hardbattle reproachfully.

"It's the honest truth!" insisted Mr. Hardbattle, making a sweeping gesture with his arm. "There's magic in every corner of my shop, Miss Quint. All you need to do is take a good look!"

Holding up her hands in mock surrender, Miss Quint gave a weary sigh. "It's up to you if you want to indulge in a little make-believe," she said, "but please don't involve me. I won't be joining in." Having said her piece, Miss Quint rooted around in her bag. She pulled out a women's magazine, which had orange seeds stuck to its cover, and started to leaf through its pages.

While Miss Quint was occupied with women's matters, Mr. Hardbattle treated Arthur to a tour of his shop. They walked in and out of every alcove, with Arthur admiring both the books and the quantity of dust. When they had finished surveying the bookshelves, Mr. Hardbattle told Arthur all about The Smell and introduced him to Trunk the elephant, the black cat bookends, and the flock of origami sheep. Raindrops continued to slip down the windows as Arthur and Mr. Hardbattle talked and talked.

"So this Mrs. Trinket knew all about magic, did she?" asked Arthur.

"Oh yes," Mr. Hardbattle said. "She's an authority on it. I was advised to let the magic be, and over the years more and more arrived. I daresay there's more magic here in my shop than in every county south of the Thames!"

"Cool!" said Arthur.

"It is rather marvelous, yes," Mr. Hardbattle agreed. He was thrilled to have finally found a customer who shared his opinion that the magic was wonderful.

"This is the best shop I've ever been in!" blurted Arthur excitedly. "I'll come here every day after school. Could I do that, Mr. Hardbattle? Would you mind?"

Mr. Hardbattle paled. He produced a smile although he felt like groaning. The conversation with Arthur had been so pleasant that Mr. Hardbattle had not wanted to spoil things by admitting that the magic was a curse as well as a blessing and that in the next few weeks—barring a miracle—he would have to kick the magic out or become homeless himself.

Mr. Hardbattle took off his horn-rimmed glasses and wiped them carefully on a clean corner of his handkerchief. When he replaced his glasses, his eyes met Arthur's eager gaze.

"I haven't been totally honest with you, Arthur," he said humbly. "There's something I need to explain . . ."

Chapter four

The Search Begins

Miss Quint heard whispering. She closed her magazine. In her experience, people tended to whisper when they wanted to pass on a secret or a tasty morsel of gossip, and Miss Quint was partial to both of these things. Without wasting another second, she got up from her chair and followed the irresistible sound of hushed voices. Emerging from between two rows of bookshelves, she glimpsed Mr. Hardbattle and Arthur standing close together by the cash register, talking up a storm.

As she approached them, Miss Quint managed to hear a snatch of their conversation.

"Problem? What problem?" she asked, forging her way into their midst.

Arthur and Mr. Hardbattle stopped talking and stared at her. The interruption had caught them off guard. Neither of them knew how to answer Miss Quint's question. It would be difficult to explain about the new landlord's ultimatum without mentioning the magic in which Miss Quint did not believe.

"I'm pleased to see you've abandoned your game of Let's Pretend," Miss Quint said, undaunted by their mute response. "So, what were you discussing, hmm?"

Arthur opened his mouth and closed it again, and Mr. Hardbattle hooked his thumbs in the pockets of his vest. He wet his lips but did not say anything.

Their silence only succeeded in making Miss Quint even more curious. She studied their troubled faces for a moment, then her sharp eyes slid downward to a letter lying on the desk. "What's this?" she asked and reached out her hand. Before she could pick up the letter, however, the magic intervened.

On the desk was a carton full of thumbtacks. The moment Miss Quint's fingers touched the letter, they leaped out of their carton, rose high into the air, and drummed into the letter with bulletlike speed. Miss Quint barely managed to snatch her hand away in time. Once she had recovered from the shock of almost having her hand impaled on the desk, she noticed that the thumbtacks had landed in formation, spelling out a four-letter word.

"MYOB?" Miss Quint said, puzzled. "What's that supposed to mean? MYOB? That's not a word. That's a load of nonsense—"

"Actually, it's an abbreviation," Arthur interrupted

helpfully. "The letters MYOB stand for 'mind your own business.'"

Miss Quint was speechless for a moment, then she said, "Of all the nerve!" and flushed with embarrassment. "Mr. Hardbattle, are you going to let those . . . those thumbtacks speak to me like that?"

"I'm awfully sorry, Miss Quint," Mr. Hardbattle said. He leaned over the desk and reprimanded the thumbtacks. "Back to your box, you little rascals!" he said, shaking his finger sternly, which was as close to chewing them out as he was going to get. "Miss Quint is a friend. She may read my letter if she wants."

The thumbtacks sprang out of the letter and regrouped in midair, then rained into the carton, falling like pennies down a chute.

"I suppose you're going to tell me that those thumbtacks got from here to there and back again . . . by magic," said Miss Quint uneasily.

Mr. Hardbattle nodded. "That's the long and short of it."

"I . . . I know I saw them with my own eyes," Miss Quint said in a halting voice, "but I can't bring myself to believe in magic. I can't! The idea's . . . well . . . *preposterous*." Miss Quint was so involved in her thoughts that she did not cast more than a fleeting glance at the cat, which had jumped onto the desk and was strolling toward her. Being fond of cats, Miss Quint extended her hand to stroke it and got a horrible shock when she discovered that it was made of wood.

"Where's its fur?" she asked, knocking her knuckles against its coat.

Her disrespectful conduct failed to charm the bookend, which hissed at Miss Quint and returned to its shelf. She watched the black cat rise onto its hind legs and press its paws against a book, mirroring the stance of its pair.

Miss Quint turned to Mr. Hardbattle. A tight smile flickered across her face.

"First, magic thumbtacks . . . and now a magic bookend! All right, I believe you. It is magic—it must be. You were telling me the truth."

For the briefest of moments, Miss Quint thought about leaving the shop right there and then. It was not that the magic unsettled her so much as the realization that, in scorning its existence, she had made a fool of herself. However, Miss Quint was not in the habit of running away from bad situations and, besides, her skirt was still damp and she wanted to know what the letter said.

A gentleman to the core, Mr. Hardbattle did not say, "I told you so." He merely patted Miss Quint's arm and offered to make a fresh pot of tea. Remembering how Mrs. Trinket had catered to his bewilderment when he had found out about magic, he resolved to put several teaspoons of sugar in Miss Quint's cup.

In the next quarter of an hour, in between gulps of

tea, Arthur and Mr. Hardbattle told Miss Quint everything. She was most upset to learn that Mr. Hardbattle might have to close his shop.

"Money is the root of all evil," she said, wincing as she sipped her overly sweet tea.

"I couldn't agree more. Money's a nuisance," said Mr. Hardbattle, "but the cold hard truth is that I need to make more of it!"

Arthur was in favor of encouraging customers into the shop by making a big to-do about the magic. "It could be like the Ferris wheel at a fairground," Arthur explained. "Magic would be your big attraction. It would draw people in."

"A crowd-puller? Ah, I see," said Mr. Hardbattle, nodding. "I prefer the bumper cars myself, but I see your point. You think that magic would attract more customers."

"Yes, that's what I think," said Arthur. He got up from his chair and began to pace the floor, enlivened by the idea that was taking shape in his mind. "I bet if we told everyone that you had magic in your shop, they'd be fighting each other to get through the door. I could make posters to put in the window, and Miss Quint could hand out flyers. Loads of people would come and you'd be rich," he finished confidently.

"Problem solved, eh?" said Mr. Hardbattle.

"Yeah!" said Arthur, beaming.

Miss Quint glanced up at them both. "It wouldn't work," she said, "if we're being realistic."

"What do you mean? Why wouldn't it work?" Arthur was crestfallen. He looked to Mr. Hardbattle for support, and his stomach turned over when he saw the pained expression on the old man's face.

"It's an unfortunate fact," said Mr. Hardbattle tenderly, "that most people aren't as open-minded as you are, Arthur. They're scared of things they don't understand, and they shy away at the drop of a hat. The Smell would put most people off. Finicky people would hate the dust, and nervous types would scream and run at the first hint of anything magical."

Arthur slumped into his chair and folded his arms. "Human beings are quite disappointing, aren't they?" he said.

At five thirty, they were forced to admit that none of them could think of a scheme to make more money while the magic was still in the shop.

"It looks as though I'll have to get rid of it," Mr. Hardbattle said.

Arthur nodded dismally. "It looks that way to me too."

"And me," said Miss Quint. "I wondered when you'd both see sense. Do you two have any idea what it's like to be homeless?"

Arthur shook his head and Mr. Hardbattle looked

shamefaced. They had both forgotten that Miss Quint's home had been destroyed by fire.

"I felt bereaved at first, and I took some time off work," she said. "But when my leave of absence was up, I found I couldn't go back—not to the way things were, to the life I'd had before the explosion. For the past three months I've been trying to think of what I should do next. Every day Mirabel says she wishes I'd hurry up and decide, but it isn't easy to know which way to turn when you've had your roots pulled up."

Almost moved to tears by Miss Quint's emotional speech, Mr. Hardbattle said that he had come to a decision and that he did not want to risk losing his home or his livelihood. He agreed to discuss the practicalities of evicting the magic, but only if Miss Quint would consent to lower her voice.

"I wouldn't want the magic to get wind of what we're up to. It might not take the news very well," he explained.

In deference to Mr. Hardbattle's wishes, the remainder of their conversation was conveyed in whispers. They discussed the sorts of places where they thought the magic would feel most at home and then tried to think of buildings in Plumford that might fit the bill.

Together they came up with a handful of suggestions, which included a boarded-up pub, a toolshed, and a soccer stadium. Arthur wanted to go and look at them that instant, but Mr. Hardbattle said that it was getting far too late. Reminding Arthur that his family must be expecting him home, Mr. Hardbattle promised to visit each place on their list the very next day.

"And I'll come too!" said Miss Quint. "I've nothing else to do!"

When Arthur turned up at Hardbattle Books on Thursday after school to find out how the two of them had fared, he was disappointed to learn that none of the places had passed the test.

"The pub wasn't derelict," Miss Quint explained, warming her cold fingers on a mug of steaming tea. "It was getting a facelift by the brewery that'd just bought it . . . and the toolshed was far too small and constantly in use."

"As was the stadium," Mr. Hardbattle said as he glanced at the list in his notebook. "The house by the river was the best of the bunch. It was old and run-down and seemed ideal, but unfortunately we were wrong about it being empty. An old fellow lives there with a German shepherd. I asked him how he'd feel about sharing his home with some magic, and he said I was a madman and threatened to call the police!"

Having ruled out Plumford, it was clear that they would

have to look farther afield. They each thought of all the places they had ever visited and tried to come up with a new list of buildings with potential for storing magic.

Mr. Hardbattle found some large-scale maps, which he thought might help to jog their memories, but despite poring over them, no one could come up with any ideas.

"I can only think of an old slate mine," said Arthur, who had been to Wales on vacation the year before. "But *Wales* is no good for *English* magic, is it?"

"There aren't a lot of options!" Mr. Hardbattle said. "I'll have to go on trips to nearby towns and villages until I get lucky and find a suitable place."

"That's a bit random," said Miss Quint. "It could take you ages! How long have we got?"

They read through the letter from Piers Honeycomb again. (Despite being punched with holes, it was still legible.)

"It says we've got six weeks," said Arthur. "The rent is due on June tenth."

"That'll zoom by in a flash!" said Mr. Hardbattle. He groaned. "We need a better plan. Can either of you think of one?"

They all thought very hard, but their effort was not rewarded. Eventually, Arthur announced that he was due home for dinner.

"We need some more thinking time," he said as he

wound his scarf around his neck and pulled on his rain slicker. “I’ve got soccer practice tomorrow after school, but on Saturday morning I’m not doing anything. I bet one of us will have thought of a good idea by then!” He picked up his schoolbag and opened the door of the shop. “Let’s meet here at ten thirty, okay?”

Chapter five

A Trip to the Newsstand

On Saturday morning, right after breakfast, Arthur wandered down to the bottom of the yard, where he always went when he needed space to think. Time was running out. He was meeting his new friends at the bookshop at ten thirty and he had not thought up a single idea for where to relocate the magic. Despite concentrating hard, Arthur's brain came up with zilch, so he got up from the grass and went back indoors, intending to ask his family's advice.

In the kitchen, his mother and his older sister, Penny, were clearing away the breakfast things.

"Say you're tired of something, right," said Arthur, "and you want to find it a new home—a good home—but you haven't got much time. What's the quickest way of doing it?"

Arthur had been so caught up with this quandary that

he had forgotten to wipe his shoes on the doormat. It had also slipped his mind that he was holding a guinea pig.

Neither of these things escaped Arthur's keen-eyed mother. The dirt on the floor worsened her mood, and the presence of the guinea pig caused her to jump to entirely the wrong conclusion.

"A guinea pig isn't a plaything that you can cast aside when you feel like it," she told her son sharply.

Arthur gaped while his mother hammered her point home.

"Cuddles and games in the yard are only part of keeping a pet. I warned you that you'd have to clean out the hutch twice a week, and you children assured me that you didn't mind. If you agree to do a thing, you should stick to it. Your guinea pigs are staying right here."

"But—" began Arthur.

"End of story!" said his mother, and she turned away from him to open the door of the fridge.

Arthur's feelings were hurt. He was astounded that his mother could think he would want to give away his two beloved guinea pigs. He stroked the dainty ear of the guinea pig in his arms, which was nibbling a neat hole in his sweater.

"You've got it all wrong, Mom!" he said in injured tones. "I wasn't talking about Quasimodo or Peanut. It's my friend. He's got something he wants to get rid of.

The thing that he wants to find a new home for isn't alive. Well . . . not exactly."

His mother made an exasperated noise and complained that he had not made himself clear. Then she turned back to the fridge, rearranging the food to make room for the milk. "*I* don't know what your friend should do," she muttered. "Why doesn't he ask his *own* parents?"

Penny was loading the dishwasher and reading a library book at the same time. She was a person of many talents, and being able to concentrate on several things at once was one of her most enviable skills.

"When I wanted to sell my CD collection," Penny said, turning a page of her book with one finger and slotting a dirty dish in the rack, "I put an advertisement in the *Plumford Gazette*."

Arthur felt a rush of adrenaline flood through his veins. "Advertising! What a fantastic idea! Thanks, Pen! That's the answer!"

He rushed outside and ran to the end of the yard, where he dropped Quasimodo into the hutch with his mate, Peanut. In the shed next to the guinea pigs' living quarters were bundles of newspapers, tied with string and waiting to be recycled. He found a copy of the *Plumford Gazette* and turned to the narrow-columned section near the back. This part of the newspaper was called the classifieds. Items that people wanted to sell were grouped under headings such as Cars, Domestic Pets, and Furniture and Furnishings.

Arthur's bicycle was leaning against five others. He stuffed the *Gazette* into his saddlebag and wheeled his bicycle up the path.

"I'm off!" he yelled as he passed the back door. "I'll be back by lunchtime! See you later!"

Mr. Hardbattle almost jumped out of his skin when Arthur burst into his bookshop a full hour earlier than had been arranged. Neglecting to ask Mr. Hardbattle if *he* had had any ideas, Arthur recounted his own enthusiastically.

"You want to advertise . . . in newspapers?" Mr. Hardbattle was not convinced. "I don't think *The Times* would print that sort of advertisement, Arthur."

"Oh," said Arthur, trying not to feel discouraged. "What about some other paper . . . or a magazine, perhaps? Let's go and do some research."

"Now?" Mr. Hardbattle said. "What about my customers?"

"What customers?" said Arthur. There was no one in the shop.

Feeling a little browbeaten, Mr. Hardbattle walked to the door and flipped over the sign so that it said

CLOSED. Then he put on his hat and coat and allowed Arthur to lead him to the newsstand on the next street. It was a small shop but, despite being the size of a beach hut, it stocked hundreds of newspapers, comics, and magazines. These were crammed onto shelves from ceiling to floor. In order to find the publication of your choice, a lot of rummaging was usually involved.

"We need to think carefully about the type of person we'd be appealing to," Mr. Hardbattle said. Despite initial doubts, Arthur's idea was beginning to grow on him.

"What about *Homes & Gardens*?" asked Arthur. He held up a magazine.

"The people who buy *Homes & Gardens* like their houses to be spick-and-span," pointed out Mr. Hardbattle. "We need someone with lower standards who doesn't mind if their furniture's shabby or if their yard goes to seed."

"But they have to be *kind*," insisted Arthur, wanting the magic to have a considerate caretaker. "Old ladies are kind," he said, pointing to the cover of a magazine featuring a gray-haired lady in a cashmere cardigan, holding a Persian cat.

"Something more unorthodox—that's what we should be looking for," Mr. Hardbattle said, burrowing under a pile of sticker albums. "A magazine for oddballs who believe in the weird and wonderful, like witches and crop circles . . ."

They decided to take out ads in *Kindred Spirit*, *The Lady*, and *Farmers Weekly*. Mr. Hardbattle purchased a copy of each magazine and a bag of peppermint-flavored sweets, which he felt would aid them in putting together their advertisement.

"Have a peppermint," he said in the doorway of the newsstand.

"Cheers," said Arthur, taking a huge, round sweet out of the bag and popping it in his mouth.

Cheeks bulging, they marched back to the bookshop and, once they had put their hands on pencils and paper, got down to business. It took longer than they thought to write the advertisement. Arthur was not that bothered about the wording, but Mr. Hardbattle was a perfectionist when it came to composing even the briefest piece of writing. The task was made even harder by the arrival of Miss Quint, who insisted on putting her two cents in. It took until midday to come up with an advertisement all three of them were satisfied with.

FREE TO GOOD HOME!

MAGIC REQUIRES TRANQUIL, RUN-DOWN RESIDENCE TO LIVE IN FOR THE LONG-TERM. HOMEOWNER MUST BE KIND AND RESILIENT. THOSE OF A HOUSE-PROUD NATURE NEED NOT APPLY.

PLEASE CONTACT: MR. M. G. HARDBATTLE OF HARDBATTLE BOOKS, MEADOW STREET, PLUMFORD, EAST SUSSEX.

They had to wait weeks rather than days for their advertisement to be printed in the three magazines. By the middle of May readers were starting to reply, and soon mail pelted Mr. Hardbattle's doormat daily. After sifting through the letters, Mr. Hardbattle put aside twelve with potential. Of the remaining replies, eight were from time-wasters, three were from family or friends inquiring about his health, and the last—on perfumed notepaper—was from Mrs. Elizabeth Trinket, who expressed the hope that Mr. Hardbattle knew what he was doing.

Late on a Friday afternoon toward the end of May, Mr. Hardbattle, Arthur, and Miss Quint had a conference.

"Twelve possibilities," Mr. Hardbattle murmured, moving toward a map of Great Britain, which he had tacked to the wall. "They all sound promising, but, of course, they'll have to be checked out. What's the name of the first place, Arthur?"

"Somersham," said Arthur, taking the letter from the top of the pile. It was from a Mrs. Jean Passworthy who lived in a small cottage in the countryside.

"That's in Suffolk," said Mr. Hardbattle, taking the cap off a marker. He found Somersham on the map and drew a thick red circle around it. "Read out the next place, Arthur, please."

By the time they finished, the map looked as if it had contracted chickenpox.

"One of the places is nearby," said Arthur, smearing the red ink with his finger as he pointed it out on the map. Several miles northeast of Plumford was a village called Thornwick.

Miss Quint looked up from a letter she had been reading. "Arthur and I could tackle that one for you, if you like."

"Good idea!" said Mr. Hardbattle, staring at the map. His eyes moved rapidly behind his horn-rimmed glasses. "Common sense dictates that I should hop from one place to the next, but that would mean I'd have to take at least a week off of work," he said, "and I dare not leave the shop for any length of time. There's no telling what mischief the magic might get in to."

"You need someone to shop-sit!" concluded Arthur. "I'd do it if I didn't have to go to school."

Mr. Hardbattle's hazel eyes widened, and after smiling at Arthur he shifted his gaze to Miss Quint. "I wonder, dear lady, if *you'd* consider helping me?" he said. "Your duties wouldn't be too burdensome. You'd just need to keep an eye on the shop, feed Scallywag, and see that Trunk's spirits don't sink too low."

Miss Quint considered his proposal for a moment or two, then with a determined nod of her head she said, "I'll do it!"

The prospect of looking after the shop prompted Miss Quint to take a walk around it. "This place could do with a woman's touch," she said, running her finger along a dust-caked shelf. "I assume you'd be offering me room and board. I'll break the news to Mirabel right away. I could move in as soon as you like."

"Great!" Arthur said and glanced at Mr. Hardbattle, who, to his surprise, looked less than pleased.

It had not occurred to Mr. Hardbattle that Miss Quint might want to move into his shop. He had lived on his own for more years than he could remember, and it filled him with horror to think of someone else hanging her clothes in his wardrobe and having a bath in his tub. He felt it was only right to warn Miss Quint about the inconveniences she would have to put up with.

"The mattresses are lumpy and the toilet makes a gurgling noise. And there are spiders—huge fellows—and no television set. Oh, and the windows must not be opened more than a crack for fear of disturbing the dust."

Miss Quint did not bat an eye at the mention of these aggravations. "It sounds like a palace compared to Mirabel's!" she joked. Then she unzipped her handbag and drew out a pen. "So, that's settled. Good. Where's your notebook, Mr. Hardbattle? I think it's high time we discussed your trip."

The spiral-bound notebook was produced, and Miss

Quint began to compile a list. "You'll need to work out your route beforehand and plan where you're going to stay each night," she said, scribbling down each thought as soon as it occurred to her.

Mr. Hardbattle was rather annoyed to have his expedition organized for him. However, he was too polite to say so, and he had to be satisfied with contributing the odd remark: "My camera needs new film . . . I'll have to shine my shoes before I go . . . Motion sickness pills—they're a must . . . I'd better take a flashlight. Oh, and a pair of overalls."

Arthur thought of five or six suggestions of his own, the best of which was an evaluation sheet that he offered to draw up.

"This way, every building gets a score," Arthur explained as he started to draw lines on a sheet of paper. "I'll list lots of categories, and each of them can be marked out of ten. We'll also need columns for total, percentage, and rank." In minutes, an impressive-looking table had taken shape. After writing THE BEST PLACE FOR MAGIC TO LIVE IN? in large, untidy letters at the top of the page, Arthur glanced up at Mr. Hardbattle and grinned.

"If only my homework were this interesting!" he said.

Chapter Six

Company for Miss Quint

Having been persuaded to travel by bus (which was free to all holders of a senior citizen's pass), Mr. Hardbattle dangled the keys of the van above Miss Quint's outstretched palm. He did not seem to want to let go of them. As he stood in the doorway of the bookshop, suitcase at his feet, he gave her the low-down on getting the best from his much-cherished vehicle.

"Let her engine turn over before you put her in gear, and go easy around corners. Try not to yank the steering wheel if you can help it. Keep an eye on the temperature gauge. Don't let her overheat. Oh, and remember to check her oil. She gobbles it up, the greedy girl."

"What is it about men and cars?" said Miss Quint to no one in particular. She snatched the keys from Mr. Hardbattle's grasp and shooed him away. "Go on, you old fusspot! You'll miss your bus!"

"My instructions!" he fretted. "You haven't mislaid them? Oh, and say good-bye to Arthur for me."

"No," said Miss Quint patiently. "And yes, I will."

"Poor chap!" said Mr. Hardbattle. "He'll be in Geography now with that buffoon, Mr. Beaglehole. I do hope our map of South America was up to snuff. You'll take an interest in his homework, won't you, Miss Quint?"

"Yes . . . yes," Miss Quint muttered. "Off with you, now! Not a word more. Go and find a new home for the You Know What—and don't lose any sleep in the meantime. Your shop is in safe hands."

Mr. Hardbattle had not walked more than half a dozen steps when he heard a mournful whine coming from an upstairs window. Scallywag's spotted muzzle was poking through a Venetian blind. That morning, sensing that something was up, she had followed her master all over the house, then lain down by his suitcase, her head on her paws. When the time had come for Mr. Hardbattle to leave, it had been necessary to shut her in an upstairs room or she would undoubtedly have bolted after him.

There had been no need to go to such lengths with Trunk. Fond of Mr. Hardbattle though the elephant was, he had never been known to stray from his shelf, haunted by the fear that his forgetful little mistress might return without him noticing.

"Cheerio, Scally, old girl! I'll be back in a week or so!" shouted Mr. Hardbattle, wiping a tear from his eye. He walked to the corner of the road and stopped to wave before vanishing around it.

"Okay!" said Miss Quint, shutting the door of the bookshop. The bell jingle-jangled with a note of melancholy. "He's off. Now, I'm sure I saw some fruitcake in a cupboard in the kitchen. Time for my late-morning snack, I think."

Miss Quint soon stamped her personality on the shop. Though she had promised not to polish or vacuum, she made changes. In the shop, she tidied as much as she dared, putting books in order on the shelves and filing paperwork. She organized the cash register, finding a shilling among the change, which had long since ceased to be legal currency.

Upstairs in the living quarters she was just as thorough. Beds were aired and floors were swept lightly with a dustpan and broom. Everything expired in the kitchen cupboards was thrown away. Miss Quint baked bread. She made marmalade and jam. The mop was encouraged to slosh water a little more tidily over the floor, and the salt and pepper shakers were asked not to empty themselves over every dish (they always had a tendency to be overly generous). She used up leftovers and fed vegetable peelings to the dog. On the third day, when the magic ran amok, she turned the second-to-last stair into sponge cake topped with custard. Her arrival brought order and thriftiness, and the magic did not know quite what to make of her.

For the first few days she kept herself busy. Then boredom set in.

A people person, Miss Quint's whole purpose for being was to chat, and there was not much of that in a bookshop whose average clientele was three customers per day. Scallywag could be relied upon to wag her tail, sigh, yawn, bark, and scratch at the door, but that was the limit of her communicative powers. The origami sheep could only bleat repeatedly, and Trunk did not say anything, having a trunk and a pair of tusks but sadly no mouth. Miss Quint yearned to be asked to hand-deliver books, and when she received a request she made the most of it, keeping the customer talking on their doorstep for as long as she could. However, these opportunities were few and far between.

For the most part, Miss Quint had to content herself with listening to Mr. Hardbattle's old transistor radio, but after a while, the magic would change the station at vital moments in news bulletins and afternoon plays, and it also developed the habit of turning the volume up and down. Eventually Miss Quint grew so annoyed with the magic that she returned the radio to the bathroom cabinet where she had found it.

Without fail, Arthur dropped by every day after school. Trunk barely acknowledged him, but both Scallywag and Miss Quint viewed Arthur's arrival as the highlight of their day. Scallywag greeted Arthur by tugging at his trouser legs (the only bad habit she had retained from puppyhood). There was a brief interlude while Scallywag fetched her lead, then copious tail wagging until he took her for a walk. Miss Quint's form of welcome was more demure but no less enthusiastic. Watching for Arthur from the window, she was always ready at the door to let him in. She took his bag, hung up his coat, and asked about his day before telling him in great detail about her own.

While Scallywag and Arthur were taking their walk to the park, Miss Quint occupied herself with pouring him an orange juice, putting cookies on a plate, plumping the cushion on the wing chair that was Arthur's usual seat, and setting out his workbooks and pencil case on a small oak table. On his return, she babbled to Arthur until he asked her to stop so that he could start on his homework. Miss Quint was no scholar. She had been an average student, but she did her best to assist him. She found books on relevant subjects on the shelves and made what she thought were helpful suggestions, but otherwise she respected his wishes and tried to leave him alone (never fully succeeding).

It was a Thursday afternoon, almost four days after

Mr. Hardbattle's departure, when the solitary lifestyle of a bookseller finally defeated Miss Quint.

On that Thursday in May, Arthur's schoolbag was bulkier than normal. With vacation week coming up, he wanted to get most of his homework out of the way so he could help Miss Quint in the shop and, more important, travel with her to Thornwick. In Thornwick there lived a lady named Mrs. Carruthers, who had offered to make room for the magic on her farm.

Arthur had two tests to study for, a page of math to plow through, and he needed to finish a project that required drawing diagrams (not his forte at all). Scallywag's walk was short that afternoon—to the top of the road and back—and Miss Quint was disappointed to find that Arthur was most unwilling to take part in even the briefest conversation.

"You haven't touched your juice!" she said to Arthur, who was hunched over the little oak table, coloring something in.

"Sorry, Miss Quint," mumbled Arthur. He picked up the glass and drained it without taking his eyes or his pen off the half-filled-in page in his workbook.

"What's that you're drawing?" Miss Quint asked, attempting to peer over his shoulder.

"A subduction zone," said Arthur, his scribbling getting more feverish.

"Biology?"

"Geography," he said and tensed. Tactfully, Miss Quint withdrew.

Not having been a conscientious student, Miss Quint found it hard to understand Arthur's devotion to work. She had been more than happy to scrape through exams, get mediocre grades, and take home less than glowing reports. Her school days had been one long period of chatting too much and narrowly escaping detention.

Miss Quint began to wonder if she was the problem. Arthur seemed to get on famously with Mr. Hardbattle. Perhaps Arthur buried himself in schoolwork so that he would not have to talk to a gossipy, middle-aged female (charming and youthful-looking though she thought she was). Miss Quint was perfectly aware that she did not know what boys liked to talk about, not having any children or nephews of her own. She found herself wishing that Arthur were a girl. It was obvious that she and a girl would have so much more in common. There would be endless opportunities for long, intimate chats, and they could play cat's cradle, bake together, and sing songs.

Arthur pushed aside his diagram of a subduction zone and opened a book with dog-eared pages, which was dotted with math problems.

Bored and deflated, Miss Quint wandered around the bookshop, picking up books and reading random paragraphs. In one book, she found a passage about some children playing and decided to read it aloud, but quietly so as not to interrupt Arthur.

It was an old book called *High Jinks*, which had been written in the 1950s. In the part she read out loud, the central characters (a boy named Reginald and his best friend, Keith) were leaping like daredevils from one playground device to the next. Also in the snippet was an unnamed girl who, in contrast to the energetic boys, was not moving at all. She was standing by herself beside some railings, waiting for a turn on the swings.

"If that little girl were here now," Miss Quint said, pressing her finger on the place in the book where the girl was mentioned, "we'd have a super time, I'm sure. I bet she wouldn't want to waste her time doing *homework*." Miss Quint looked dejectedly over her shoulder at Arthur. "If only that little girl was here right now. Oh, how I wish she was!"

Making wishes out loud was a risky business in a building filled to the brim with magic, but Miss Quint, who had barely glanced at Mr. Hardbattle's instructions, did not know that. Ever so slowly and faintly, a light-colored apparition started to glow in a corner of the shop. Miss Quint did not see it. She had closed the book containing the playground scene and moved on to another one. The hazy, foglike blur morphed into a figure, which grew bolder in color with every minute that passed.

Trunk was the first to see the girl. The sight of her

made his black felt eyes try to pull away from their blobs of glue. When he realized that she was not *his* little girl, his surge of joy turned to bafflement. He had not heard the bell and could not understand how the girl entered the shop. Trunk examined his ears with his soft, plump feet to check that the stuffing had not fallen out of them.

"Oh! H-hello," said a startled Miss Quint, when, after several minutes, she peered through a gap in a bookshelf and saw a person standing in the farthest corner of the shop. Being less observant and not as alert as Trunk, she could not be sure if the bell had rung or not. But, in any case, it was clear that her afternoon had improved vastly. A customer had come in.

Miss Quint walked briskly around the blocks of teetering shelves. She felt she should speak to the customer face-to-face rather than hold a conversation through a tiny space with the chance that she might breathe in a shelf's worth of dust.

"Good afternoon!" said Miss Quint, nearing the corner where the person stood. "How nice of you to visit our establishment."

"Hello," said the customer, sucking the end of her braid.

Miss Quint's heart leaped. What a stroke of luck! She had wished that a little girl would join her in the bookshop and here one was!

The girl stared at Miss Quint solemnly. Under thickly

powdered, pastel blue lids, Miss Quint's eyes took in the plain, chubby-cheeked, listless girl in front of her. The little girl was not quite the pretty, charismatic child that she had had in mind but, as Miss Quint had come to learn, you could not always have everything. She gave the girl her brightest smile.

"How can I help you, cherub?" she said.

Chapter Seven

A full Shop

When asked what kind of assistance she needed, the girl was not forthcoming. She seemed able only to shrug her shoulders and say "Don't know." Eventually, Miss Quint was forced to resort to guessing games.

"You've come to buy a storybook about ponies. Am I right?" she asked.

"Don't know," said the girl. Her eyes were big and expressionless.

Miss Quint tried a different tack. "Perhaps you're lost. Did you find yourself on your own, and come in here to ask for help?"

"No," said the girl dully. "I'm not lost—I'm waiting."

"Waiting for what, dear?" Miss Quint was flummoxed. "For someone to find you? Your mommy, perhaps?"

"I'm waiting . . . for a turn," said the girl.

"A turn?" said Miss Quint.

"On the swings."

Miss Quint was taken aback. "But the park's a good

distance away. I don't understand. It won't do you much good to wait here." She thought the girl might not be too bright. Miss Quint touched her gently on the arm. "This isn't a *play* area. This is a bookshop, dear."

The girl stared.

"What's . . . your . . . name?" asked Miss Quint, speaking each word slowly.

"Don't know," said the girl.

Miss Quint's patience deserted her. "Don't be ridiculous! You must know what your name is! Everyone knows that. Now, think!"

The girl's front teeth bit nervously into her bottom lip. "I don't know what my name is," she said. "It doesn't say."

Miss Quint was close to having a hysterical fit. "What do you mean, 'it doesn't say'?"

"In the story," said the girl, biting her lip harder.

"The story? What story is that?" Miss Quint fell silent. Suddenly, everything the girl had said slipped into place and made perfect sense.

"Good gracious!" she said, seizing the girl by her shoulders. "It can't be possible! I'm crazy to believe it! You're the girl I wished for. The girl in the book!"

The girl would have shrugged if she could have managed it, but Miss Quint's hands were like clamps.

"I'll get you an orange juice and a chocolate cookie. Would you like that?" Miss Quint asked sweetly. She fussed over the girl, retying her hair ribbons and making flattering comments about the color of her eyes (which were an unattractive, murky blue). "I'm sorry I was curt just now," Miss Quint said, pressing her cheek against the girl's. "I didn't realize who you were. I know this bookshop is magic, but I never thought it could make wishes come true!"

With an arm around the girl's shoulders, Miss Quint led the nameless child across the shop floor and up the stairs to the kitchen, where she laid out a feast. When they came down again, Arthur was closing his books and zipping up his pencil case, having made a satisfactory start on his homework.

"I'm off now, Miss Quint," he said breezily. "It's almost dinnertime. Thanks for the juice and stuff." His gaze landed on the solemn girl holding Miss Quint's hand. She could only be a year or two younger than he was, but she was dressed like a kindergarten child. She had on a gingham dress, white ankle socks, and sandals. Her hair was tied with ribbons and dangled down in thin brown braids.

"Who's this?" he asked.

Miss Quint gave a tinkling laugh and squeezed the girl's hand. "That's what I've been trying to find out!" she said. "I've decided to call her Susan."

Arthur frowned. His head was still congested with algebra, but he was sure that what Miss Quint had said did not sound right. Had she just announced, gleefully, that she had renamed someone's child? He was half inclined to get to the bottom of things, but his brain felt too overloaded to do any more thinking. Besides, it was a Thursday, which meant there were fries, eggs, and beans for dinner. Thinking that the girl was a customer and that he must have been too absorbed in his homework to hear the bell jingling when she arrived, Arthur made his excuses.

"Mom freaks if I'm late," he said, stuffing all his books and school gear into his bag. "Can't come tomorrow. Got to take Bubbles to the vet's right after school. He's our cockatiel. I'm the only one he hasn't tried to bite. We're going to my granny's on Saturday morning, but I'll come around in the afternoon. You'll keep it free, won't you, Miss Quint, so we can check out that farmhouse? Bye, then."

"Good-bye, dear!" said Miss Quint gaily, untroubled by Arthur's news that he would not be able to come to the bookshop until after lunch in two days' time. What did it matter now? She had magicked up the perfect companion for herself!

Miss Quint tired of Susan long before Saturday afternoon came.

It was not that Susan was badly behaved. In fact, Miss Quint had never met a more compliant child. Susan did not throw tantrums, or sulk. She accepted the name Susan without a word of argument. She made no demands, did as she was told, and never left Miss Quint's side, trailing after her like a loose thread.

Conversations were one-sided. Miss Quint would think up an interesting topic upon which Susan would have nothing to say. She had no opinions of her own and no amusing anecdotes to share. It quickly became apparent that Susan lacked any kind of personality, but when Miss Quint had another look through *High Jinks*, the book from which Susan had been spirited, she realized that the girl's blandness was not her fault. It was the author who was to blame. Susan was mentioned only once in the whole book, standing by the railings in the park in the section that Miss Quint had read aloud. She was a girl waiting for a turn on the swings and nothing more. There was no fuller description. She was a blank slate.

For an outspoken chatterbox like Miss Quint, having the constant company of a dreary, soulless person was the worst sort of torture imaginable.

When the telephone rang on Friday morning, Miss Quint rushed across the shop to answer it, muttering "Hallelujah!" under her breath. The caller was an awkward old man named Mr. Wax, who had caused offense to every other bookseller in the county. He spoke to

Miss Quint in a rude and demeaning way, but she did not care at all. In fact, she almost broke down with relief to finally talk to someone with opinions.

Mr. Wax wanted three books to be delivered: "Not this afternoon. Not next week. Right this minute, thank you, miss." If the books were in a damaged state when they arrived, he would, apparently, see to it that Miss Quint was fired from her job.

Glad to have the chance to escape from the bookshop for an hour or two, Miss Quint locked up Hardbattle Books and herded her two helpers into the bottle-green van. Scallywag rode in the back with the books, and in the passenger seat sat Dreary Susan (as Miss Quint had gotten into the habit of calling her).

Mr. Wax lived in an isolated cottage twenty miles outside of Plumford. It had once been surrounded by a large, thriving community—until Mr. Wax moved to the area and upset everyone.

The excursion did them all good. Scallywag had a long sniff of a gatepost while Miss Quint stood on Mr. Wax's doorstep and refused to let him bully her. On the way back, Susan almost displayed excitement when she saw a herd of cows in a field.

The afternoon crawled by with slothlike heaviness, enlivened only by the antics of magic. One of the ducks from the painting of Lake Tahoe flew into the windowpane and had to be revived with a drop of peapod wine (nothing else seemed to do the trick); the paper clips linked themselves together and went on a march; and the black cat bookends spent several hours stalking a pincushion mouse. Wherever Miss Quint went, her new friend, Susan, followed. No customers came and the telephone did not ring. After unsuccessfully attempting to unwish Susan, Miss Quint had an attack of guilt. Vowing to be nicer to the girl, she asked her what she would like for dinner, but, predictably, Susan did not know.

They went to bed early, when it was still light. Miss Quint had cleared out a storage room for Susan to sleep in. Her bed was an old canvas cot, but Miss Quint had found a feather quilt and a thick sweater, which made a fine pillow.

By lunchtime on Saturday, Miss Quint had nearly gone crazy in the absence of stimulating company. She had watched in vain for customers since nine o'clock, but none had arrived. It was a sunny day in May and the people of Plumford evidently had better things to do than poke around in dark, dingy bookshops that smelled unpleasant. It reached the point where Miss Quint could no longer bear the poor companionship of Dreary Susan. If she could not unwish the girl, then she would have to wish for some different people to join them both—adults, this time, with fully rounded characters and plenty of life experience. She took down books from the shelves and started to leaf through them, looking for anyone who sounded vaguely interesting.

Going through exactly the same motions she had done before, Miss Quint pressed her finger on the character's name that she had selected and wished out loud that they could be with her. The magic in the bookshop did not disappoint. People began to appear gradually, just as Susan had done. An eminent politician materialized in one of the wing chairs, wearing a top hat and a monocle; a parlor maid bobbed a curtsy by the fireplace; a shoe shiner took shape in a kneeling position, a tin of boot polish and a cloth in his hands. Thrilled by the emergence of each character, Miss Quint wished for more and more companions. Dutifully, the magic obliged.

Scallywag was ecstatic. Her tail wagged itself into a blur as she ran up to each new arrival, then sat at their feet and leaned against their legs, inviting them to stroke her. Susan loitered shyly by the cash register, not possessing Scallywag's talent for mingling. Trunk, meanwhile, was in a tizzy. He paced up and down his shelf, his gray ears flapping as he shook his head unhappily. There had not been a single jingle-jangle of the bell and yet the bookshop was filled with customers. He did not know how it had happened, not having a proper brain (even magic stuffing has its limitations), but he felt uneasy and was convinced that something was terribly wrong.

The bookshop had never been so full. By the time

Miss Quint had summoned her final guest, the floor was almost impossible to see under the many feet. There was a mixed assortment of footwear on display, every pair of which was buffed by the shoe shiner over the course of the afternoon. Unlikely characters chatted together (who would have thought that an actress, a bellhop, and a mountaineer would have anything in common?), and Miss Quint swanned and sashayed among them all, her face frozen in rapturous delight.

When Arthur turned up at ten past three, he could barely get through the door. He was amazed to find the bookshop heaving with customers, and by the look of the headwear on the hat stand they were a diverse bunch.

Miss Quint accosted Arthur before he had crossed the doormat. She thrust a shopping bag and a list into his hands. "And here's my purse!" she said, having to shout to make herself heard over the tumultuous din. "I haven't got nearly enough in my cupboards to provide these good people with tea."

"Since when have we started feeding customers? Mr. Hardbattle didn't put *that* in his instructions," Arthur protested worriedly. "And where did all these people come from? You haven't decided to have a sale, have you, Miss Quint? What would Mr. Hardbattle say?"

"Shush about Mr. Hardbattle!" ordered Miss Quint, growing more irritated with Arthur by the second. "He left the bookshop in my charge, didn't he?"

"Well, yes," admitted Arthur, "but he wanted me to look after it too." Arthur peered past Miss Quint and frowned. "Are these the sort of people he'd want in his shop? No one seems to be looking at the books or buying anything. That guy over there's wearing armor AND he's got a great big sword. You were going to close the shop by three. Tell them you're closing and throw them out. Mr. Hardbattle's counting on us to take a look at that farmhouse. You promised we'd go there *today*."

"Something more pressing's come up," said Miss Quint. "Our trip will have to be postponed. Stop scowling, Arthur. A little delay won't matter. Mrs. Carruthers said in her letter that we could pop in any day we liked. We'll go tomorrow instead."

"Don't suppose I've got much choice, do I?" Arthur said.

"No, so chin up! You're being a party pooper!" Miss Quint dropped her purse into the shopping bag and gave Arthur a firm push. "I've put bread and butter on the list, and fillings for sandwiches, and some cakes and pastries as well. Don't be tempted to get anything cheap or out of a jar. No peanut butter or chocolate spread or anything like that. There's a high government official and a duchess among this crowd."

"Can't *you* go?" complained Arthur, who did not derive much pleasure from grocery shopping. "There are so many aisles. I won't know where anything is."

"Take Susan with you," said Miss Quint, who had become aware of a familiar, irksome presence sidling up to her. "She'll be very helpful, I'm sure."

"Her again?" said Arthur, recognizing the girl in the gingham dress as the one he had seen two days before. "Why has she started to hang out here? Hasn't she got a home to go to?"

Miss Quint glared at Arthur with just the right degree of displeasure to make him back out of the door.

Arthur glanced resentfully at the girl who had been foisted on him. "Come on, then, what's-your-name," he grumbled.

"It's Susan!" she said and tried to hold his hand.

"Quit it!" said Arthur, horrified. "Hold this if you want to hold something!" He pushed the shopping bag into her arms and started to walk away. "Let's go, Suze. We've got a lot of shopping to do."

"All right," Susan said amiably, "but afterward, do you think there'll be time to play on the swings?"

Chapter Eight

The Tea Party

Miss Quint turned out to be wrong about Susan. On the shopping trip she was not helpful at all. While Arthur dashed up and down the aisles, hunting high and low and checking things off the list when he found what he was searching for, Susan ambled after him, clutching the shopping bag to her chest and gazing at everything in awe. When they had arrived at the supermarket, Arthur asked her to find a few items, but it was almost too painful to watch her floundering without a clue, and in the end he gave up and took the task upon himself.

As they traipsed back to the bookshop, each holding one handle of the bulging shopping bag, Arthur kept giving Susan curious, sidelong glances. She was the oddest girl he had ever met. Her dress sense was disturbingly nerdy, but it was her strange behavior that concerned him most. Susan was not a talkative person and she tended to stare a lot. When she did speak, she often used old-fashioned words and phrases he had heard his granny utter from time to time. Everyday sights like people talking on cell phones would cause her to stand and gape, and the roar of a motorcycle would make her jump out of her skin. She seemed to be like a tourist from a faraway place, and Arthur's heart, which had hardened toward her, slowly began to soften.

After ten minutes of stumbling along the pavement with their achingly heavy load, Arthur thought they deserved a rest. He remembered that Susan had asked if they could stop at a playground and, despite the mile or so it added to their journey, he decided to take her to the park.

Since it was a warm day, the playground was busy, and they had to wait in line to have a turn on the swings. Susan did not seem to mind. In fact, she looked completely content and at ease standing in a line with the other more fidgety children. It was as if she had finally returned to the environment in which she felt most at home.

When her turn came, she spent the first minute kicking her legs out in front of her, then quickly bending her knees. Gradually she gathered momentum, soaring higher and higher; the chains that held the swing squeaked and clanked under the strain.

"Thank you, Arthur," said Susan when she had finished her turn and left the swing wobbling enticingly, awaiting the bottom of the next eager child. Susan's face, which was usually blank or conveying puzzlement, was lit up like a sunbeam.

"That's all right," said Arthur, smiling. "It beats making tons and tons of sandwiches, which I bet is how we'll be spending the rest of our afternoon."

The tea party was a resounding success. Arthur and Susan were recruited to pass things around, and the guests happily nibbled on the inviting range of sandwiches that the children had indeed been roped into making. It had not escaped Arthur's notice that the customers were a motley crew. He had already spotted the guest who was wearing a breastplate and gauntlets (which the man had to remove in order to eat a cream puff). It appeared that several others had opted to come in fancy attire as well.

Returning to the kitchen to refill a plate of sandwiches, he wondered yet again where Miss Quint had found these people and how she had attracted them into the shop. He wanted to confront Miss Quint with these questions, but she proved difficult to pin down. As soon as he spied her and pushed through the crowd to talk to her, she slipped away to the opposite side of the room, almost as if she were avoiding him.

Arthur and Susan were reunited at the kitchen sink

after all the food had either been eaten or dropped on the floor. Susan turned on the faucet.

"The cucumber sandwiches were popular," commented Arthur.

"Everything was," observed Susan, putting on yellow rubber gloves and dipping her hands into the sink. And it was true; in no time, their entire bag of groceries had been polished off.

"Mrs. Doasyouwouldbedoneby said she liked the éclairs the most." Susan selected a sponge and began to clean a plate.

"Mrs. who?" asked Arthur, a dishtowel clutched in his hand. "Was that really her name?"

Susan nodded.

"I've heard that name before," said Arthur, picking up the plate Susan had stacked in the drainboard. "Mrs. Doasyouwouldbedoneby. Yes, I've seen it written down. Was she the lady in black?" he asked.

"Oh no!" said Susan. She tossed her head twice, flicking her braids behind her so their ends did not dangle in the soapy water. "The lady in the black coat was Nurse Matilda."

"Nurse Matilda?" exclaimed Arthur. "Are you sure?"

"Yes," Susan said. "I heard her say so." Since she had gone on the swing, Susan had acquired a new decisiveness. She lifted a pile of plates from the counter and let them sink gently into the water.

"But Nurse Matilda's not real," said Arthur, confused. "She's a made-up person. My sister, Beth, drew a picture of her for school. The picture's stuck to our fridge. I'm certain Nurse Matilda is a character from a book."

Susan shrugged and busied herself with her sponge.

"Oh, good, you've made a start." Miss Quint popped her head around the kitchen door to check that the dish-washing was under way. "Hasn't it been a wonderful afternoon?" she said.

"Not especially," Arthur replied. He wiped a plate with exaggerated care and placed it on some others on the counter.

"You're a plucky pair," said Miss Quint with admiration. "As a reward for all your hard work, how would you like a trip to the beach? We could take the van to Plentiful Sands!"

"Sounds nice," snapped Arthur. Normally, he would have been thrilled at the prospect of a day at the beach, but the eager-to-please note in Miss Quint's voice merely added to his worries about the peculiar customers down-stairs. He eyed Miss Quint with growing unease as he dried a handful of teaspoons. "When are your guests going to leave?" he asked.

Miss Quint's face turned azalea pink.

"Yes," joined Susan. "When *are* they going home? I'm tired, Miss Quint. I think I'd like it if they went."

"Soon, I hope," said Miss Quint, her smile beginning

to lose its radiance. "I'm feeling a bit spent myself. This hostessing business takes a lot out of you. I'll hint around that it's time they took off. All right?"

From the kitchen on the first floor, Arthur and Susan heard the bell jingle-jangle time and time again. When they had finished cleaning up and were confident that all the customers had left the shop, Susan peeled off her gloves and Arthur threw down his towel. Together they raced downstairs.

When they reached the bottom step, Arthur and Susan saw that the bookshop had emptied itself of everyone who did not belong there. They flung themselves into the chairs by the fireplace, greatly relieved.

Relaxing after a busy afternoon was not something that Scallywag, Trunk, and Miss Quint seemed able to manage. Rather than flopping into the chair behind Mr. Hardbattle's desk, Miss Quint stood fretfully beside it, staring out the window at some unseen spectacle in the street. Scallywag was similarly ill at ease, but she was seated on the doormat with her head tilted and her ears pricked. The only part of Trunk that was visible was the knot in the end of his tail. Unlike the other two, he was not preoccupied with whatever was outside. He had traveled the length of his shelf and hidden behind a flowerpot, which was a sure sign that everything had gotten to be too much.

"What's up with everyone?" asked Arthur.

Susan shook her head. "Don't know."

Arthur got up from his chair. He passed Scallywag, who was now lying down, making snuffling noises at the bottom of the door, and walked to the window to see what had secured Miss Quint's interest. She flinched when Arthur edged up beside her but did not avert her gaze. Arthur squinted through the layers of age-old grime on the window and was shocked to see a large group of people assembled on the sidewalk outside. He might have supposed they were holding a protest, but as far as he could tell they were not carrying signs. He rubbed his sleeve on the glass to see more clearly.

"Miss Quint," he said after a minute, peering intently, "why are all your guests standing around outside the shop? Why haven't they gone home?"

Miss Quint gave a feeble moan. "I've wished and wished that they'd go," she said, more to herself than to Arthur.

"Perhaps we should call them a taxi," Arthur suggested practically, "or rather, a whole fleet of them."

Miss Quint sighed and patted her nostrils with a handkerchief. "I'm not sure they'd be able to pay the fares," she said, "and I don't have any money to lend them. I've only got pennies left in my purse. Everything else went toward food for the party." Miss Quint turned to face Arthur. Her cheeks had lost their healthy pink tinge. She looked drained and tearful and, unusually for Miss Quint, she appeared to be at a loss for words.

"Who are those people?" asked Arthur suspiciously. "Magic wasn't involved in their coming here, was it? You haven't done anything stupid?"

Miss Quint blanched. "Susan, dear!" she called in a high, quavering voice. "Would you be a good girl and run upstairs to fetch the keys from my bedroom so I can lock up the shop?"

Susan jumped to her feet. "Yes, of course I will, Miss Quint," she said and trotted up the steps.

Arthur's suspicions deepened when he saw the bunch of keys Miss Quint had requested hanging from her belt.

"But, Miss Quint—," he began.

"I know," she said, following Arthur's befuddled gaze. "I wanted Susan out of the way. I think it's time I owned up."

Guilt-ridden and contrite, but not so humbled that she left out the part about how lonely and miserable she had been, Miss Quint confessed that the guests at her party had been characters from books. She explained to Arthur that she had only needed to wish for them to be real and the magic in the bookshop had done the rest.

Arthur was tongue-tied with fury, but after a moment he found his voice. "Miss Quint!" he raged. "Mr. Hardbattle *said* you mustn't! What's the point of instructions if you won't read them? I can't *believe* this! What were you thinking?" When he had calmed down, Arthur ran his fingers through his hair. "So, what are we going to do?"

Miss Quint took a hopeful peek outside. "They might go in a minute," she said.

"Go? Where to?" said Arthur, exploding with anger again. "You can't just put them out on the street and expect them to fend for themselves! They'll end up living in cardboard boxes. They might be mugged or kidnapped, and that guy with the sword is bound to take someone's head off if he keeps swinging it around like he's doing now. You'll have to get them back in here and undo all your wishes."

"Don't you think I've tried that?" whined Miss Quint. "I did my best to unwish Susan, but as you've seen she's still flesh and blood."

"*Susan*?" Arthur took a step back. "You mean she's one of *them*? You're telling me that I've been out shopping with a fictional character?" His astonishment melted away as the realization sank in. "Does she know?" he asked quietly.

Miss Quint shrugged her shoulders. "She seemed to when we first met, but I think she's forgotten. That's why I got rid of her just now. I thought she might be upset to be reminded."

A flurry of movement outside caught Arthur's attention.

Somebody new had joined the throng, and that someone was wearing a helmet and a sharp black uniform.

"Oh heck!" said Arthur. "It's the police. We're in big trouble now."

Chapter Nine

A Spell of Unwishing

Afterward, Arthur was forced to admit that Miss Quint had been magnificent. He had been the resourceful one who thought up the idea, but she had acted as the linchpin, without whom the plan would not have been possible to execute.

At first Miss Quint doubted that she was up to the challenge of fooling a policeman, but Arthur assured her that it was worth a try. She had made an unpromising start, tottering out onto the street in her high-heeled shoes, waving weakly, and shouting, "Yoo-hoo!" However, Miss Quint had held her nerve and gone on to charm the pants off the humorless policeman. Lying through her teeth, she managed to convince him that the milling crowd was a motley group of book-lovers who were waiting for a famous author to turn up to sign his latest book.

The policeman had been surly to begin with, and, perhaps to save face, he had insisted on confiscating the knight's sword with the words "Simmer down, sir, and hand it over. Knives are for chopping vegetables, not for carrying . . . and . . . and the same goes for swords and all."

The knight had been unwilling to give up his shining steel blade, and there might have been a scuffle (in which the policeman would surely have made out worse) if the politician in the black top hat had not stepped in. Fitting his monocle to his eye, the fictional government official from North Lonsdale said some fine and eloquent things. No one fully understood what these meant, but his distinguished tone of voice had the desired effect. The situation was diffused, the knight gave up his sword, and both parties were persuaded to shake hands.

Fooling a policeman was a minor challenge when compared with unwishing a roomful of people.

"So, how exactly did you go about each wish?" inquired Arthur after they had gotten rid of the policeman and herded all of Miss Quint's guests back into the shop. (Scallywag was best at this because she was part sheepdog.)

Miss Quint dispatched Susan to put the kettle on the stove and get the cups and saucers out before applying her mind to Arthur's question.

"Well, let's see . . . um . . . I picked out a book and turned its pages until I found a character that seemed . . . *promising*. Then I put my finger on their name and wished."

"And when you tried to unwish Susan, what did you do?" asked Arthur.

Miss Quint was about to give her reply when a fictional fishmonger attempted to involve her in a conversation about whelks. Miss Quint excused herself politely and pulled Arthur to a more secluded section of the shop. She chose the most cobwebby corner, which was a no-go area for all arachnophobes.

"What did you ask me, Arthur?" she said. "How did I go about unwishing Susan?" Miss Quint struggled to remember. "I was finding her annoying. She wouldn't leave me alone, you see. I whispered it under my breath, I think, so she wouldn't hear. I said, 'I wish this darned girl would go back to her book,' or something similar."

Arthur regarded her critically. "You didn't find the book or point at her name, then?"

"She didn't *have* a name, but no, I can't say that I did," Miss Quint admitted. "Do you think that would have made a difference?"

"I don't know," said Arthur, fishing a spider out of his hair, "but Mr. Hardbattle said that magic won't be bossed around. If you'd asked more nicely, or been clearer about what you'd wanted it to do . . ."

"I think it's worth another stab," Miss Quint said, and

Arthur was quick to agree. "Although there's one slight snag," she added, glancing around the dusty shelves.

If Miss Quint had been thinking straight and had not been in such a desperate hurry to people the bookshop with suitable companions for herself, she might have set aside the books she had used, piled them all together, and put them somewhere safe. But Miss Quint had been swept up in the excitement of the moment and thrust the books back, willy-nilly, on the shelves. If she and Arthur were to match each tea party guest to the book from which they had been summoned, it was going to take a very long time.

"Let's start with Nurse Matilda," said Arthur, dropping to his knees and scanning the shelves in front of him. "She comes from a book with the same name. The author's somebody Brand."

It took them twenty minutes of scrutinizing spines to find it.

"Aha!" said Arthur, handing Miss Quint a yellow jacketless book. "Here you are. You take that and I'll watch Nurse Whatshername to see if she disappears." He sought out the ugliest old lady in the room, who was dressed from head to toe in black.

"Poor Susan!" he said, distracted by the sight of his fellow dishwasher passing behind the old woman, her arms supporting a heavy tray. "She's *still* handing out cups of tea."

"I hereby solemnly declare," Miss Quint asserted in a singsong voice, keeping to one constant note as if she were chanting a canticle in church, "that I really do regret wishing that this lady, Nurse Matilda, would pop out of this book and be a real human. I'd be forever in your debt, not to mention eternally grateful—"

"That's groveling," Arthur interrupted. "I don't think the magic would be too impressed by that."

"All right, then," said Miss Quint testily, reverting to her normal way of speaking. "I'd be *obliged* if your good self . . . selves . . . whatever you are . . . could grant me another wish and put this Nurse Matilda person back where she came from."

Miss Quint triumphantly removed her finger from the page she had chosen. "How was that?" she asked.

"A bit long-winded," said Arthur bluntly. "We've got thirty-eight more to go."

"Thirty-nine," said Miss Quint, correcting him. "You've forgotten Susan."

Arthur grunted. "Does she seem paler to you?"

"Who, Susan?" asked Miss Quint. "I wouldn't say so. She seems to have gotten some sun today. Her nose has gone all freckly."

"Miss Quint, I wasn't referring to Susan," said Arthur, suddenly feeling weary. "I meant the old lady."

Stretching her neck, Miss Quint looked over to where Nurse Matilda was lecturing an elderly, bearded clergyman who had laid claim to one of the wing chairs. Every now and then she poked the old man in the ribs with her stick to ensure that he stayed awake. "Well, bless me!" exclaimed Miss Quint. "I do believe she's gone gray around the edges!"

Miss Quint and Arthur grinned at each other and watched to see what would happen next.

Her jaw continuing to exercise itself, Nurse Matilda slowly ebbed away, fading into nothingness like a dawn mist. The clergyman's head fell forward onto his chest and remained there. No stick jabbed him between his ribs to interrupt his nap because Nurse Matilda had dematerialized.

"Job done!" said Arthur. "Well, almost." He gazed around the shop, his eyes flitting from person to person. They would all have to be dealt with in the same laborious way. The enormity of the task ahead was daunting, but Arthur felt upbeat. "What's the next book we've got to look for, Miss Quint?" he asked.

It went quite well to begin with. Fifteen guests were removed from the shop without any hitches. All of them took their leave gradually, like aspirins dissolving in water. The other guests were untroubled by their departure and assumed that their acquaintances had gone outside for a breath of air or upstairs to use the bathroom.

At six thirty, Arthur made a phone call home and asked his mother if he might be allowed to sleep over at his friend's house that evening. With six children to look after, a cockatiel, two guinea pigs, and a salamander, not to mention a scatterbrained husband, Arthur's mom could not be expected to remember the names of all her children's friends. She expressed no surprise when Arthur told her that his playmate was named Susan.

"Susan? Fine, but you'll have to come back home for your pajamas and your toothbrush," she told him.

Things started to go awry when Arthur left to collect his things. He had brought his bicycle and was not away for long, but winds can change in an instant and large clusters of magic are just as fickle. With Scallywag asleep on a rug by the fireplace, Susan dozing on the bottom stair (worn out from her tea-making duties), and Trunk still refusing to come out from behind his flowerpot, Miss Quint was left to cope alone.

She had her first inkling that the magic was starting to misbehave when a ballet dancer vanished with a bang. Up until that moment, every character had faded gently, over a period of minutes. But the instant Miss Quint wished for the dancer to disappear, there was an ear-splitting crack, the ballet dancer was engulfed by smoke, and when it cleared there was nothing left of her.

The other guests did not react well to this event. Everyone threw up their hands in surprise, most of the ladies screamed, and the gentlemen—depending on their upbringing—said "Yikes!" or "Good heavens!" or "What in the world was that?" All over the shop there was the sound of breaking china as dropped teacups and saucers shattered on the floor. Susan ran to fetch a broom and dustpan, Scallywag dashed upstairs after her, and Miss Quint hid, not knowing what to do.

After about a minute and a half, an idea came to her. "Marvelous!" declared Miss Quint, striding into the frightened crowd. "Excellent! Superb! What an amazing stunt!" Expecting the others to believe that the ballet dancer's sudden disappearance had been some kind of spectacular trick was wildly optimistic and, at first, they stared at her as if she were mad. Refusing to abandon her plan, Miss Quint kept up the pretense, and slowly the crowd began to relax and smile and join her in remarking upon the wondrous nature of the ballet dancer's feat. Soon they had separated into little groups and resumed their former conversations.

A little while later, when Miss Quint had picked the next person to unwish and had the right book open in her hands, she paused, afraid that the same alarming exit would befall this person too. She weighed this fear against the knowledge that she could not afford to dilly-dally. There were still around twenty guests to evict from the bookshop, and if she did not get on with the job she would find herself unwishing people into the early hours.

Taking a deep breath, she put her finger on the character's name and pleaded with the magic to do as she asked. "And I'd rather you did it without all that razzmatazz this time."

The magic outdid itself, but not in the way that Miss Quint had hoped.

Instead of getting fainter, the character that she had unwished (a cook with an apron tied around her waist) grew fatter. The unfortunate woman swelled to three times her normal size, and the squeals and exclamations of those watching her were matched in volume by zinging sounds as the buttons on the woman's dress detached themselves and shot across the room. A lone thumbtack emerged from its carton and began to circle her like a fly. She flapped at it with her pudgy hands, but it zigzagged out of reach. It hovered in midair, then with a rapid dive it struck, puncturing the cook and making her pop like a balloon. The thumbtack dropped to the floor. Nothing of the cook remained.

Pandemonium followed. A group of ladies cowered in a corner, and there was screaming and shouting and lots of running back and forth. Miss Quint's attempts to calm everyone merely made things worse and, grouping themselves together, the bulk of the guests made a rush for the door.

Fortunately, Arthur came back just at that crucial moment.

"Stop them, Arthur!" cried Miss Quint. "Bar their way! Pull the bolts across!" She steamed toward him in a fright-ful panic. "Whatever you do, don't let them escape!"

Chapter Ten

Meddling and Muddling

In an agitated state, Miss Quint lobbed the door key at Arthur. It sailed over the heads of the stampeding guests and, timing his jump to perfection, Arthur snatched it out of the air. He turned around quickly and locked the door, then slipped the key into his pocket before the others could do anything about it.

"Boy, give up that key and stand aside!" the official from North Lonsdale bellowed pompously. "A policeman must be summoned at once. Betsy the cook has been murdered!"

"Right in front of our eyes!" said the parlor maid, clutching the politician's arm and trembling. "It were *'orrible.*"

"'Twas not an honorable death," said the knight, sounding aggrieved. He curled his gauntleted fist and placed it over his heart. "Betsy deserved a bloodthirstier end. I myself desire to have my gizzards slashed open and my eyes gouged from my head."

"*Gross!*" muttered Arthur.

Everyone thought the knight's comments were in poor taste and it was agreed that, in the future, he should keep his ideas about noble ways to die to himself.

"The key, you little brat!" roared the official impatiently. "I demand that you hand it to me this instant. If you refuse, I shall have no choice but to search your person."

"Alas! If only I had my sword," bemoaned the knight, slapping his empty scabbard and cursing in Old English. "I would smite this young churl's head from his shoulders with one blow—"

"Enough of that sort of talk!" interrupted Miss Quint, appalled by the threats being leveled at Arthur, who was only a schoolboy after all. She elbowed her way through the unfriendly mob. "Leave the boy alone!" she yelled. "There'll be no smiting of heads or searching of persons or running to the cops for that matter. You've all got your facts wrong. There hasn't been any murder! Your friend Betsy the cook is just fine." Miss Quint waved the dog-eared paperback book in her hand. "Betsy isn't dead. She's just been returned to her story!"

Miss Quint's explanation did not seem to convince the outraged crowd, which was growing more restless by the minute. None of them seemed to recall that they were characters, borne out of the imaginations of authors. They refused to believe that any of them belonged between the pages of books, and they stuck steadfastly to their theory that the cook had been murdered.

"Betsy blew up and exploded. We all saw her," piped up the shoe shiner.

"She did *what*?" said Arthur. "What's been going on, Miss Quint?"

"It's the magic," whispered Miss Quint, squeezing past the final few guests and reaching Arthur's side at last. "It hasn't been behaving. Things have gotten out of hand." She told him what had happened to the ballet dancer and then described the sequence of events that had led to the bursting of Betsy.

"Yikes!" Arthur said. "We're in a pickle."

Miss Quint chewed her lip worriedly. "I don't dare unwish another one. This group will go berserk."

With his back pressed against the door and a small army of angry, fearful people advancing toward him, Arthur decided he needed to take action.

"They're really ticked off," he said to Miss Quint. "I'd better do something or this could get nasty." In an appeasing gesture, he raised his hands above his head and asked them to listen to what he had to say.

"Okay, I believe you," Arthur told them. "Something upsetting has happened to Betsy. You're right. We should get the police involved. I'll phone them now. Everyone stay calm." Arthur edged past the hostile crowd and hurried over to where the telephone rested on the desk. He picked up the handset and, holding down the button switch, he cut off the dial tone and spoke to a dead line.

"Is this the police?" Arthur said to nobody. "Hello, this is Arthur Goodenough. I'd like to report a murder, please. I'm calling from the bookshop on Meadow Street. You'll come immediately, won't you? Thank you very much." Pretending to look relieved, he put down the receiver and smiled at the crowd, which was on edge. "The Plumford police are on their way," he said.

Ignoring the clapping and cheering that greeted his announcement, Arthur dashed to join Miss Quint by the door. He got to her in the nick of time. Her face had been paralyzed by shock and she was swaying unstably, about to faint. "Miss Quint!" whispered Arthur, putting an arm out to steady her. "Don't panic! The police aren't really coming. It was a bluff."

By now, Arthur and Miss Quint were getting used to dealing with sticky situations. They stood in a conspiratorial huddle beside a display of baseball books and talked in hushed voices.

"It's a shame we can't unwish them all in one try," lamented Miss Quint, anxiously shifting her weight from one high heel to the other.

"Hey! I think you've got something there," said Arthur. "Why don't we split them into groups? We could put the groups in different rooms and call them in here when we're ready for them. I bet we could manage to unwish three or four people at once. That way no one would see any funny disappearances and get worked up."

Miss Quint gave an awestruck gasp and patted Arthur's shoulder. "Great idea," she said. "That would certainly speed things along."

Arthur nodded. "They're expecting the police to arrive, don't forget. It's important that we get rid of these people quickly. If we take too long, they might get suspicious. The only problem is, I can't think how to persuade them to split up."

"Party games!" Miss Quint cried out exultantly.

"Huh?" said Arthur.

Reaching behind his head, Miss Quint plucked a book from the shelf and grinned at him. The book was called *Popular Party Games*. She turned to its index and ran her finger down the columns. "Blind man's bluff, charades, postman's knock, the thimble . . . This should keep them busy. We could put Susan in charge."

Arthur was doubtful. "Do you think they're in the mood to play games?" he asked.

"Oh yes!" Miss Quint waved a dismissive hand. "We could tell them that it'll keep their minds off Betsy until the police get here. They'll go for it. I know they will. We could even have a hangman tournament. Who can resist one of those?"

"Um . . . I'm not even sure what that is," said Arthur, scratching his head. He peered warily over his shoulder. Miss Quint's voice was getting very loud and squeaky. In his opinion, she was becoming overexcited.

"Don't worry, Arthur. Leave it to me," said Miss Quint. She tweaked his nose. Then, clutching the book, she bustled off, calling out Susan's name. "Where are you, cherub?" she cried. "I've got a little project that I want you to help me with!"

Much to Arthur's astonishment, the guests did not object when Miss Quint asked for their attention and explained to them why she thought it might be a good idea if everyone joined in some games. Perched on a pile of old musical scores, Susan had her nose in *Popular Party Games* while Miss Quint delivered her spiel. There was a slight interval while the guests decided which groups they wanted to be in. When they had made up their minds, Miss Quint stepped behind Susan and gripped her shoulders.

"This is Susan, everyone," said Miss Quint. "She'll be supervising your games while my young friend, Arthur, and I will be preparing a special treat for you."

Having been briefed on her task, and with the copy of *Popular Party Games* wedged under her arm, Susan took each of the six groups to their allotted rooms and explained the rules of the games Miss Quint had selected. Susan then flitted from room to room to check that everyone had enough paper and pens and that they were all obeying the rules. From the ripples of laughter heard throughout the house, the games seemed to be providing light relief.

The first four groups were summoned, one by one, to the shop's first floor and, working as an effective team, Miss Quint and Arthur sent them back to their books with a minimum of fuss.

The fifth group to be unwished contained the knight. Miss Quint was glad to be seeing the end of him, as he had shown himself to be hotheaded and reckless. Having watched the knight participate in a game of hangman, Susan reported that he was a terrible cheat as well.

The knight and his two companions lined up in front of Arthur and Miss Quint, expecting to be rewarded with a treat. Arthur had two books opened in front of him, and Miss Quint held *A Tale of Derring-do*, the book in which the knight's story was told. Placing their forefingers on each of the character's names, Arthur and Miss Quint wished them back into their stories. Magic achieved this by spinning them like tops while they faded into nothingness.

Feeling a strange tingling in her palms, Miss Quint glanced down and saw *A Tale of Derring-do* reducing in thickness until it was only a few pages long. "Oh, dear!" she said as the reason for this new, compact version dawned on her. "We sent the knight back without his sword." She turned to the last page and her face twisted in revulsion.

"Let's see!" said Arthur, pawing at the final page.

"No!" Miss Quint told him sharply. She slammed the book shut. "It's not the sort of thing your mother would want you to read. Let's just say the knight got what he wanted."

"Ohhh," said Arthur in a drawn-out breath. "You mean his gizzards and—ugh!—his eyeballs . . ."

"I don't wish to discuss it," said Miss Quint. "Call the last group, please."

When it came to the sixth and final group, a problem arose. Miss Quint and Arthur could not find the books they needed, even though they hunted on every shelf and in every corner of the shop.

"Oh, never mind," said Miss Quint tiredly, sending the people away again. "We'll move on to Susan, shall we? Well, that's a funny thing," she said, her hand hovering above a column of books. "I'm sure I put Susan's book on top of these others." Arthur and Miss Quint searched and searched, but finally they were forced to admit that they could not find Susan's book, *High Jinks*, either.

By nine o'clock the three remaining guests had played so many games of cards that they were heartily sick of it. Susan brought them downstairs, where they confronted Miss Quint and asked her where the police were.

"Oh, the police have come and gone," Miss Quint

told them casually. "They dusted for fingerprints and cordoned off the crime scene . . . and . . . and then they uncordoned it because they'd solved the murder and they've gone now, so everything's done. Nothing to worry about at all."

"Who did it?" asked one of the men.

"And where, pray, is everyone else?" asked a well-dressed woman.

Miss Quint's stockpile of lies was all used up and it was left to Arthur to spin a story. "*They* did it," he said. "All the others did. They're not here anymore because they've been taken away for questioning!"

Miss Quint gaped at Arthur admiringly while the two men and their female companion expressed their shock. Susan was so traumatized that she started to cry. Hearing a little girl's sobs, Trunk peered around his flowerpot.

"There, there, sweetheart!" Miss Quint said soothingly. She pulled Susan toward her and embraced the distraught child. "It's been a long day, hasn't it? I think it would be sensible if we retired for the night."

"Where are we all going to sleep?" asked Arthur.

Miss Quint relinquished Susan and looked thoughtfully at the assembled group.

"Mrs. Voysey-Brown can have my bed," she said, "and Susan won't mind snuggling down in the storage room. She's slept there for the last two nights. I'll put Mr. Blenko and Mr. Claggitt in the spare room. You can take the couch on the landing, Arthur, and I'll sleep down here in one of the chairs. I know it's not ideal, but it's only for one night."

Arthur raised his eyebrows at her questioningly.

"We'll have them all back in their books in the morning," she whispered. "You'll see."

Chapter Eleven

Blenko and Co.

On Sunday morning, Arthur rolled off the couch where he had spent the night and wandered into the kitchen in search of breakfast. The females of the household were already there. Miss Quint was pouring coffee, Susan was forever setting the table, and, mesmerized by the smell of frying sausages, Scallywag was getting under everyone's feet. A motionless figure languished in a chair in the midst of all the activity. She had curled black eyelashes and unbrushed hair and seemed to be asleep.

"Um . . . hi," murmured Arthur.

Susan looked up and gave him a smile. "Hello, Arthur! Did you sleep well? I did, like a log."

"How ghastly for you. *I* shouldn't care to resemble a log, even in repose," sneered the woman in the chair, speaking in a lazy drawl.

Susan's cheeks reddened. She turned to get more knives and forks.

"Arthur, could I trouble you to hand this cup of coffee to our guest?" asked Miss Quint, putting on a refined accent. "Mrs. Voysey-Brown is in *films*," she added, breathless with admiration.

Arthur was not surprised to hear it. Mrs. Voysey-Brown was a strikingly handsome woman and she looked very much like an actress despite being clothed in Miss Quint's raggedy old robe.

"Thank you, darling," purred Mrs. Voysey-Brown, revealing her eyes, which were violet blue. She raised the cup of coffee to her painted lips and took a delicate sip.

"Morning, Mr. Claggitt!" she said as a bearded colossus strode into the room. He reached the kitchen table in two strides and sat down.

"Slept in," said Mr. Claggitt, shaking his bobble-hatted head. Unlike his friend, he had bothered to get dressed. He was wearing a sweater, a parka with a fur-lined hood, pants made from waterproof fabric, and hiking boots. "Wanted to check out the terrain before breakfast," he said. "Thought I'd do some exploring later."

"You like walking, do you?" asked Arthur, who had come to enjoy exercising Scallywag every afternoon.

"Walking?" Mr. Claggitt poured scorn on Arthur's remark. "Do I look like a sissy to you? I'm a mountaineer, boy! I've scaled all the greats: Everest, K2, Kanchenjunga. Wanted to see what Plumford had to offer. Was hoping to glimpse a peak or two from my window."

"There's a hill in Victoria Park," said Arthur.

"Really?" Mr. Claggitt said with interest. "What gradient are we talking about?"

"Oh, I don't know," said Arthur, "but it's pretty steep. My crazy friend Ollie skateboarded down it once and busted his kneecaps."

"Breakfast is served!" announced Miss Quint. She forged a path through the crowded kitchen with two plates of appetizing food in her hands. "Give Mr. Blenko a call, would you, Arthur?"

Arthur went to the door and was on the verge of shouting up the staircase when he saw a young man in a reddish-purple uniform strolling down the steps, sniffing the air.

"Breakfast, eh?" said the man, skipping down the last few steps and patting the newel post as he passed it. "This ain't such a dive after all!" The young man winked at Arthur and proceeded to introduce himself. "Me friends call me Jimmy," he said, shaking Arthur's hand.

"Mine call me Art," said Arthur, preoccupied with Jimmy's attire. Jimmy was dressed like a drummer boy in plum-colored pants edged with gold piping, a close-fitting jacket, and a round, brimless cap.

"Want to know 'bout me uniform, do you, Art? I'm a bellhop, ain't I? London's finest." Jimmy brushed his jacket sleeves and grinned at Arthur's bemused face. "A bellhop's a feller who works in a 'otel. When the bell's rung we 'op to it, carrying cases and opening doors."

"Like a sort of servant," muttered Arthur.

"Ain't they sausages I can smell?" said Jimmy, pushing past Arthur. "Outta the way, chum! Let me at that nosh!"

Breakfast was a riot. The three more senior members of the group gathered at one end of the table and Jimmy the bellhop seated himself at the other, flanked by Arthur and Susan. Mr. Claggitt talked the most. In a voice that never dipped below the volume of a foghorn, he regaled the two ladies with stories of his hair-raising adventures in the world's most hazardous mountain ranges. He hardly ever paused for breath, but when he did, Mrs. Voysey-Brown was ready with a dry, sarcastic comment. Miss Quint barely said a word. She was far too busy frying more food and refilling the mountaineer's plate to make any contribution to the conversation, although she did find time to shoot scathing looks at Jimmy, whose table manners were dreadful.

Everyone ate at different speeds. Mr. Claggitt tucked into his helpings of sausages, eggs, and tomatoes with gusto, more than making up for Mrs. Voysey-Brown's poor appetite. A thin, willowy person, she picked at her plateful of food like a finicky cat and spent the duration of the meal dabbing at the corners of her mouth with a napkin. Miss Quint snatched mouthfuls of food here and there.

At the other end of the table, the children finished their meals long before Jimmy Blenko had gobbled down his. Jimmy was a born entertainer. He knew a bunch of jokes and rattled them off, one after the other, keeping Arthur in stitches. Susan giggled too—on the rare occasion that she managed to understand one. An excellent mimic, Jimmy started doing impressions of all the staff and clientele, from the rich to the riffraff, who passed through his hotel.

When breakfast was over and Susan and Miss Quint were bent over the kitchen sink doing the dishes, Arthur changed out of his pajamas and went downstairs, intent on having a look around the shop in search of the missing books, *Tinseltown Ticket*, *Rockfall!*, and *Champagne for Geraldine*. Miss Quint told him that she had a look at daybreak, when everyone else was still in bed. Her search proved to be fruitless, but Arthur hoped to do better.

The bookshop was quiet and undisturbed. Everything was in its proper place. The books were filed correctly, the black cat bookends stood symmetrically on either side of Ibsen's plays, and the ducks in the painting of Lake Tahoe were asleep with their heads tucked under their wings. The only lively presence was Trunk. He was frolicking back and forth on his shelf, curling up his trunk and shooting it straight out again, like a party horn. His behavior was very out of character. Arthur asked the elephant if something was the matter but, of course, having no mouth, Trunk was unable to answer him.

After half an hour, Arthur abandoned his hunt for the books, which were still nowhere to be found, and made his way toward the stairwell. Before he could reach it, however, Arthur heard the sound of feet tramping down the stairs and was soon joined by Miss Quint (who was closely followed by Susan), the three new house-guests, and Scallywag.

Miss Quint was carrying a shopping bag and Mr. Claggitt had a plaid blanket tucked under his arm. Mrs. Voysey-Brown was wearing a pair of borrowed sunglasses.

"The weather forecast is great!" declared Miss Quint. "It's a shame I never got around to buying a new swimsuit. Still, there's more to being beside the sea than swimming. All set, Arthur? Plentiful Sands, here we come!"

Arthur gaped at Miss Quint in disbelief. "We're not going to the seaside *today*!"

Susan's face fell immediately. "Aren't we?" she said. "Why don't you want to go, Arthur? Miss Quint says there are castles built out of sand and fish made from jelly and watery things called waves."

Feeling like a jerk, Arthur struggled to explain. "It doesn't mean we can't go another day," he said. "It's just that today Miss Quint and I had made plans. We need to have a look around a farmhouse. It's urgent. We've already put it off once."

Susan started to sniff. Within seconds, Arthur found himself accused of making her cry.

"What did you expect me to do with them?" Miss Quint whispered fiercely in Arthur's ear. "I've got to entertain these people *somehow*. They've been promised a day at the beach. I can't suddenly change my mind!"

"Face facts," said Mr. Claggitt, slamming his hand onto Arthur's shoulder. "You're outvoted, sonny boy!"

Miss Quint drove and Mr. Claggitt blocked out half the windshield with a map and made a terrible navigator. For a seasoned explorer, he did not seem to understand the basics of map reading. He urged Miss Quint to take shortcuts through barbed-wire fences, in between trees, and over railway tracks, until Miss Quint was able to get the message across that in England, when journeying in a car, one was required to travel on roads.

"Up and over," Mr. Claggitt advised whenever they came to a traffic circle. "Go, go, go!" he shouted when the traffic lights were red.

The odds were against them arriving in one piece with Mr. Claggitt in the passenger seat, but they did eventually reach their destination without so much as a scratch, mostly thanks to Miss Quint's cool head and the well-marked signposts.

Plentiful Sands was well named. The cove arched in a golden crescent for miles and miles. It was not quite summer, but the sun was out and the weather was pleasant enough to entice the usual horde of day-trippers, who were prepared to don their bathing suits at the first sighting of a patch of blue sky.

There was a place that rented deck chairs, and an ice cream stand, but Miss Quint told the others, regretfully, that she could not afford any extra treats. She spread the tartan picnic blanket over the sand and gave them each a paper bag containing their lunch, explaining that they would have to make do.

Jimmy had other ideas, it seemed. Kicking off his shoes, he sauntered down the beach and returned with a beach ball, a deck chair, and two straw sun hats for the ladies. Later in the afternoon, on another jaunt, he came back with a bucket, shovel, and six ice-cream cones. Arthur and Jimmy played around with the beach ball, spraying sand everywhere, getting hot, pausing for a dip in the sea, and then starting their ball game all over again.

They were not the only members of their group to enjoy themselves.

Never one to let the chance to wade pass her by, Miss Quint took off her tights and ventured down to the water's edge. While she was swishing around in the water, Scallywag thundered across the sand and launched herself into the waves, barking with insane delight. Susan was more reserved than the other two and would only allow the foam to tickle her toes.

Mr. Claggitt hung around for a short while, moaning that the beach was far too flat. As soon as he sighted some cliffs in the distance, he was off. He weaved a route through the sandcastles and seaweed patches in his parka, weatherproof pants, and hiking boots.

Mrs. Voysey-Brown confided to the others that she was more of a St. Tropez type of person. She hogged the only deck chair and hid underneath her wide-brimmed hat for the entire afternoon. To amuse herself, she criticized people's swimwear, and she flatly refused to help Susan look for seashells along the shore.

"Really, darling, have some sense," she told the disappointed child. "Famous actresses don't get their ankles wet in public!"

All in all, it was a thoroughly enjoyable day and they were sad to see it end. They waited until the setting sun almost touched the horizon before they plodded from the beach and piled into the van. They were sticky and sunburned and had sand between their toes, but no one could remember having had a better time.

When they pulled up outside Hardbattle Books, Arthur yelled a hasty good-bye and rode home on his bicycle. It was left to Susan and Miss Quint to organize supper. The sea air seemed to have sapped everyone's strength, and most of them were too tired to lift their forks to their mouths. Once the meal was out of the way and the others had trooped off to bed, Miss Quint tidied up the kitchen.

Crouching down to pick up a napkin that had fallen onto the floor, Miss Quint spied a small pile of letters under the kitchen table. It was Scallywag's job to collect the mail from the doormat every day, and while she was fairly successful at this, she was not so adept at delivering it to Miss Quint. Consequently, it was not unusual to find letters scattered all over the house.

Miss Quint retrieved the pile of mail. There were three brown envelopes and a postcard.

She laid out the mail on the table in front of her, then opened the three brown envelopes first. Two were bills and one was an order. Finally she looked at the postcard. On its front was a picture of a pier, which was described as being in Great Yarmouth. She turned the postcard over and saw that Mr. Hardbattle had sent it. The weather in East Anglia he described as "good" and the food as "rather chewy." He mentioned that Arthur's method of rating the buildings had been working well and listed the rankings thus far. Miss Quint noted with a sharp breath that only one of the eight places he had visited racked up a score of more than 40 percent.

Contained in the final few sentences were the words

Miss Quint had been dreading: *Will be returning Tuesday eve. I assume all is well. Kind regards, Mr. H.*

Miss Quint was not the sort of person to swear. "Oh knickers!" she said, reaching for a chocolate cookie.

Chapter Twelve

Arthur Manages

The next morning, Arthur skidded to a stop outside the bookshop. He flung his bike on the sidewalk and knocked insistently on the door until his knuckles hurt. The reason for his urgency was the call from Miss Quint. She had telephoned his house very early that morning, before any of the Goodenoughs were up, and left a rambling, incoherent message on the answering machine. He had recognized her voice, high and hysterical though it had been, and he heard her say his name and also the phrase "We're in for it." As it was a vacation week, Arthur was able to head straight over to Hardbattle Books without the worry that it would make him late for school.

He gave up knocking and pushed open the mailbox slot instead.

"Hello!" he yelled through the slender gap. "Is anyone there? Miss Quint, can you hear me? Are you all right?"

Arthur heard a muffled exclamation and saw a familiar

floral pattern pass across his vision. He recognized it as the print of the dress Miss Quint had been wearing the day before. There was the sound of a key turning in a lock. Arthur let go of the mailbox flap and waited for the door to open.

"Miss Quint, you look strange," he said. For a person who took pride in always dressing neatly, she had let her standards slip. She stood in the doorway, bleary-eyed. Her dress was creased, her hair was wild, and on one side of her face were telltale creases indicating she had been resting on something uncomfortable. Her appearance suggested to Arthur that she had not been to bed.

"Oh, Arthur!" said Miss Quint dramatically. She beckoned him inside. "We're in trouble."

"What have you done now?" asked Arthur, lingering warily in the doorway. "You haven't been making any more wishes—"

"No. Perish the thought!" Miss Quint said, shuddering. "It's Mr. Hardbattle. He's been in touch. He's coming home tomorrow, and from what he said in his postcard, I don't think the places he's seen have been much good."

"What a bummer!" said Arthur.

"He's pinning his hopes on us," yammered a panic-stricken Miss Quint, "and we haven't gotten our act together and looked around that farm yet!"

Like Miss Quint, Arthur felt at fault. He had had no

choice but to go to school during the week, and on Saturday his schedule had been full (what with the visit to his granny's and the tea party), but Arthur knew, just as Miss Quint did, that Sunday had been free, and that they should have spent it checking out the farm at Thornwick instead of at the beach having fun.

"We should not have left it so late," he said. "But I don't really get why you called in such a tizzy. We've still got time to go to the farm."

"You've forgotten about our other problem," said Miss Quint. "Our four other problems, to be precise."

"Oh, you mean the book characters."

Miss Quint nodded and wrung her hands. "Can you imagine what Mr. Hardbattle will say when he finds out about Susan and the rest of them? I've been thinking that we might try to conceal them in the attic, but I can't see Mr. Claggitt being cooperative. He's too outdoorsy to agree to being penned in."

"Ah! It's all making sense now," said Arthur. "*They're* the reason why you're in such a state and phoned my house so early this morning! You're scared of Mr. Hardbattle finding out that you broke his rules." Arthur heaved a sigh of relief, which turned into an enormous yawn. "I don't understand why you're making such a fuss. All we've got to do is find their books and do some unwishing."

"That's easy to say, young man, but not so easy to

do," said Miss Quint. She pulled her fingers through her unkempt hair, giving herself a crooked part.

"Yeah, all right," accepted Arthur, finally condescending to step inside the shop. "It might take some work to find those books, but it wasn't worth dragging me out of bed. I rode really fast to get here, and I haven't even had breakfast yet. Mom was going to make pancakes. We hardly ever have those . . ."

Arthur stopped grumbling and gazed around the shop in amazement. It was in total disarray. Books had been tossed on the floor and wedged into places they did not fit. They were no longer arranged in any logical order. It looked as if a whirlwind had swept through the shop, leaving a scene of devastation in its wake.

"Oh, Miss Quint!" said Arthur, turning with his mouth hanging open. His eyes rested on Trunk, who seemed to be just as shocked as he was. The elephant stood at the nearest end of his shelf, immobile and blank faced, with his trunk outstretched.

"This is *bad*," said Arthur. "Why didn't you say so? The magic's really flipped out this time. It must have made one heck of a racket last night. No wonder you look as if you haven't slept."

"I haven't!" said Miss Quint. "I've been awake for hours. You see, the magic didn't make this mess. I did."

"You!" blustered Arthur, glaring at her angrily. "What on earth for? Have you gone nuts? It's lucky Mr.

Hardbattle's not back yet. He'd have a fit if he knew what you'd done."

"Don't tell him! You must not tell him!" pleaded Miss Quint. She sank to the floor and started to cry, fishing up her sleeve for a handkerchief. "I panicked!" she wailed. "I've been looking for those blessed books all night long. They're not here, Arthur. I'm certain of it. I've searched *everywhere*. There isn't a nook or a cranny that I haven't poked around in. *Tinseltown Ticket*, *Champagne for Geraldine*, *Rockfall!*, and *High Jinks* must all have been sold."

"If we'd sold them we would have written their sales in the ledger," pointed out Arthur.

"They must have been stolen, then," Miss Quint said miserably.

"Stolen? No!" said Arthur, aghast. "Borrowed, maybe."

"Whatever's become of them, they're gone!" Miss Quint lamented. She screwed up her face and dissolved into tears. The sight of Miss Quint falling apart was far more alarming to Arthur than seeing the bookshop a terrible mess.

"Don't cry!" he said, patting her shoulder awkwardly. He began to collect some books from the floor. "We'll have this place tidied up in no time, and things will sort themselves out. You'll see."

Miss Quint sobbed a little louder. She did not show

that she appreciated Arthur's attempts to comfort her. Nor did she raise a finger to help him pick up the books. She seemed determined to sink into a deep depression.

Trunk was still in a catatonic state, standing as rigidly as a pointer dog that had just scented a pheasant.

"Why don't you have a word with poor old Trunk?" said Arthur. "He's not looking well. He could use some cheering up."

Miss Quint shook her head and did not get up. Fearing that she might stay slumped on the floor in a wretched heap for the remainder of the morning, Arthur made further suggestions to encourage her to get to her feet. "Perhaps you'd feel better if you took a bath or changed your clothes or had something to eat," he offered brightly.

"I'm not hungry," mumbled Miss Quint. "After supper I ate a whole package of chocolate cookies."

"Suit yourself!" said Arthur, his patience exhausted. He turned his back on her and stooped to retrieve some books from under a chair. There was only an hour and a half until the shop was due to open, and he could not afford to waste any more time attempting to perk up Miss Quint.

Arthur tried to ignore his growling stomach and immersed himself in his back-breaking task. The magic did not assist him. In fact, it made his job harder by changing the weight of the books—they were either so heavy he could barely lift them or so light they kept floating out of his reach. If he lost his temper, the magic reacted by irritating him even more. He was dive-bombed by the ducks, assailed by the rubber bands, and at one point rooted to the spot while two dozen thumbtacks played tag around his feet. Gradually he learned that if he ignored the magic's hijinks, it was far more likely to leave him alone.

By a quarter to nine the shop was remarkably neat, and Arthur felt he deserved a medal as well as a giant stack of pancakes. As he looked around, reflecting upon his achievement, he noticed that Miss Quint had gone. Avoiding the thumbtacks, which had formed a circle and were whizzing counterclockwise at a mesmerizing speed, he stepped wearily up the staircase in search of some breakfast.

The smell of burned toast came from the kitchen. When Arthur went in, he found Jimmy, Mr. Claggitt, and Mrs. Voysey-Brown seated at the table. They were grasping cutlery impatiently and Susan was scurrying between them with a plate of charred bread in her hand.

"Lightly toasted, I said, not singed!" grumbled Mr. Claggitt, smearing his toast with great lumps of marmalade.

Jimmy laughed, took a slice, and scraped off the worst of the burned bits with a knife. "Just like me ma used to make!" he said.

"No, thank you," said Mrs. Voysey-Brown when Susan held out the plate to her. "Darling, I feel I should point out that cooking is not your thing. Be an angel and open a window, would you? Before we all expire from the fumes."

They were delighted to see Arthur.

"Any good with a frying pan?" Mr. Claggitt asked him. "The Quint woman's deserted us, and Susie's efforts aren't cutting it."

Having spent the best part of an hour cleaning up the bookshop on his own, the last thing Arthur wanted to do was to cook breakfast for everyone.

"How about some cereal?" he said, producing a box from a cupboard and filling a jug with milk from the fridge. He noticed Susan's downcast face and gave her a friendly nudge.

"Don't let them get to you, Suze," Arthur whispered. "You just need some practice, that's all."

When breakfast was almost over and the remnants of the toast had been crunched up by Scallywag, Miss Quint appeared at the kitchen door. She had changed into her nightgown, and looked jaded and gray. "You'll amuse yourselves, won't you?" she mumbled tiredly. "I'm off to bed. I'm exhausted."

Leaving the others to mutter discontentedly, Arthur followed Miss Quint onto the landing and grabbed her arm. "Who's going to open the shop?" he asked.

Miss Quint focused her red-rimmed eyes on Arthur. "Won't be good for anything till I've had some sleep," she said. "Shop'll have to stay closed. Can't be helped."

Arthur groaned. Miss Quint's ill-timed nap meant the shop would be unmanned *and* their trip to the farmhouse would have to be postponed *again*. The excursion to Thornwick could be put off until the next morning, but losing a day's profits seemed stupid when every penny was so important.

"Where are the keys, Miss Quint?" Arthur asked suddenly. "Me and Suze and Jimmy, maybe . . . we can look after the shop."

Miss Quint led Arthur along the landing to the broom closet. Not wishing to sleep in the chair downstairs during daylight hours, she had transformed the closet into her bedroom. Three sofa cushions from the couch served as her mattress, and draped over these was a sleeping bag.

After quickly rummaging through the pockets of her dress (which dangled from a hanger on the doorknob), Miss Quint found the shop keys and pressed them into Arthur's hands. "Do whaddever you want," she said thickly and gestured that he should go.

Arthur unlocked the door at nine o'clock sharp and sat down at the desk, awaiting the first customer. The cash register occupied the left-hand side of the desk. Next to it was the ledger in which every sale was recorded. Lined up by an inkwell were the thumbtacks, staples, and assorted writing implements. Arthur picked up a pencil, intending to play tic-tac-toe with himself, but the pencil would only write Latin words and phrases, so he swapped it for a crayon that wasn't as headstrong.

Susan felt purposeless without Miss Quint to follow around, and when Arthur asked her if she would give him a hand in the shop, Susan said yes right away. Showing gumption that she had not displayed before, she started to put some maps in numerical order. Arthur had hoped that the other three would help out too, but they revealed soon after breakfast that they had other plans.

Jimmy, Mr. Claggitt, and Mrs. Voysey-Brown said they were going to spend the day touring the sights of Plumford. Arthur considered this a bad idea. He hated the thought of the three book characters roaming the town unchaperoned, but there was little he could do to stop them. He argued that, apart from a Saxon church and a bungalow that had been the birthplace of a famous comedienne, there was nothing of interest to visit. However, the three grown-ups would not be persuaded to change their minds.

Mr. Claggitt wrenched open the door with a powerful tug, causing the bell to reverberate like an alarm. "Best foot forward!" he said determinedly, as if he were setting out on an expedition rather than a walk around a small English town.

"Good-bye!" called Arthur. "Be careful, won't you? Don't get lost!"

Business was not brisk in the bookshop. By midday, Arthur had served one person, who asked if the shop stocked washing machines. After lunch, Arthur was inspired to give the windows a wipe so that people passing by would be more likely to come in. This proved a successful ploy. Four customers entered the shop in the afternoon. One returned a book for a refund, one purchased a book on trains, and the other two (a husband and wife) were scared away by a rug, which kept altering its pattern while they were looking for a book on stamps.

By closing time, Arthur had decided that a career in retail was not for him. He glared enviously when the three sightseers returned in a buoyant mood. Mrs. Voysey-Brown's neck was swathed in a new silk scarf and the two men sported gold-colored wristwatches. It seemed that fictional money was accepted in Plumford's stores just as readily as the regular kind.

Miss Quint surfaced after nightfall, by which time Arthur had gone home and Susan had put herself to bed.

The next day, Arthur detected a change in Miss Quint. She was waiting at the door of the shop to let him in when he turned up at a quarter to nine. She welcomed him with her arms outstretched; Arthur retreated swiftly, not wishing to receive a hug. Only when the threat of an embrace had subsided did he feel it was safe to draw closer.

"I'm sorry, Arthur!" Miss Quint said. "I was a nitwit yesterday, wasn't I?"

"Not a nitwit, exactly," said Arthur.

"I let you and Susan run the shop all by yourselves. A couple of kids!" she said. "It wasn't right."

With his hands stuffed in his pockets, Arthur leaned against the doorpost. "We managed," he said nonchalantly. "We sold one book and a lady brought one back. There were holes in all the pages. Pin-sized holes."

Miss Quint frowned. "Those thumbtacks are devils. I've half a mind to lock them away. There's an old tin in the kitchen that would hold them—"

"Please don't!" said Arthur. "They wouldn't like that. The magic was well behaved yesterday, on the whole."

"Oh, all right," Miss Quint conceded. "I promise I won't lock them up." She gave his shoulder a friendly squeeze. "I've been a ninny. I'll admit that. Worrying about the trouble I'll be in when Mr. Hardbattle gets back from his travels! I should have remembered what a nice man he is. Not the sort to blow his top. Thank heavens I went to my meeting of the Women's Institute last night. They set me straight. Gave me a good talking to."

"You told your friends about the shop?" asked Arthur.

He stopped leaning against the door and stood up straight. "You explained about the magic? And they believed you?"

"I mentioned bits and pieces," Miss Quint told him.

When Arthur had tried to tell his friends at school about the magic, they laughed in his face and said he was crazy.

"And they didn't think you were nuts?" he asked.

"Naturally not," replied Miss Quint. "They were very supportive, in fact."

Precisely what had been said at the meeting was never disclosed because, at that moment, Susan appeared at Miss Quint's shoulder, holding a cardboard box in her arms and Scallywag on a leash.

"Ah, there you are!" Miss Quint said. She moved the children and dog out of the shop and onto the sidewalk.

"What's in the box?" asked Arthur.

"Books, of course," replied Miss Quint. She felt in her pocket for the door key. "They need to be delivered to a house in Rabbit's Cross. I thought it'd be nice if we all went, and on the way back we paid a visit to a friend in the countryside—"

"Mrs. Carruthers at Down-the-Ages Farm!" cried Arthur.

Miss Quint winked at Arthur, and Arthur winked back.

Susan, who was standing between the pair of them,

realized that something had happened that she had not understood. "Why did you and Arthur twitch your eyes like that?" she asked.

"It's because we know a secret," said Miss Quint as she slotted the key in the lock.

"Can't we tell her?" Arthur begged.

Miss Quint raised her eyebrows at Arthur and turned to give Susan a long, hard look. "As you're a good girl, and not the type to tattle, Arthur and I will tell you all about it on the way."

Overjoyed, Susan skipped on the spot. "Ooh! Thank you! I won't spill the beans. That's a promise, truly it is!"

Arthur chuckled to himself. He felt glad. By now, he considered Susan a friend, and it seemed unfair to keep the problem of the magic a secret from her. As long as Susan did not learn that the magic had been responsible for bringing her to life, he did not think that involving her in their project would be ill-advised.

Letting his gaze wander from Susan's flushed, excited face, Arthur glanced to his left, and his smile faded rapidly.

"Miss Quint," he asked in a puzzled voice, "where's the van?"

"Right there in the road where I parked it," replied Miss Quint, twisting the door key with a flourish and dropping it into her pocket.

"Um . . . it's *not*," said Arthur.

Annoyed at having her word doubted, Miss Quint

looked up. She gasped with shock when she saw the empty portion of road next to the curb.

"Oh my goodness!" she exclaimed. "It's been stolen!"

Chapter Thirteen

Ups and Downs

"Mr. Hardbattle worships that van!" Miss Quint said. She clapped her hand to her mouth in dismay and spoke through her fingers. "He'll blame me. He will! He'll spread it around that I'm useless. He'll kick me out and no one else will want to employ me. If Mirabel won't have me back, I'll be destitute!"

Arthur shook her elbow. "Miss Quint, you're getting ahead of yourself. A minute ago you were saying how nice and kind Mr. Hardbattle is. It's not your fault the van's been stolen."

Susan set down the box of books on the sidewalk, and knelt beside Scallywag to give her a pat. "Gosh!" she said. "What rotten luck! We won't be going to see your friend at Down-the-Ages Farm, now, will we?"

Arthur smiled at her sadly. "Not unless we all sprout wings and fly there, we won't," he said.

"Like pigeons?" said Susan. "Golly, wouldn't that be fun? I wish I did have wings. I wish . . ."

Almost before the words had left her mouth, Susan bent one arm behind her back and began to scratch her shoulder blades. "Ooh! I think I've been bitten by something. I can feel lumps," she said.

"No, it couldn't happen," said Arthur. "We're out of the shop. You locked the door." He grimaced at Miss Quint and she glared angrily back at him.

"Why did you have to put that idea in her head?" scolded Miss Quint as she peered at Susan's back. Two knoblike growths had burst through Susan's dress.

"Me?" said Arthur. "What about you? Why didn't you tell her she shouldn't wish?"

They stared at each other stubbornly and then, without saying a word, they seemed to accept that awarding blame would not achieve anything.

"How do you think it could have happened?" asked Miss Quint. "Did the magic squirm through the keyhole?"

"Perhaps it was in the drainpipe," said Arthur, "or maybe a cloud of magic wafted outside when you closed the door."

Susan stood up. She twisted her neck as far as it would go in order to see the peculiar bony stems that were protruding from her back. They grew thicker and longer, with threads swelling along them like teeth on a comb. "What are those horrid things?" she asked, biting her lip and blinking back tears. "Ooh, they hurt like the dickens. Take them off!"

"They're wings, dear," Miss Quint said as the slim, pale threads blossomed into tawny feathers. Scallywag backed away from Susan, barking huskily.

The wings grew at a staggering pace, and in no time they were beautifully curved and fully formed. Each wing was huge, easily matching Susan's height. The feathers were the same shade of brown as her hair, not unlike an eagle's.

"You wished for them," explained Arthur to Susan. "Say you've changed your mind. Unwish them quickly, Suze, before they fly away with you."

"T-take them off me!" begged Susan as the wings flexed and began to flap. They displaced so much air that Arthur was nearly knocked off his feet.

Susan was frightened. She gulped and sniffed while tears began to stream down her cheeks. Arthur and Miss Quint had to shout to make themselves heard above the rasping, rhythmic wing beats. They unwished as earnestly as they could, but it did not appear to have any effect. Nevertheless, they kept trying.

The wings flapped harder. Susan gave a high-pitched scream as both feet lifted off the pavement. Jerking her roughly with every beat, the wings took her higher. Her heel clipped the top of a mailbox and she tried to catch hold of a lamppost. Moments later her toes loosened some roof tiles, and then there was nothing above her but sky.

"Stop unwishing!" yelled Arthur, clutching Miss Quint's arm and gazing above him at Susan's shrinking figure. "She's too far up. If we unwish her wings now, she'll never survive the drop!"

They watched in helpless wonder as the great brown wings carried Susan in her gingham dress and sandaled feet over the rooftops of Plumford and out of sight.

"We'll have to go after her," said Arthur, his face taut with worry. "Do you think we should wish for wings too?"

"No," Miss Quint said firmly. "We'll go on the bus."

Miss Quint unfastened her handbag and, after delving deeply, she drew out a crumpled bus schedule and consulted it. "Aha!" she said. "The 48A stops at Thornwick. Down-the-Ages Farm is on the outskirts of the village, and that's where the wings will have taken her."

The bus was not due at the stop at the end of the road for seven minutes, so Arthur judged that there would be time to run inside the shop and tell the others where he, Miss Quint, and Susan would be for the rest of the morning. However, on reaching the second floor, he found the kitchen empty. Too well mannered to wake them up, Arthur scribbled a message on the back of an envelope and propped it against the bread box. He thought about calling the police to report the stolen van but decided that it might cause too much of a delay. Catching the bus to Thornwick was what mattered most of all. A missing van was a petty crime compared with Susan's abduction.

Miss Quint paid the bus fare (she had been to the bank and refilled her wallet). They chose seats near the window so they would have a better chance of catching sight of Susan in the sky. Scallywag whined until Arthur pulled her onto his lap. The ride was a bumpy one, but neither Miss Quint nor Arthur complained. They figured their journey must be arguably more comfortable than Susan's.

In actual fact, once Susan had recovered from the shock of her own pair of wings transporting her into the atmosphere, she stopped crying and started to enjoy herself. Having no tail feathers (for she had not wished for those) meant that the flight was not smooth, but her wings did their best to keep her the right way up and swooped to avoid wisps of cloud, which were cold and clammy, and soared when they found an amenable current of air. It was freezing cold in the sky, and the wind's gusts pummeled her and filled her ears with noise, but Susan had never felt more alive. When she summoned the courage to look below her, the view of all the fields and lakes and houses reduced to geometric shapes and bold, stark colors made her eyes swim with tears of delight. Flying, she decided, was not so very different from riding on a swing, only there were no chains and no plastic seat, and the distance from the ground was rather more awe inspiring.

Susan's fear returned when she began to lose height. As the wings took her downward, the minuscule features of the landscape grew larger and more recognizable, and she started to dwell upon both the perilous manner in which she was hanging in the sky and the scary realization that she would soon be landing.

With a stomach-turning dive and a flurry of wing beats, Susan's wings delivered her to the ground. They avoided a flock of sheep, an oak tree, and a roof of thatch, but it was not a textbook landing by any means. As her toes touched down, Susan panicked, tripped, and tumbled head over heels. Fortunately for her pride, there was no one nearby to witness her clumsiness. Susan lay still for a moment and caught her breath, then she patted herself all over and was relieved to find that all her limbs were intact.

When Susan got up from the patch of grass, her wings folded against her back. She looked around curiously to see where she had arrived.

Not far away was a large white, timber-framed building, which had a plump, thatched roof and tiny windows, and closer still was a giant tree with a sturdy trunk and tapering branches, partly obscured by clusters of frilly light green leaves.

Susan decided to head for the house. It stood to reason that where there was a building there would be people, and if Susan was to find out where she had landed and how she could get home again, she would need to ask someone for help. Susan guessed that she could not rely on the wings to return her to Meadow Street. Although they were joined to her body, they moved of their own accord, and she could not be sure they would do as she asked.

Encumbered by her huge wings, Susan made her way across the field, through a gate, and into a cottage garden. She walked along a dirt path, past beds of unruly plants, until she reached a wooden door that was ajar. Susan had to open it wide before she could squeeze herself and her wings through the narrow entranceway.

Inside she found a dark, low-ceilinged room with a flagstone floor. There was a bench, a table, a fireplace, and not much else. The lack of possessions made Susan think that the people who lived in the house must be poor. She was just about to call out and ask if anyone was home when a tall, bearded man ducked under a doorjamb and took a few steps into the room. He froze when he saw Susan and consulted his watch.

"You're early!" he said. "Make yourself scarce, kid, and come back in half an hour, okay?"

Susan was too astonished to move. She did not understand why this man had been expecting her. Could he have mistaken her for someone else?

"Kid? What kid?" called another voice. "Dave! Them goats got loose again or what?" At first all that Susan saw was a linen cap. Then a woman in a brown dress bustled into view.

"Gawd!" she said when she clapped eyes on Susan. "Where'd you spring from? It can't be ten o'clock!"

"It's not," said Dave, sitting down on the bench, "so, please, Lind, don't pester me to show this little girl around." He swung his long legs up onto the table and crossed his ankles.

"But, Dave—" said the woman, shooting Susan a regretful look.

With a shrug, Dave reached inside his tan vest, pulled out a newspaper, and opened it up. "Listen, just because that nutcase Gary decides to let someone in early, it doesn't mean we've got to start work, all right?"

Dismayed by the couple's less than friendly welcome, Susan clasped and unclasped her hands. "I'll go, okay?" she asked.

"No, don't be silly!" Lind took Susan's hand. With a nod of her head, she gestured toward Dave, whose face was obscured by his newspaper. "Don't you pay any mind to that old grump! Come on, hon, I'll show you around the farm."

"This is a farm?" cried Susan. "Golly! Do you mean to say that this is *Down-the-Ages* Farm?"

Lind led Susan toward the door. "Well, course it is, babe!" she said. "Don't you know where you've been brought?"

As they stepped outside, swapping the dimly lit room for bright sunshine, Lind noticed Susan's wings for the first time. "Wow!" she said. "They're neat. My little niece has got a pair too."

Susan was amazed to hear that someone else had wings. "I thought I was the only one," she said.

"Nope, wings are popular with little girls," Lind told her. "Emily's are pink with sparkly glitter. She's got a tiara to match—and a wand. Wears them all the time. Even to the dentist's."

"Really?" said Susan, suddenly feeling less self-conscious.

They walked a little way before pausing by a clump of mint where the path divided into two.

"Now," said Lind, squeezing Susan's hand. "What do you want to try first, hon? Being pulled on a cart by a draft horse or making some cheese?"

Chapter fourteen

A Stinging Attack

Susan's tour of Down-the-Ages Farm lasted half an hour, and by the end of it she found that she had learned a lot. She knew, for instance, that Lind was short for Lindsey. She also knew that Dave and Lind did not live on the farm and were not husband and wife, as Susan had supposed. The farm was a museum. It was owned by a man called Dr. Godfrey Webb and had been opened to demonstrate to its visitors what life on a farm had been like down the ages (hence the farm's name). Lind and Dave were employed by Dr. Webb to impersonate a couple from centuries past, and they spent their working week showing members of the public around the various rooms or "time zones" in the farmhouse. The hall was medieval, the kitchen late Tudor, and upstairs mainly Victorian. The museum was open six days a week between the hours of ten and four, teas were served in the granary, and dogs were allowed on leashes.

Throughout Susan's tour, she was the museum's only

visitor. She walked two-thirds of the site with Lind, stopping at the cattle shed that housed two oxen, the pigsty where four Tamworths rooted in their troughs, the stables where the draft horses lived, and the dairy where butter and cheese were made. At ten o'clock, Gary, who sat in a shed at the museum's entrance, opened the shutters and let the visitors in. Muttering her apologies, Lind went back to the farmhouse and Susan continued the walk around the farm on her own.

She liked the goats but was fonder of the sheep, and she spent a good long while watching the lambs wriggling their tails and leaping around in a madcap manner. It was the bees, however, that Susan liked the best.

The beekeeper, whose name was Pam, told Susan that the bees' cone-shaped homes were called hives and that bees knew when bad weather was coming and that bees would only sting you if you made them angry.

Pam asked Susan about her wings and when Susan told her how they had grown, she did not seem surprised. "I thought as much," Pam said. "It's no good to make wishes in the wrong sort of places. I know that from experience. When I was ten, I wished for chocolate fingers and I think you can guess what happened . . ."

Apart from Susan, the only visitors to Down-the-Ages Farm were two families with children and an old, white-haired couple with a rotund dog. None of the adults, apart from Lind and Pam, made any remarks about

Susan's wings, although she did get the feeling from time to time that alarmed looks were being cast in her direction. Without exception the children found the wings deeply fascinating, and one small boy named Jarrett thought he had the right to tug at them and to yank out the longest, most lustrous feathers.

"You're being a pest," Susan hissed at him. "Go away, little boy!"

It seemed that Jarrett was not only a nuisance to Susan. All around the farm she heard his mother shouting, "Jarrett, don't touch that!" and "Jarrett, get down! You'll hurt yourself!" and "Jarrett, I won't tell you again!" except, of course, she did, because Jarrett was a boy who did exactly what he wanted and never took any notice of what his mother said.

When Susan had seen everything, she decided to seek out Lind and ask her how she might get home. On her way to the farmhouse, Susan passed the granary and wished that she had some money to spend on a cup of tea and a cinnamon bun.

Then, for the second time that day, her wish came true.

"There she is!" shrieked a voice, and Susan looked across the field to see Miss Quint waving her hands and Arthur and Scallywag racing toward her along a dirt road. Scallywag reached Susan first, but Arthur was not far behind.

"You all right?" asked Arthur.

Beaming, Susan said, "Yes, thanks. Boy, am I glad to see you! How did you get here without the van?"

"We . . . took . . . a bus," said Miss Quint, who was slightly out of breath, not being quite as in shape as her companions. She kissed Susan's cheek and glanced around impatiently. "Where's this café, then? The man at the entrance told us about it. I think we all deserve to sit down and have a bite to eat."

Over three pots of tea and an equal number of cinnamon buns, Susan told the others about her flight and all that she had seen and heard at Down-the-Ages Farm. When she finished, it was Arthur's and Miss Quint's turn to speak. They described their journey by bus and admitted the reason why they had wanted to visit the farm in the first place.

They explained to Susan what magic was and that the magic in the bookshop needed to be moved elsewhere. They managed this in the time it took for Susan to eat her bun, and while she licked the icing off her fingers they told her of the advertisement, Mr. Hardbattle's trip, and the letter from Mrs. Carruthers. Susan was a trusting, impressionable girl, and she believed every word. She liked the idea of going on a quest.

"Can we find Mrs. Carruthers *now*?" asked Susan, taking one last sip from her teacup and rising out of her chair.

"Yeah, let's go!" said Arthur, following Susan's lead. "I don't think it'll be too hard to track her down."

They made the decision to split into two groups and reconvene twenty minutes later on a bench beside the hen house. Arthur agreed to comb the fields with Scallywag, and Miss Quint said that she and Susan would make inquiries in the farmhouse and the stables. When the time came to meet up on the bench, acute disappointment was etched on all their faces.

"I suppose this woman does exist," said Miss Quint, taking off her shoes and massaging her feet.

"They only know each other's *first* names," grumbled Arthur. "It's going to be tougher to find her than I thought."

They sat on the bench in dejected silence, watching the chickens scratching in the earth, when a shout rang out across the farm.

"Help me, someone! Jarrett's gone missing!"

Arthur, Miss Quint, and Susan rushed to help Jarrett's mother at once, and the other family, the couple with the dog, and Pam, Lind, and Dave, who had all been within earshot, sped to offer their assistance too.

Jarrett's mother was of the opinion that her son had been kidnapped, but this was shot down by the rest of the group, who had seen enough of Jarrett to be sure that no one in his or her right mind would want to go anywhere near the boy.

"Let's spread out and look for him," suggested Pam. "We've got fifty acres to cover, so we'll have to be as quick as we can. He's only five years old. He could be in danger."

"I don't know why I'm botherin' to help out," muttered Dave, striding toward the cattle shed. "That little kid put chewing gum in my beard."

As the group scattered, Susan remained where she was. She had had an ingenious thought and, as luck would have it, her wings had come up with exactly the same one. The best way to track down Jarrett in the fastest possible time was to carry out a search by air.

Susan's wings unfolded and shook themselves, and she braced herself to withstand the pull on her shoulder blades, which would come with every beat the wings made. The wings began to flap, stretching higher and wider until they had reached the required speed to lift Susan off the ground. None of the search party saw her take to the sky because they were far too busy looking in feeding troughs and behind hay bales for the missing boy.

When the wings judged that Susan had risen to a sufficient height, they started to sweep through the air in a wide circle over the farm.

She saw Arthur moving toward the sheep pen with Scallywag at his heels, and other human shapes that she could not identify all running from one place to the next like worker ants. She picked out the stables and the farmhouse, and then in the farthest corner of the plot she saw whom she was looking for.

Jarrett was standing by the beehives, striking at the air with his fists, and as the wings swooped to carry her lower, Susan could hear his yells and squeals. She recalled Pam's advice: that bees were calm creatures unless you made them angry. Over the course of the morning, Jarrett had annoyed almost everyone at the farm—and now it seemed as if he had met his match.

Before she could worry about the likelihood that she would be stung, the wings plunged her through a cloud of buzzing dots. Susan stretched out her arms and grabbed the tormented boy. Then the wings flapped hard, driving the bees away and taking Susan and Jarrett up into the clear, cold air, free from angry bees and their painful stings.

Holding on to Jarrett was not easy or pleasant. True to form, he was uncooperative—pinching and kicking Susan and shouting for his mom. Eventually, the horror of being high up stopped Jarrett from squirming, and his roars quieted to a murmur.

Luckily, the wings brought them to earth again within minutes. The landing was chaotic. Both children ended up lying on the ground with their limbs inelegantly splayed. Susan got to her feet first and seized Jarrett's hand so he could not run off and get into further mischief.

They had landed behind a barn, which was used to

store farm machinery. Susan walked around it, struggling to keep hold of Jarrett, who was straining to get away.

She spied Dave in the distance and waved to get his attention. Soon the others arrived. Jarrett's mother smothered him in kisses and cried over the red marks on her son's arms, which showed where the bees had vented their displeasure. She complained to Pam the beekeeper but met resistance.

"My bees aren't bad-tempered," insisted Pam. "They must have been provoked." She took hold of Jarrett's hand. "You come along with me, young man, and I'll put ointment on those stings. Maybe this little encounter will teach you to keep your hands to yourself in the future, eh?"

Not receiving the sympathy Jarrett felt was due to him, he thrust an accusing finger at Susan.

"That girl grabbed me and hurt my arms. Then she flew me up into the sky. If she'd dropped me I would've gone *splat*." Jarrett ended with a feeble attempt at a sob.

No one believed his claim (except Arthur, Miss Quint, and Pam, who stayed silent). The old couple shook their heads and muttered a rhyme about tattletales, and Dave lifted his lip in a sort of snarl. Lind glared and pushed up her sleeves, and a couple of children snickered.

"That's naughty!" said Jarrett's mother, turning on her son. "Well . . . all the other things you did today were naughty, but lying about this lovely girl who saved you from those bees is really, extremely naughty, Jarrett. Mommy isn't pleased with you."

Jarrett scowled and kicked a tuft of grass with the toe of his sneaker. As he was led away between Pam and his mom, he turned his head and stuck out his tongue at Susan.

"Do it back to him!" urged Arthur; so Susan did.

Later, when Pam found them to thank Susan for stopping Jarrett from being stung all over, she assumed that Miss Quint was Arthur's and Susan's mother.

"Your youngsters are a credit to you," said Pam, seizing Miss Quint's hand. "I'm Pam . . . Pam Carruthers, by the way."

"Mrs. Carruthers! You're Mrs. Carruthers? Woo-hoo! We've finally found you!" Arthur was so excited that he did a cartwheel—badly—almost kicking Susan in the face.

Pam was somewhat startled. "You've been looking for *me*?" she asked.

"Almost all morning!" said a beaming Miss Quint. Their handshake became more vigorous. "We're friends of Mr. Hardbattle, the owner of Hardbattle Books."

At the mention of Mr. Hardbattle's name, Pam's expression changed to one of elated surprise. "Good gracious!" she said. "The advertisement in *Farmers Weekly*! I should've guessed you had something to do with the bookshop when I met Susan! It's not every day you bump into a girl with magic wings!"

When all had been revealed, and Pam and Miss Quint had stopped laughing at Arthur's remark that their handshake might qualify as the longest one in history, Pam led them to a patch of woodland that was out of bounds to the public. In a clearing in the middle of the woods was a one-story cabin where a woodsman had once lived. Dr. Webb had the idea to include the cottage in the tour of the farm, but once he realized that lots of visitors traipsing through the woods would upset the woodland creatures, his idea, along with the planned renovation of the cottage, had been scrapped.

"What do you think of it?" asked Pam with a grin.

The cottage was small, but its roof was in good condition and its unglazed windows had shutters to keep out the wind and the rain. There was a well and an outhouse behind the cottage, and a garden overwhelmed by weeds.

"Ooh! Isn't it dark?" said Susan when Pam pushed open the door and everyone trooped inside.

Arthur and Miss Quint were complimentary as they walked from one room to the next. Not having realized they were looking for somewhere run-down, Susan was surprised to hear them rejoicing over the size of the spiders and laughing when a rickety old bedframe collapsed.

Their voices became livelier with every minute that passed, and when they had completed their tour of the cottage and emerged into the sunshine again, Arthur and Miss Quint could not contain their jubilation.

"Talk about filthy!" said Arthur. "That cottage was really dusty and there were hundreds of crawly things!"

"Quite unfit for human habitation," said Miss Quint. She turned to Pam and hugged her. "We're agreed: it's *perfect*!"

When possible dates for transferring the magic had been discussed, Pam borrowed the horse-drawn cart and took them to the bus stop, where they hopped on the express bus back to Plumford, which ran every hour. Sitting was uncomfortable for Susan, so she stood in the aisle and clung to a pole. She envied Arthur and Miss Quint. They had found seats together and were talking about the cottage and the look of joy that was bound to appear on Mr. Hardbattle's face when they revealed their marvelous news. Susan had to endure all the other passengers' stares. She was relieved when the bus reached the stop outside the toy store, which was only a short walk from Hardbattle Books.

"As soon as we get in, we'll unwish those darned wings," Miss Quint promised Susan as they stepped off the bus. "The magic's been left to its own devices for the whole morning, so it should be in a receptive mood."

"I'll be glad to be rid of them," said Susan, dragging her feet tiredly as she walked beside Miss Quint. "But I feel very lucky to have had the chance to fly. It scared the daylights out of me, but it was fun all the same."

Arthur was walking slightly ahead of the others

because Scallywag had sensed she was nearing home and had started to pull on the leash. "I think you were very brave today," Arthur told Susan over his shoulder.

"Do you?" said Susan. Her cheeks reddened. "Gosh!"

"After we've unwished the wings, I suppose we'd better call the police and tell them about Mr. Hardbattle's stolen van," said Arthur, walking backward for a few paces.

Miss Quint let out a groan. She had forgotten about the van. She had been on a high ever since she and Arthur had solved the problem of where to relocate the magic. She had even convinced herself that Mr. Hardbattle might be persuaded to overlook the fact that wishes had been made in the shop, contrary to his instructions. Knowing how much Mr. Hardbattle loved his van, however, Miss Quint realized that no amount of good news could make up for its disappearance. She was about to agree with Arthur that the police should be called when they turned into Meadow Street and saw a familiar bottle-green van parked outside the bookshop.

"Well, I never!" declared Miss Quint. "The thieves have brought it back!"

Chapter fifteen

Laying Down the Law

The van had a scratch on its hood, a dented hubcap, and a muddy bumper. Miss Quint was appalled at these discoveries because she knew how highly Mr. Hardbattle prized his vintage delivery vehicle. She guessed that it would take a great deal of detective work to find out the identity of the lowlife who had taken the van, but she turned out to be wrong. The culprits—there were three of them—owned up to the crime immediately without showing any remorse at all.

"But you're not insured, you don't know how to handle her, and, more important, you didn't ask!" railed Miss Quint.

The three law-breakers took no notice of her and continued with their card game. They had pulled up some chairs and were playing poker at Arthur's homework table.

"Texas Hold'em?" Mr. Claggitt asked his companions.

"Yep," said Jimmy, fanning the cards in his hand.

Miss Quint reached between the two men and snatched the keys to the van, which she had spied on the table soon after she set foot in the shop.

"It's tantamount to stealing," she told them sternly.

Mr. Claggitt stopped examining his cards to give Miss Quint a cursory glance. "Nonsense, woman!" he said. "We only borrowed it!"

"Borrowing implies that you gained my permission, which you most certainly *did not*," Miss Quint said. She broke off an irritated stare and stepped aside to let Arthur pass through the doorway and onto the street. He had been instructed to fetch a sponge and bucket of water from the kitchen and to do what he could to restore the shiny appearance of the van's front bumper.

"Really, lady!" said Jimmy, sorting his cards. "It ain't worth getting all worked up! We brought your van back, didn't we?"

"You did, but not in the same condition," Miss Quint pointed out. "And, for your information, the van isn't mine. It belongs to Mr. Hardbattle, the man who owns this shop."

"All this talk, and it ain't even hers!" Jimmy murmured to his friends, rudely rolling his eyes.

It was obvious from their behavior that they did not believe they had done anything wrong and were only too willing to forget the whole affair. But Miss Quint refused to be sidelined and would not let the matter rest. She insisted that the houseguests come clean and admit to her why they had taken the van.

"Mr. Claggitt here rose early and suggested that we drive into the country," said Mrs. Voysey-Brown in her trademark drawl. A smile thinned her lips at the remembrance of their adventure. "It was such fun being out and about when everyone else was tucked in bed!"

"It's habit," Mr. Claggitt said. "A good mountaineer's always up before sunrise. Finest part of the day."

"But what did you *do*?" asked Miss Quint.

Mr. Claggitt grunted. "Stretched our legs. Looked at the scenery."

"Had a look around some fancy homes," Jimmy said.

"And now we'd like to be left alone to get on with our game," said Mrs. Voysey-Brown, glaring coldly at Miss Quint. "So why don't you stop being such a frightful bore and make us something to eat?"

The trio began their card game, and Miss Quint's fighting spirit faded. "You're not to take it again," she told them, pocketing the keys. "Mr. Hardbattle's due to arrive home this evening, and I want him to find his van exactly where he left it!"

Cheerfully swinging an empty bucket, Arthur reentered the shop. He had scrubbed the front bumper of the van until it gleamed. When he had poured the dirty water out, he saw a glittering object in the gutter and picked it up.

"Anyone lost a piece of jewelry?" Arthur asked. He unfurled his fingers to show them his find. The brooch was in a bow shape, set with round, white gems.

"Ooh!" exclaimed Susan. "Isn't it pretty!"

"Are those diamonds?" asked Miss Quint. She bent to get a closer look, but before she could examine the brooch, a hand shot out and grabbed it.

"It's mine!" said Mrs. Voysey-Brown, and she pinned it to her dress.

The card game continued until, crowing triumphantly, Jimmy won the hand. He asked if anyone else wanted to join in the next game, and Arthur, who liked to play cards at school during break, told Jimmy to deal him in. He enjoyed playing poker, but he was less enamored with the game of fifty-two-card pick-up, which involved Jimmy throwing the whole deck of cards up in the air and telling Arthur to get down on the floor and pick them up. When they first met, Arthur thought Jimmy was funny, but after enduring his pranks and taunts for three straight days, Arthur had begun to tire of him.

While Arthur played cards, Miss Quint escorted Susan to the kitchen, where she checked her skin for beestings. Finding only one, Miss Quint dabbed the sore spot on Susan's knee with cool, white cream. Then she progressed to the much more difficult task of unwishing Susan's wings. She guessed they would have a greater chance of success if they concentrated their efforts in the areas of the bookshop where the largest, smelliest clusters of magic were to be found.

For their first attempt to get rid of the wings, Miss Quint stood Susan in the bathtub, where magic could always be counted upon to make a nuisance of itself (pulling out the plug when someone was having a bath was a favorite prank). Despite their best efforts, unwishing the wings in the tub did not work, so Susan and Miss Quint moved on to the pantry and afterward to a corner of the landing that smelled particularly rank. They also tried to get into the attic but found that it was locked.

It was only a matter of time before the magic began to interfere in the card games downstairs. Just as Arthur was about to lay down a royal straight that would have won him the game, the ace changed itself into a two; later when he had collected two queens, they skipped across the table and plunged back into the pack. Soon afterward, Arthur lost interest in playing and went in search of Susan. He found her leaning against the couch on the landing, both wings still attached.

"I thought you were going to unwish those," said Arthur, flopping down next to her. (Miss Quint had replaced the couch's seat cushions, fortunately.)

"We tried," said Susan. "We both did our darnedest."

"Given up, have you?" said Arthur. "Where's Miss Quint now?"

Susan flapped a hand in the direction of the kitchen.

"She's busy making sandwiches for Mrs. V-B and the rest of them. She said they didn't deserve to be fed and shouted at me when I tried to help."

"Don't take it personally," said Arthur to Susan. "It's not you she's mad at, it's that selfish bunch downstairs."

Stroking the ribbon on one of her braids between her forefinger and thumb, Susan nodded solemnly. "She's angry because they went off in the van," she said.

"Yes," agreed Arthur, "and she hasn't got much patience today, with Mr. Hardbattle coming home soon." He stared at Susan's wings and frowned. "It's going to be awkward enough to tell him about his four extra houseguests. Those wings of yours will be even more of a problem to explain. Let's try to get rid of them, shall we?"

Arthur was inspired to stand Susan on the stair that turned to custard from time to time, and it was here that the magic finally yielded to their demands and took away the wings. It was a long, drawn-out process, each wing vanishing one feather at a time. When her ordeal was over, Susan was left with two gaping holes in the back of her dress, so they went to Miss Quint, who got her needle and thread and sewed them up. She did the best she could, but the stitches looked messy and they wrinkled the material. Miss Quint promised that, after their meal, she and Susan would go to a thrift shop to buy Susan some new clothes.

"What time did Mr. Hardbattle say he'd be home?" asked Arthur.

Miss Quint did not seem pleased to be reminded. "His postcard said in the evening," she said. Then she pulled Arthur to one side and lowered her voice. "I've been thinking, Arthur . . . I'm going to tell him that Susan is my niece, and the others are friends of mine from out of town."

Arthur did not like the idea of lying to Mr. Hardbattle. "Couldn't we just tell him the truth? Okay, he'll be annoyed when he realizes we've broken his rules, but when he sees the fine place we've found for the magic, he's bound to forgive us."

Miss Quint was skeptical of Arthur's plan. "We'll see," she said uncertainly, "but whatever we tell him, that little trio will have to improve their manners. Mr. Hardbattle won't let them stay if they act all high and mighty."

Having missed lunch, they had a little snack at three thirty, which was eaten in a tense, strained atmosphere. When the last morsel had been consumed, Miss Quint asked for everyone's attention and unfolded a list of dos and don'ts that she had compiled after her conversation with Arthur.

"Just lately," she told them, eyeing the adults stonily, "I have noticed that certain members of the household have been getting rather uppity. You may be staying as guests here, but that does not give you license to do whatever you want."

There was an uncomfortable silence. A bulging vein pulsed on Mr. Claggitt's forehead. Next to him, Mrs. Voysey-Brown inspected her nails. Farther down the table, between Arthur and Susan, Jimmy attempted to balance a teaspoon on the rim of his cup, giving the impression that he was not listening.

"I've drawn up a list of rules," Miss Quint said, "which I will pin to the cupboard above the sink. It would be in your best interests to read them. You've had it easy for far too long. From now on, I'll expect you to help with the cooking and cleaning, and the making of the beds, and on no occasion will you be permitted to get behind the wheel of Mr. Hardbattle's van."

Miss Quint's announcement was greeted with several murderous looks. Then Mr. Claggitt stood up. Muttering under his breath, he began to clear the table, scooping up armfuls of plates and cups and dumping them in the sink. He turned on the faucet, and water poured from them in gleaming rods. Miss Quint's apron would not fit around his middle and the rubber gloves split as soon as he tried to put them on.

"Here's a dishtowel for each of you," Miss Quint said, handing a linen cloth to Jimmy and Mrs. Voysey-Brown. Jimmy grinned and draped his around his shoulders like a cape, but Mrs. Voysey-Brown was more reluctant and would handle her towel only with the tips of one finger and thumb.

Leaving them to their chore, Miss Quint led Arthur and Susan downstairs. The children were a little in awe of Miss Quint after her showdown with the three grown-ups, and they hardly dared to open their mouths.

"What's up with you two? Cat got your tongues?" Miss Quint said when they reached the shop floor.

They both shook their heads and Susan giggled nervously.

"That was some talking-to you gave them," said Arthur.

Miss Quint seemed flattered by Arthur's remark. She smiled self-righteously and primped her hair so that it curled neatly against the collar of her blouse. "Yes," she said. "It went pretty well, I thought. It was high time I stopped pandering to those idlers and told them what was what."

She walked to the door and unlocked it, then turned over the sign, which told the public that they were open.

Susan followed behind her as if she were Miss Quint's shadow and, when she got up the nerve, she tugged on the woman's sleeve.

"Miss Quint," she said, "might we go shopping for my new outfit now?"

"Yes, I think so," said Miss Quint. She glanced around the shop to check that it was tidy enough for customers to be able to browse with ease. "Will you be all right on your own, Arthur?" she asked. "We won't be more than an hour."

Arthur assured them that he was perfectly capable of managing without them, and Scallywag banged her tail against a table leg to communicate that she would be on hand should her canine skills be required.

Arthur was quite happy to be left in the bookshop on his own. It gave him a feeling of importance. At home he was the third of six children and he had siblings who were funnier, smarter, and cuter than he was. At school he felt even more ordinary. In a class of thirty-one, there was nothing about his average grades or his modest athletic ability to make him stand out. However, in Hardbattle Books on this particular afternoon, Arthur was solely in charge. It was possible, in the space of an hour, that customers might come in, and if they had a question, Arthur was the one whom they would need to rely on to answer it. He felt calm, confident, and ready for anything.

When the bell jingle-jangled, his reactions were even faster than Trunk's. He jumped to his feet and waited to see if the customer would ask for assistance. Faintly, through the ceiling, he heard the sound of breaking china, which told him that the others had not yet finished the dishwashing.

"I'm looking for a book," said the customer, getting

straight to the point. "The title's . . . oh, my sainted aunt!" The man blundered forward and covered his mouth. "GOODENOUGH!" he bellowed. "WHAT IN HEAVEN'S NAME ARE YOU DOING BEHIND THAT DESK, BOY?"

Arthur came close to wishing that the ground would swallow him up. The customer that he had been so looking forward to helping was none other than Mr. Beaglehole, his least favorite teacher.

Chapter Sixteen

From Bad to Worse

Scallywag would not stop growling. She did not have to be told that the man who had come into the shop was not a nice fellow at all. She objected to the thumps his boots made on the floor and the cloying, musky smell that oozed through his clothes. When he leaned over her master's desk and made loud, angry noises at the kind boy who took her for walks, Scallywag came very close to sinking her teeth into the man's leg.

"Steady!" murmured Arthur. He placed his hand on Scallywag's head and her growl acquired a less threatening tone. Mr. Beaglehole was not the sort of man you wanted to mess with. If Scallywag's teeth so much as brushed against Mr. Beaglehole's jeans, Arthur had no doubt that he would drag Scallywag down to the police station, where he would insist that he had been savaged by a dangerous dog.

"Come out from behind that desk, Goodenough!"

commanded Mr. Beaglehole, wrinkling his clean-shaven face into a sneer.

Arthur might have obeyed him if Scallywag had not been sitting, firmly and loyally, on his feet, preventing him from taking even the smallest step in any direction. "I . . . I'd prefer to stay here," said Arthur, which was the truth. It made him feel more secure to have a three-foot-wide piece of furniture between himself and his overbearing teacher.

Mr. Beaglehole folded his muscular arms and shot Arthur a disconcerting smile. "I suppose you think you can do as you please because we're not at school?"

Arthur found the courage to nod. As Mr. Beaglehole so helpfully pointed out, teachers had no power over their pupils outside the school gates. Arthur started to feel a bit braver. His teacher was not wearing his usual school attire of slacks, a short-sleeved shirt, and a stripy tie. Dressed in jeans and a T-shirt, Mr. Beaglehole was slightly less intimidating.

"Where's the real assistant?" barked Mr. Beaglehole.

Arthur drew himself up to his full height. "I can help you if you have a question," he said.

Mr. Beaglehole snorted with laughter. "You?" he said. "A pimply little twelve-year-old?" Abruptly, Mr. Beaglehole's scornful smile disappeared. "I've changed my mind," he said. "I demand to see the manager. It's shameful to keep a customer waiting, and I'd also like a word with him about the smell in here. Rotten eggs, if I'm not mistaken. Very unhygienic."

Scallywag continued to growl, her body trembling against Arthur's shins.

"The manager's away," said Arthur coolly, "and I'm minding the shop for Miss Quint because she had to step out. Oh, and you got my age wrong. I'm thirteen."

Mr. Beaglehole breathed in sharply. "Insolent twit!" he snarled. "You won't be as flippant on Monday when I reveal the results of that last test I gave you. In the meantime, I want to know if you have a particular book. It's called *The Future Is Nuclear* by Aidan Schmidt."

Arthur was not prepared to unseat Scallywag in order to search for a book for a man he despised. "We don't have that," said Arthur as confidently as he could.

"I'd like it ordered in that case," said Mr. Beaglehole. He did not offer to pay up front; instead he moved toward the door. He paused on the doormat and glanced over his shoulder at Arthur. "You are aware, aren't you, Goodenough, that it's against the law for a person your age to work in a store?"

"Yes," said Arthur stiffly. "I'm not being paid."

Mr. Beaglehole's arrogant grin made Arthur feel anxious.

"I've got my eye on you, Goodenough," Mr. Beagle-hole told him, and left.

As soon as he had crossed the threshold, Scallywag

ran to the door and barked to let the man know he had not been welcome and would be wise never to come in again. Trunk ambled along his shelf so he could give Arthur a look of deep sympathy.

"I know," Arthur said with a sigh. "It's just my luck to have a moron for a teacher."

Behind Mr. Hardbattle's desk were dozens of files, which listed most of the books still in print in England. Arthur sifted through them. When he found *The Future Is Nuclear*, he filled out an order form and put the lower half in an envelope ready for someone to mail.

He wondered if Mr. Beaglehole had chosen that title on purpose to annoy him. Arthur did not approve of nuclear power. He thought there were far better ways of making energy and had worked hard on a presentation about it for his geography class that term. He had gone into great detail about solar panels, wind turbines, and other amazing ideas, and he had hoped to get at least a B. Predictably, however, Mr. Beaglehole had failed to be impressed and gave Arthur a D minus minus, which was the lowest grade he had ever handed out.

When the bell jingle-jangled for the second time that hour, Arthur stayed seated. Harboring a vain hope that a friendly customer had just arrived, he glanced across to see who had come in and instantly experienced a jolt of panic. A policeman stood in the doorway and, if Arthur was not mistaken, it was the very same member of the force who had confiscated the knight's sword just a few days before. Arthur thought about hiding, but he was too slow. The policeman had already spotted him and was marching toward him like a soldier on a parade ground, swinging his arms stiffly and sticking out his chin. When the stout little officer halted with a *stomp-stomp* of his feet, Arthur half expected to be honored with a salute.

"Young sir," said the policeman, giving a nod. He took off his helmet and wiped his sweaty brow with a handkerchief.

Arthur stood up gingerly. His legs felt as if they had turned to cotton. "Did Mr. Beaglehole send you?" Arthur asked nervously. "I'm not working, honest. I was just sitting in this chair because my legs were tired. I'm not an employee or anything like that."

"What are you talking about, boy?" the policeman said. "Mr. Beagle-who?" He unbuttoned his collar and scratched his neck. "I was sent here by my sergeant. I've come to give you a warning."

Arthur gulped. He had never been in trouble with the police before. He racked his brain to think what he had done in recent weeks that might be construed as a crime. It was possible that he had ridden his bike on the sidewalk, and he remembered throwing an apple core under a hedge. Would he be given a ticket? He dreaded to think what his mother would say.

The policeman stared at Arthur with a concerned frown. "You've gone a peculiar color, boy. If I were you, I'd open a window and get some fresh air in here. I've never seen a place so smothered with dust, and there's a funny odor—smells like tripe. Now, where was I? Ah, yes. Shoplifting. There's been a spate of it in these parts. My sergeant has told me to put you shopkeepers on alert. Have you had anything stolen in the last week or so?"

"Um . . . no, I don't think so," said Arthur, not wanting to mention the missing books in case it prompted some awkward questions. He smiled at the policeman, relieved that the purpose of his visit had not been to tell Arthur off.

"Well, keep your eyes peeled, won't you?" said the policeman. He put on his helmet and fastened his collar. "If you see anyone shifty, call the station and ask for me. My name is Officer Chubb."

Arthur assured Officer Chubb that he would follow his advice, then he escorted the policeman to the door. The magic had kept a low profile while the policeman had been in the shop, but Arthur could not count on it to remain inconspicuous for very much longer. He did not know if magic was against the law, but he had a feeling that Officer Chubb and his sergeant would not approve of it.

"Phew!" said Arthur when the policeman had gone. Arthur closed the door firmly and pressed his back against it, praying that no more customers would come in before Miss Quint returned. He did not think his nerves could stand another shock in so short a space of time.

He checked his watch. There were fifteen minutes to go before the hour was up. He moved away from the door and wandered around the shop, looking for a book to browse while he waited for Miss Quint and Susan.

When the bell jingle-jangled two minutes later, Arthur ducked down and hid. From the innermost recesses of the children's section, he could not see around the corner to the doorway. However, if he stretched his neck and leaned to the left, he could get quite a good view of Trunk. The elephant's ears had raised themselves up like hoisted flags, and Arthur watched as they fell into folds again, as they always did when the newcomer did not prove to be his little girl. The elephant continued to peer in the direction of the doorway and then, instead of staying where he was, he ran quickly along his shelf and dived behind his flowerpot. Arthur knew this did not bode well, and neither did the low rumbling sound emanating from Scallywag. A quick glance told Arthur that her hackles were up and she was baring her teeth. Whoever had just come into the bookshop had been scary enough to alarm a dog and a stuffed elephant. Arthur took off his belt, slipped it through Scallywag's collar, and tied her securely to a table leg. He crouched low beside her and hoped that the person would think the shop was not staffed and go away. Arthur heard the creak of shoe leather and the rustle of clothing; he almost jumped out of his skin when he heard somebody cough.

It was a dry, artificial sort of cough. Arthur knew people only coughed like that to get somebody's attention—or to check whether anyone was around. Could the person who had just entered the shop be the shoplifter Officer Chubb had warned him about? While Arthur skulked behind shelves of children's books, was the mystery person filling grocery bags with Mr. Hardbattle's stock?

Arthur realized he could not hide any longer. He had been entrusted to look after the bookshop, and it was his responsibility to guard against theft. Stealthily, Arthur stood up and tiptoed out of the alcove. If there was a thief in the bookshop, Arthur wanted to catch him red-handed.

The man who stood in the doorway did not strike Arthur as the criminal type. He was young and had an open, friendly face. He wore overalls and workman's boots, but his sideburns and his tuft of dark hair shaped like a shark's fin implied that he was more stylish than his clothes suggested. Arthur could not understand why Scallywag and Trunk had taken such a dislike to the man. He looked harmless enough. He did not have any grocery bags or huge pockets in which to stuff stolen goods, and he was not acting in a threatening or suspicious way.

All the man was doing was standing on the doormat with his hands in his pockets, sniffing the air.

Arthur walked up to him without a shred of fear. "Hello!" he said. "Can I help you?"

The man gave a lopsided smile and stepped forward to shake Arthur by the hand. He seemed to smell strongly of detergent.

"Afternoon," he said. "My name's Dexter Bland and no, man, I don't need your help—but I think you could use mine."

Arthur was bemused. "Oh, really?" he said.

"I'm in the extermination business," said Dexter.

Not seeing how this affected him, Arthur said, "Good for you."

"Pest control's another name for it," said Dexter. He reached into a pocket in his overalls and put on a pair of thick, padded gloves. "I got a report that Hardbattle Books had an infestation—something making holes in the pages of your books—and by the smell of this place, I'd say you're knee-deep in cockroaches."

Arthur took half a minute to digest what Dexter had said. He remembered that a fussy, middle-aged woman had brought back a book, complaining that its pages were riddled with holes. At the time, Arthur had been sure that the makers of the holes had been the thumbtacks.

Trying to see the humor in the situation, Arthur gave a nervous laugh. "You're mistaken," he said. "We don't have cockroaches here. Someone's been playing a joke on you."

Dexter took up a determined stance. "Don't give me that, pal. This nose of mine has never been wrong. There's a mighty powerful stench in here, and I know roaches when I smell them."

Arthur tried to explain that, although there was a smell, it was a misleading one and that what Dexter's nose detected was actually magic. His rushed explanation made no impression on Dexter.

"Listen, buster," Dexter said to Arthur. "A shop full of roaches is a health hazard. They'll have to be gotten rid of. It's as simple as that." He turned and walked out of the bookshop but was back again within seconds. In his arms he held what looked like a gigantic vacuum cleaner with a suction hose and a telescopic tube. Arthur realized with horror that it was large enough to suck up all the magic in the shop.

"NO!" cried Arthur. He tried to push Dexter out of the door. "You can't use that in here!"

"Oh yeah?" said Dexter, standing firm. "Just you watch me, kid."

Chapter Seventeen

The Pied Piper of Plumford

Arthur was not a coward by nature, but he knew when he was beaten. One glance at the mammoth, cockroach-eating monster in the pest control man's grip was enough to tell him that he stood no chance against it on his own. He could have run upstairs to ask one of the guests to intervene. Mr. Claggitt was the obvious choice. A hulking, strong, barrel-chested mountaineer would undoubtedly cause Dexter to think twice before he switched on his machine. However, Arthur's instinct told him not to bother with the guests upstairs. He felt that, in a crisis, it was probably best to enlist the help of people whom you judged to be the most dependable. It was purely for this reason, and not because of any streak of cowardice, that Arthur dodged past Dexter Bland and sprinted up the street.

The panic that had built up inside him made Arthur run so fast that he reached the end of Meadow Street in one minute flat. He waited at the intersection with Milestone Lane, where the best of Plumford's thrift shops were to be found. Surrounded by a forest of much taller bodies, it was difficult for Arthur to see every person as they passed. To give himself a better view, he scrambled on to a mailbox (which would have earned him a lecture if Officer Chubb had caught him). From Arthur's new vantage point, he looked in every direction, searching for the familiar faces of Susan and Miss Quint.

With each second that ticked by, Arthur grew more anxious. He tried to blot out the vision in his mind of Dexter Bland's machine consuming all the magic in the shop. Arthur's vision disintegrated when someone tugged on his pant leg, and a man's voice cut through the hubbub on the busy street corner.

"Good heavens, Arthur! Why are you standing up there?"

Fighting to keep his balance, Arthur glanced below him and saw a gray felt hat and a raincoat draped over somebody's arm. On the sidewalk, next to a pair of light brown shoes, was a suitcase. Arthur closed his eyes and felt relief flood his veins. Then he sank to his haunches and grinned at Mr. Hardbattle's upturned face.

"Boy, am I glad to see *you*," said Arthur.

"And I you," replied Mr. Hardbattle, frowning. "But the reason escapes me why you'd want to stand on a mailbox of all things."

"I didn't have a stepladder handy," joked Arthur, his broad grin widening. Then, remembering Dexter Bland, his mood turned serious again. "There's an emergency back at the shop," he said, jumping down from the mailbox. "We have to get there right away. The magic is in danger."

Seventy-year-old Mr. Hardbattle proved in the next few minutes that he was no slouch when it came to running. As they hurried together along the sidewalk, dodging shoppers, Arthur revealed what had happened while he had been minding the shop.

"What a pest!" Mr. Hardbattle said of Dexter Bland as he panted and puffed in Arthur's wake, clutching his suitcase and raincoat. "I'll kick him out of my shop. I'm the owner. He'll have to do what I say!"

Over his shoulder, Arthur expressed his view that that plan might not work. "Dexter's very strong willed. It's unlikely he'll notice!"

"Pig-headed fellow, is he?" said Mr. Hardbattle, his fury increasing. "How do you propose we stop this madman, then?"

"Don't know," Arthur replied. "That's why I hurried out to get help!"

They slowed to a walk as they drew nearer to the bookshop, each of them thinking hard about how they could prevent the exterminator from emptying the shop of magic. Parked next to Mr. Hardbattle's green van was a much larger vehicle, Day-Glo orange in color with PEST PULVERIZERS painted boldly on its side.

Mr. Hardbattle eyed Dexter's van with distaste. "What a vulgar automobile," he said.

Arthur cupped his hands around his eyes and peered through the bookshop's window to see what was going on. "There's Dexter!" said Arthur. "He's crouching beside his machine. I can see his white overalls."

"Overalls?" Mr. Hardbattle scratched his head. "That's the sort of uniform they wear, is it? Hmm . . . Well, if this Dexter chap won't listen to a lay person, perhaps he'll take notice of a pest control expert like himself."

Arthur watched curiously as Mr. Hardbattle knelt down on the sidewalk and rummaged around in his suitcase. The old man withdrew a pair of blue paint-spattered overalls.

"Here they are!" Mr. Hardbattle said, shaking them out and unbuttoning them. "I took them with me on my trip to protect my clothes. Thought that some of the places I'd look at might be a little grimy." Before he closed the lid of his suitcase, Mr. Hardbattle folded his raincoat and put it on top of the rest of his things. Then, once he had fastened the clasps on his case, he got up from the ground.

"What's the plan?" Arthur asked him eagerly.

"I'm thinking," Mr. Hardbattle said as he stepped into

the overalls and buttoned them over his shirt and trousers. “I’ll need an alter ego. What about Alan the Insect Man?”

Arthur regarded the old man in his scruffy new garb. “I think you look like a Bert,” he said after a moment’s consideration. “What do you think of Bert the Bug Blaster?”

Mr. Hardbattle frowned. “Er . . . it’s . . . well, it’s . . .”

“Question is,” said Arthur, ignoring the fact that his suggestion had not been seized upon, “*how* do you blast the bugs? Where’s your equipment? Dexter’s got a ginormous machine.”

“Our approach? Yes, that’s a stumbling block,” admitted Mr. Hardbattle. “We’ll have to put on our thinking caps and come up with something quick.”

After thirty seconds of unbroken silence, Arthur scowled and let out a sigh. “It’s those thumbtacks’ fault,” he complained. “If they hadn’t hopped all over that lady’s book and made holes in it, we wouldn’t be in the mess we’re in now.”

“It’s not the name Bert I object to,” mused Mr. Hardbattle, who had seated himself on the doorstep of the shop. “It’s the method of dealing with the bugs . . . I mean, *insects*. I don’t think I’d be capable of blasting them to pieces. Coaxing or cajoling is more my sort of thing.”

Arthur’s heart sank. He glanced anxiously through the

window and saw Dexter roaming the floor on his hands and knees. Mr. Hardbattle's idea of impersonating someone from the pest control industry had been a good one, but if the old man was going to insist upon some namby-pamby method to get rid of the cockroaches, Arthur could not see how their plan would work. There was no way Dexter was going to take a kind-hearted pest control expert seriously. Unless . . .

"If we had time, I could run home to borrow my sister's recorder," said Arthur jokingly. "You could be like the Pied Piper of Hamelin from the fairy tale."

Arthur was surprised when Mr. Hardbattle slapped his hands on his knees and got up from the doorstep. He walked toward Arthur with shining eyes.

"Who needs a recorder?" said Mr. Hardbattle, smiling. "A penny whistle will do just as well."

"Huh?" said Arthur. "What are you staring at me for?"

"Your whistle," Mr. Hardbattle said, holding out his hand. "I'd like to borrow it, if you don't mind."

Arthur looked at him blankly. "A whistle? I don't have one."

"You don't?" Mr. Hardbattle said, clicking his tongue against his teeth. "Gracious! What is the world coming to? When I was a boy, I was never without my penny whistle or my whittling knife or my slingshot!"

"Sorry," said Arthur. "I guess times have changed."

He emptied his pants pockets to prove that there was no whistle inside them. Mr. Hardbattle's eyes took in the collection of odds and ends on Arthur's palms.

"What's this?" Mr. Hardbattle asked, pointing at a flat plastic toy with holes at either end.

Arthur squinted at the object, which was tangled in a rubber band. He had traded a bar of chocolate for it several days before and had completely forgotten about it.

"Um . . . it's a kazoo," he said. "It makes a noise if you blow through it."

"May I?" asked Mr. Hardbattle, taking the kazoo. "It will serve very well. Now, here's what we're going to do . . ."

One minute later, Mr. Hardbattle burst through the door of the bookshop like a cowboy walking into a saloon. His sudden entrance made the bell swing so sharply that its jingle-jangle sounded like a shriek and captured Dexter Bland's attention immediately. He looked up from the floor of the shop, where he was crawling around, holding a plug attached to a long length of cable. He appeared to be searching for an electrical outlet.

"Go, Arthur . . . now!" Mr. Hardbattle whispered.

As swiftly as he could, Arthur slipped behind the old man and ran to Mr. Hardbattle's desk, almost tripping over the coils of the suction device in his haste. Once he reached the desk, he snatched up the carton of thumbtacks and went to join Scallywag, who was sitting beside the table, still tied to its leg and grumbling like a kettle coming to a boil.

"Have you seen a pest around?" was Mr. Hardbattle's opening line.

Dexter Bland locked his jaw. He narrowed his eyes and pinched his shark-fin forelock between his finger and thumb. "Who's asking?" he said.

Mr. Hardbattle grasped the knot of his tie and moved it a smidgen to the right. "People in the trade know me as Marmaduke the Cockroach Charmer."

"I've never heard that name," said Dexter suspiciously. He got up from the floor and stood in a defensive pose in front of his cockroach-eating contraption. "Your help isn't wanted, thanks. I've got this cockroach job all sewn up."

"I beg to differ," Mr. Hardbattle said, venturing deeper into the shop. "By the looks of it, you haven't even made a start!"

"Hey! This is my turf, old-timer," said Dexter, shaking his plug at him threateningly. "Go and do your cockroach charming somewhere else!"

"What's the matter, sonny? Afraid I'd do a better job?"

Mr. Hardbattle's daring talk made Arthur hold his breath, but Dexter Bland did not seem fazed, and he showed his contempt by snorting with laughter. "There's nothing more efficient than my machine," he said, setting aside the plug and grasping the telescopic tube with both hands. "I put this nozzle in cracks and crevices and suck out roaches like milk through a straw."

"Showy," sneered Mr. Hardbattle bravely, "not to mention cumbersome. I find that the old traditional methods are best."

"How d'you do it, then?" asked Dexter, sounding a little less sure of himself.

"You must've heard of the Pied Piper of Hamelin?" said Mr. Hardbattle. He stepped up to Dexter and looked him in the eye.

"Sure!" said Dexter brazenly. "Everyone in our line of work knows about the Piper dude. He's the most famous controller of pests that ever was. He lured a load of rats out of a town by playing on his pipe, then led them to a river, where they drowned."

"Go to the head of the class!" Mr. Hardbattle said to Dexter. Then he wiggled his finger in his right ear, which was the signal for Arthur to begin the next stage of their plan.

Obediently, Arthur unfolded the flaps on the carton, which he had balanced on his knees, and began to whisper instructions to the thumbtacks. This was easy because Scallywag had stopped growling as soon as she recognized her master's voice, and the only sound that Arthur had to compete with was the *swish-swish-swish* of her tail sweeping the floor.

"You're telling me you serenade the roaches?" Dexter said to Mr. Hardbattle. He smirked. "Boy, I'd love to see that! Where's your pipe, then? Let's have a tune! Put your money where your mouth is, granddad!"

"Very well," Mr. Hardbattle said. "Stand back and enjoy the show."

The sound the kazoo made when Mr. Hardbattle put it to his lips and hummed through the narrowest end could not be described as melodic. It made the hairs on the back of Arthur's neck stand up. Dexter grimaced and placed his hands over his ears, and Scallywag raised her muzzle to the ceiling and started to howl. No cockroaches appeared, which was to be expected, but as Mr. Hardbattle continued to belt out his unrecognizable tune, there was movement in the corner of the shop where Arthur was sitting. The carton on his knees gave a wobble and then, like a snake emerging from a hole, the thumbtacks jumped out of their carton and, in a long, wavering line, hopped on their little pin legs toward Mr. Hardbattle.

"There are the cockroaches!" cried Arthur, running up and down beside them so that Dexter could not get a clear look at them. "See, there they go!" he said as they followed Mr. Hardbattle and hopped two by two in a line out of the shop.

Dexter stood and gaped. "I've never seen anything like it!" he said.

"Made it look like child's play, didn't he?" Arthur

commented gleefully. "That's experience for you, I guess. Well, I bet you've got to dash off to your next appointment, Mr. Bland . . ."

With a defeated sigh and a slump in his shoulders, Dexter began to coil the electrical cord and wind it around the top of his cockroach-eating machine.

Arthur was thrilled that he and Mr. Hardbattle pulled off their scam with such ease, but he did feel a twinge of guilt for tricking Dexter so slyly. "You win some, you lose some!" he said to the pest control man as he helped him to carry his machine to his van.

When Dexter had driven away, Mr. Hardbattle emerged from behind a lamppost and gave Arthur the thumbs-up.

"Worked like a dream," said Mr. Hardbattle, walking rather gingerly because his pockets were filled with thumbtacks.

Arthur nodded and grinned. "Marmaduke was a cool name to choose. Better than Bert by miles."

"It's my first name," said Mr. Hardbattle, chuckling. "I'm glad it meets with your approval, Arthur!"

Chapter Eighteen

Miss Quint Is Dishonest

Once inside the shop again, Arthur took the thumbtacks and tipped them into their carton, while Mr. Hardbattle enjoyed a reunion with his dog. Not waiting to be untied, Scallywag slipped out of her collar and streaked across the floor. When Mr. Hardbattle bent down to greet her, she lathered his face with licks.

After a few minutes, Scallywag contented herself with lying at her master's feet, and Mr. Hardbattle straightened up and dried his face with his handkerchief. "What's become of my large-eared friend?" he asked, glancing at the shelf above his desk, which was Trunk's usual stomping ground.

"He's hiding," said Arthur. "He got scared."

"Trunk, my boy!" Mr. Hardbattle called, waving his handkerchief in the air. "There's nothing to fear. That loathsome fellow has gone. Come out and say hello!"

It was unclear whether it was Mr. Hardbattle's plea or

the jingle-jangle of the shop bell that persuaded Trunk to come out from behind his flowerpot. His trunk made an appearance first, followed by his tusks and his anxious, velvety face. Trunk's ears gave a twitch of delight when he saw that Susan and Miss Quint had returned from their shopping trip, but it was the sight of Mr. Hardbattle that gave the elephant the most joy. He lifted his trunk to deliver a trumpet blast to welcome his old friend home, but unfortunately the new arrivals in the shop had seized everybody's attention by that time, and because he could not make any sound, Trunk's fanfare went unnoticed.

It had been Susan who caused the bell to ring. She skipped through the door ahead of Miss Quint, a blissful smile on her face. In one hand she clutched a shopping bag and in the other a piece of pink paper. Her appearance made Arthur do a double take. Rather than her drab gingham dress, Susan wore a T-shirt and shorts. Behind Susan lurked Miss Quint, who had stopped dead on the doormat, panic in her eyes.

"You seem surprised to see me," Mr. Hardbattle said, raising his hat in a respectful greeting to Miss Quint.

"No!" Miss Quint said hurriedly. "It's just . . . you're early . . . and I didn't realize it was you at first. That old getup threw me. I thought you were a handyman!"

Mr. Hardbattle looked down at his overalls, which he hadn't yet removed. "I'm supposed to be in pest control," he told her and, with several interruptions from Arthur, he divulged the details of their recent adventure. While they chattered away, Susan hovered by Mr. Hardbattle's side, bursting with eagerness to introduce herself.

Eventually, Mr. Hardbattle turned to speak to her. He pushed his horn-rimmed glasses up his nose and asked, "Who might *you* be?"

"She's my niece," Miss Quint said, getting in her explanation before Arthur could admit the truth. She put an arm around Susan's shoulders and ignored Arthur's disapproving stare. "Susan needed somewhere to spend her vacation," said Miss Quint. "Her parents are too ill to look after her. They've got . . . Pollywolly disease . . . quite badly. I didn't think you'd mind Susan moving in."

It was a struggle for Mr. Hardbattle to look as if he did not mind that his home had been invaded by a second female. He was too flustered to speak at first. All he could do was smile unhappily.

"I don't eat much, and I'm helpful—aren't I, Aunt Beatrice?" Susan said.

Arthur glowered at Miss Quint even more intensely. It was plain that she had taken Susan into her confidence and persuaded the girl to go along with her deceitful ruse. Perhaps Susan's new clothes had served as bribery. Turning Susan into a liar was not something Arthur approved of; neither was trying to pull the wool over Mr. Hardbattle's eyes.

"Pollywolly disease . . . ," murmured Mr. Hardbattle,

frowning. "I haven't come across that. It doesn't sound nice." He gazed at Susan pityingly, and his voice became gentler. "Poor girl! Of course it's all right if you remain here."

After blowing out her cheeks with relief, Miss Quint clapped her hands. "That's settled, then. Arthur, have you told Mr. Hardbattle our good news?"

Arthur stopped leaning against a bookshelf and took his hands out of his pockets. "No, there hasn't been time," he said. Aware that he sounded sullen, Arthur tried to shake off his sulky mood and made an effort to sound glad. "We've found the perfect place for your magic, Mr. Hardbattle! It's an old cottage in a wood, and it's got *loads* of cobwebs!"

Mr. Hardbattle's cheeks turned a rosy shade of pink, and he clapped Arthur on the shoulder with immense pride. "That *is* a load off my mind! How splendid! Good for you! The places I looked at weren't really up to snuff. The best of the bunch was a hayloft in Devizes, but horseshoe bats and barn owls had already set up home there, and bats, owls, and magic wouldn't make good bedfellows."

"The cottage is at Down-the-Ages Farm," said Miss Quint. "Pam Carruthers suggested we move the magic in this weekend."

"But not Saturday," said Susan, her eyes widening with worry.

Arthur hesitated. "What's happening on Saturday?"

"This!" said Susan, holding up a pink flyer. "A man was handing these out in the street. He was taller than a tree!"

Arthur was baffled by Susan's description of the flyer man until Miss Quint explained that he had been standing on stilts.

Arthur took the flyer from Susan and read it. Almost immediately his face broke into a smile. "Oh yeah!" he said. "I'd forgotten it's the carnival this weekend."

"The high point in Plumford's cultural calendar," Mr. Hardbattle said. "Naturally, you children shouldn't miss it. I'd be more than willing to move the magic on Sunday." His eyes grew round and bright as a thought occurred to him. "That's the one day the shop isn't open, so I won't lose any business!"

Mr. Hardbattle took off his hat and threw it with enough precision for it to land on the hatstand. "My bookshop is saved! This calls for a celebration!" he cried. Then he picked up his suitcase and walked spryly toward the stairs.

With a squawk of alarm, Miss Quint moved like lightning to head him off. "Stop!" she shrieked. "You can't!"

"What do you mean, I can't?" Mr. Hardbattle asked. He tried to pass Miss Quint, but she prevented him from doing so. "I'm only going upstairs to put the kettle on!" he said, frustrated by her awkwardness.

"I can do that for you!" said Miss Quint soothingly. "You've been traveling all day. You must be exhausted!" She laced her fingers around the handle of his case. "Let me take your bag!" she said, trying to tug it from his grip. "I'll make tea while you sit down and put your feet up!"

Mr. Hardbattle had to admit that Miss Quint was right about one thing. He had been on the go all day, and he was certainly too weary to argue the point. Without another word of protest, he let Miss Quint relieve him of his suitcase and headed straight for the nearest chair.

While Miss Quint was upstairs making tea, Arthur sat and fidgeted. He tried to join in the conversation with Susan and Mr. Hardbattle, but he could not prevent his mind from straying to other things. He knew why Miss Quint had been eager to go upstairs. She wanted to talk to the houseguests before Mr. Hardbattle met them. She was probably asking them to pretend to be her old pals, just as she had prevailed upon Susan earlier.

Arthur looked over at Mr. Hardbattle, who was sitting contentedly in a chair with one of the bookends on his lap. Arthur yearned to tell the old man the truth, but he did not dare reveal all while Susan was in the room. He got up from his perch on the arm of a chair and paced the floor restlessly.

Within the space of ten minutes, Miss Quint returned

with a tray. Behind her, trotting down the staircase like obliging sheep, came Jimmy, Mrs. Voysey-Brown, and Mr. Claggitt.

Mr. Hardbattle heard the clatter of footsteps and glanced at the stairwell, aghast. "Miss Quint! Who in the world are these people?" he asked. "Are they your family too?'

"No!" said Arthur loudly. He planted his hands on his hips. "And they're not her friends either. They're—"

"They're relatives of Arthur's," interjected Miss Quint. She turned and nodded at each of them as they stepped off the final stair. "This is his uncle Jim . . . and aunt Dolores . . . and uncle Sidney."

Arthur was so mad at Miss Quint that he left the bookshop immediately after she introduced the three houseguests as his relations, and he did not come back until the following afternoon.

He still had a little homework to finish over the school break, and he tried to fill his time by concentrating on it. As usual, however, this was anything but easy. Everywhere he went in his house, he was confronted with loud music, arguments, giggling, or his cockatiel, Bubbles, who had developed the habit of sitting on Arthur's head. The backyard was Arthur's sanctuary but, because of the good weather, his family had taken this over too. When Arthur sat at the bottom of the yard, his brothers started a football game and clobbered him with their ball, and when he moved to the patio, Arthur's bikini-clad sisters got on his nerves by squealing as they ran past the sprinklers on the lawn.

It was late on Wednesday afternoon when Arthur admitted to himself that the best place to study was the bookshop. He moaned and grumbled about it as he packed his schoolbooks into his bag, but secretly he was glad to be returning, having missed his friends.

When he pushed open the door of the shop, Arthur discovered, to his disappointment, that Mr. Hardbattle was not there.

"He's gone in his van to Down-the-Ages Farm," explained Susan, who leaped from her chair as soon as Arthur entered the shop. She had been reading a book but threw it aside to greet him.

Miss Quint was sitting behind a sewing machine at Mr. Hardbattle's desk. The machine was an odd-shaped contraption, topped with a cotton reel. As Miss Quint turned a handle, a needle dipped in and out of some cloth in a blur.

"He wanted to meet Pam Carruthers and to see the cottage for himself," said Miss Quint over the whir of her sewing machine. "Mr. Hardbattle's such an old stickler! Let's hope he doesn't find fault with it!"

She stopped turning the handle of the sewing machine, whipped the material out from underneath the presser foot, and inspected the stitching. Arthur saw that the garment was a child's skirt and that Miss Quint was altering its length. Obviously, shorts and a T-shirt were not the only clothes purchased for Susan the day before.

Arthur had made up his mind not to speak to Miss Quint, but he found that he could not bring himself to be quite so rude.

"I've come to do some schoolwork," he said gruffly. "It was too noisy to get much done at home and the library's too crowded this week." He lifted his head and listened, but there were no sounds from upstairs. "It seems quieter than usual," he said. "Where are the three musketeers?"

Miss Quint smiled to herself. "You mean your aunt and uncles, Arthur!"

"That's *not* who they are," snapped Arthur, "and you shouldn't have said they were!" He threw his schoolbag on the floor in frustration.

Miss Quint abandoned her sewing to glare at him. "You didn't give me much choice, did you? I was all set to follow Plan A, but thanks to your little outburst, I had to invent a Plan B on the spot!"

Arthur was amazed that Miss Quint seemed to think he should be sorry for inconveniencing her. He curled his hands into fists and fumed silently.

The handle of the sewing machine revolved again. "They're out, if you must know," said Miss Quint. "I advised them to make themselves scarce. Mr. Hardbattle wasn't pleased with three more houseguests. I told him that your parents' house was too packed to accommodate them. He's agreed to let them stay here for now."

Arthur grunted and started to clear a space on his homework table. He laid out his pencils and workbooks. Susan picked up the nearest book and leafed through the pages.

"What does *abysmal* mean?" she asked, peering at a teacher's scrawl.

Arthur snatched the book back and told her not to be so nosy. Startled by his hostile manner, Susan decided to leave him alone. She went back to the book she had been reading when Arthur came in. It was called *Emil and the Detectives*.

Half an hour passed without another word spoken. The only noises were the whir of Miss Quint's sewing machine and the twangs of rubber bands as they competed in a contest to see which one could fling itself farthest across the room. Susan read her book and Arthur gnawed his pen, trying to do his homework, but he found it hard. Apart from having impossible questions to answer, there was also the distraction of the temperature. It was the first day of June and the weather was cloudy and humid. Inside the dusty, airless bookshop, Arthur felt uncomfortably warm. He untucked his shirt and took off his shoes, but neither action made him feel much cooler.

At quarter to five, he sighed and put down his pen.

"How's business been?" he asked.

"Quiet," said Miss Quint. She had finished altering Susan's skirt and was trying to put her machine away, but the bobbins had escaped from their compartment and were racing each other across the desk. "Come back here, you!" she said to the fastest bobbin, which was wound with black thread and nearing the table's edge.

"Have you had a visit from that shoplifter Officer Chubb told me about?" asked Arthur.

"No," answered Miss Quint, snatching at bobbins left and right.

Arthur wiped the sweat from his forehead with his sleeve. "I bet that other bookshop in town has had loads of customers. When the magic's gone, Hardbattle Books will be much busier . . . won't it?" His tone was faintly anxious.

Miss Quint slammed down the lid on the last errant bobbin. "Are you sure that's what you want?" she said.

"For Mr. Hardbattle's bookshop to be successful? Of course it is!"

"But where will you do your homework?" Miss Quint asked.

Arthur smiled. He checked his watch, then closed his

books and began to place them in his bag. But before he could leave for home, Mr. Hardbattle returned.

He was in a cheerful mood, having been greatly impressed by the cottage. He bid Arthur a hearty hello and handed Susan a warm bundle wrapped in newspaper, which had a fishy, mouth-watering smell.

"Fish and chips!" Mr. Hardbattle said. "You'll stay for some, won't you, Arthur? And afterward I wonder if you'd help me get down some storage boxes from the loft. I've got three or four of them, and each one's dusty and dry as a bone. They'll be perfect for transferring the You Know What when I drive it to Thornwick."

Arthur nodded. "Sure thing!"

Declaring that the fish and chips smelled scrumptious, Susan hugged the takeout package to her chest while Miss Quint went upstairs to get plates and silverware.

Arthur helped to unwrap the food and dish out the portions of haddock and chips. As he peeled away the layers of the *Plumford Gazette*, his eyes were drawn to a photograph of Officer Chubb underneath a headline that warned: ROBBERS RUN AMOCK IN PLUMFORD. Arthur read the beginning of the article, which revealed that burglaries were on the rise in the area, as well as theft from shops. The others did not have the patience to wait for him to finish reading the entire story, so Arthur folded up the page of newsprint and tucked it away in his pocket to read later.

Once their appetites had been satisfied, Miss Quint and Susan trooped off to the kitchen with the greasy paper and dirty plates. Arthur and Mr. Hardbattle went to get the stepladder from the shed. They carried the ladder upstairs and stood it under the opening to the attic. Then Arthur remained at the bottom, holding it steady, while the old man climbed up the steps. When Mr. Hardbattle reached the top step, he gasped and gave a cry.

"Well, that's a funny thing!" he said, staring at a large brass padlock inches from his nose. "I don't remember putting a lock on here! Where could I have put the key?"

After an hour of Mr. Hardbattle emptying drawers and finding every sort of key except the one that fit the padlock in question, they decided to postpone their storage box forage until the next day. It made no sense to Arthur. He got on his bicycle and rode home.

Much later on at Hardbattle Books, when night had fallen, beds were occupied, and every light had been switched off, a bumping noise startled Susan awake.

Scallywag, who had taken to sleeping on Susan's bed, woke up too. Susan put out her hand to touch the dog's shoulder and felt her stiffen. The next moment she started to growl, and then, without warning, Scallywag jumped off the bed and disappeared through the door. Susan sat up. She clutched her quilt tensely. More noises banged above her head, similar to the first. It sounded as if someone were dropping rocks and boulders onto the roof. Susan suddenly wanted the company of Mr. Hardbattle or Miss Quint. She threw back her quilt and got out of bed, but before she could reach the door of her room, somebody slammed it shut and a key turned in the lock. Susan tried the door handle, and her worst fears were realized: the door would not open. There were more thumps from above.

"Miss Quint?" called Susan. She raised her voice. "Mr. Hardbattle? This is Susan! What's all that banging? Why have you locked me in?"

She rattled the door handle once again but stopped when her ears caught a muffled shout. Susan listened more intently and heard the cries of the same two people she had called out to a moment ago. Both were demanding to be freed from their rooms. Susan gulped when she realized that all of them had been locked in.

The situation did not make any sense to Susan at first. Then she remembered the article in the paper that Arthur had been reading. Perhaps there were burglars in the house, and they had locked everyone in their rooms so that they could steal Mr. Hardbattle's books without risking capture. Susan's imagination began to run wild. She thought about the books that would be lost and the damage the burglars might do to the shop, but mostly she worried about Scallywag, who had sped off bravely to scare away the robbers and had not been heard from since. What could be done? Susan racked her brain. Arthur would know, but how could she contact Arthur when she was locked in her room? If only she could think of a way to escape!

The room's only window was already open a crack. Susan hoisted it up and leaned out over the sill. Even in the dark she could tell that attempting a jump to the ground would be madness. She would not be able to get help with a couple of broken legs! Something moved several feet away, and Susan saw a shadowy trunk and a branch with quivering leaves. It occurred to her that if she knelt on the window ledge and stretched out an arm, she might be able to swing onto the branch and climb down the tree.

But not in my bare feet, wearing nothing but my pajamas, she thought, and she hastened from the window to get dressed.

Chapter Nineteen

A Walk in the Dark

Once she pulled on a skirt and a sweater, Susan was ready to go. In her skirt pocket she shoved some change and a flashlight that Miss Quint had been kind enough to give her. With the utmost care, Susan climbed onto the windowsill and peered out into the night.

The most frightening part of the whole exercise was the beginning, when she shuffled along the window ledge and made a lunge for the branch. Hesitating was not an option. Having made her move, she was forced to leave the window ledge completely and swing from the branch by her arms. For a few anxious seconds, while she found a foothold on the tree, Susan dangled in midair and tried not to look down. She felt hanging from a tree was not half as pleasurable as being on a swing or flying through the air.

Once she had anchored herself, the actual climb was not too bad, although she was torn between sliding down the tree quickly and taking things slowly so as not to risk tearing her new clothes. She decided to slide down quickly, guessing that Mr. Claggitt would not have approved of her technique. It was more of a slither than a measured descent, but Susan's lack of expertise did not seem to matter since she reached the ground without so much as a scraped knee.

Although the moon was out, the back of the house was draped in darkness, so she switched on her flashlight and directed its beam down the yard. The beam missed the side gate but picked out the toolshed, a garbage can, a clothesline, and a high fence.

Intending to climb over the fence, Susan walked down the path, which took her past the shed. As she drew closer to the shed, she heard a scrabbling noise coming from inside. Susan was tempted to hurry by, but her inquisitiveness prevailed and, with the aid of the flashlight, she found the shed door and lifted the latch. Thrusting her flashlight beam inside, she saw that the maker of the noise was none other than Scallywag, who had been tied to a workbench and muzzled with a scarf. Susan was overjoyed to see that Scallywag was unhurt. She released the excited dog quickly, untying the rope and freeing her bound nose. Then, using the rope as a dog leash, Susan ushered the dog out of the shed and continued toward the fence.

It was Scallywag who found a way out of the yard. She went straight to a loose board and prodded it with her nose. The board swung backward and Scallywag slipped through. Tugged by the rope leash, Susan had no choice but to follow where Scallywag had gone. In order to get through the gap, she had to squeeze through sideways while sucking in. Being fairly slim, she managed it.

Fighting her way through brambles was more challenging, but eventually, covered in scratches, Susan crawled out to a clearing next to a strip mall. Keeping a firm hold on Scallywag's leash and pointing her flashlight at the ground, she made her way over the bumpy terrain of rubble and weeds. Her flashlight beam fell for a moment on a fox whose eyes shone like bottlecaps in the unnatural light. Then with a flick of its bushy tail, it was gone. Scallywag yanked Susan's arm, yearning to go after it, but Susan did not intend to be waylaid even for a moment.

Once she reached the sidewalk, Susan switched off her flashlight. The amount of light from the streetlamps was more than adequate to enable her to find her way. She walked along the street, which was flanked by terraced houses, searching for a phone booth.

Susan had no clue where Arthur lived. She had thought she might walk the streets of Plumford until she encountered a person who knew him, but she quickly dismissed this idea as time-consuming and likely to fail. The plan she had settled on was infinitely better. She remembered being told about phone booths and the books called Yellow Pages, which could be found inside them. These Yellow Pages were huge and held the name, address, and telephone number of everyone who lived locally. All she had to do was find Arthur's number in this book and call him.

It did not take Susan long to spot a phone booth. There were a few glass panes missing from it, but the all-important Yellow Pages was there. Standing on tiptoe to reach the shelf on which the book sat, Susan took it down and flipped through it, searching for the last name Goodenough. Luckily, it was not a common name in the Plumford area, and there were only two Goodenoughs listed. Goodenough, G. was a doctor and his address was at a hospital, so she knew that Goodenough, I. was the one she wanted.

Susan got out her money. She read the instructions on the telephone carefully, lifting the receiver, putting in her money, and dialing the number in the order it said. The telephone on the other end rang and rang for a long time.

Susan's heart pounded. Why wouldn't anyone answer?

"Hello?" said a sleepy voice at last.

Susan perked up. "Is that you, Arthur?"

"No, it's Arthur's mother," said the voice. "Who are you? What do you want? Don't you know what time it is?"

Susan did not have a watch, and anyway she did not

see that it mattered what time it was when there was an emergency to report. "My name's Susan," she said, "and it's really, really important that I speak to Arthur right away."

"Well, you can't," said Arthur's mother in a not-to-be-messed-with voice. "He's in bed, and if *I* were your mom, Susan, *bed* is where I would have sent you *hours* ago. It's ten minutes to midnight! Call back when the sun is up. Good-bye!"

The receiver on the other end of the line was put down with a *clunk*, and Susan was left listening to silence.

Murmuring under her breath, she replaced her receiver too and heard her change drop in the machine. "So much for that idea, Scallywag."

Although she had encountered a setback, Susan was not prepared to give up. She decided that there was nothing to do but to memorize Arthur's address and to try to find his house. The only problem with her new plan was that she did not have the faintest idea where she might find Willow Road. She would need to rely on the help of a passerby.

As Susan made her way through Plumford, she was struck by how eerily quiet it was. Most of the roads were deserted and the houses she passed had their curtains drawn, but plenty of windows were open, it being such a warm night. Through them, from time to time, Susan heard snatches of laughter, raised voices, and the tinny blare of music. A cat or raccoon crossed her path occasionally, but the presence of Scallywag kept most creatures at bay. Not knowing in which direction she should go, Susan asked everyone she met for assistance. A couple strolling arm in arm had never heard of Willow Road, and a bunch of boisterous teens were more interested in pulling her braids than providing helpful advice.

Susan's persistence finally paid off when she stopped at the door of an Indian restaurant and spoke to a man named Vijay, who had driven cabs before he became a restaurateur. He gave Susan detailed instructions to get to Willow Road. He even drew her a map on a napkin and gave her some curry to eat on the way.

Willow Road, where Arthur lived, was part of a new neighborhood. All of its roads had been named after trees, shrubs, or flowers. When Susan turned into Dahlia Drive she felt a great sense of relief. She followed the sidewalk, which wound its way through a maze of roads. Those with the grandest names were lined with large, detached houses that had garages tacked on the side and neat front lawns. On the plainer-sounding roads, the buildings were jam-packed and looked shabbier.

Susan's belief that she would find Willow Road started to fade when the rain began to fall. The drops were light at first, and Susan mistook them for winged insects landing in her hair, but soon they grew plumper and fell to the ground in a rush. Getting wet did not dismay Susan as much as the knowledge that her napkin map was softening, and Vijay's carefully written words were being turned into splotches of ink. Within seconds the map was unreadable.

A distant rumble in the sky filled Susan with even more anguish, and Scallywag answered the noise with a rumbling growl of her own. To prevent them both from getting soaked to the skin, Susan looked for a place where they could hide from the rain. She spotted a tree in someone's front yard and ran to it. She felt drier beneath its branches, but she also felt a sense of despair. Having come so far, it seemed that she would have to spend the rest of the night under the tree or wandering around the neighborhood, getting increasingly lost.

The next moment a car swept past, its windshield wipers quickly flitting back and forth. Susan was caught in the car's headlights and raised her hand too late to shade her eyes against their glare. She was still blinking to get rid of the brightness when she heard a squeaking noise and the sound of a skidding wheel.

A voice called out, "Why are you standing there, dopey?"

Susan looked up and thought, for a moment, that she must be dreaming. A few feet in front of her, sitting astride his bike, was Arthur. He grinned at her and pushed his long bangs out of his eyes. "Don't you know that standing under a tree in a thunderstorm is one of the stupidest things you can do?" he said. "If lightning strikes that tree, you'll be fried to a crisp!"

His words were lost on Susan, who had not yet recovered from the shock of Arthur appearing. "How'd you know I was here?" she asked.

"I used my psychic powers!"

Scallywag whined to be stroked and Arthur leaned down to oblige. "Found you, didn't I?" he said. "You woke up the whole house with your phone call, Suze. I heard Mom say your name and guessed that something weird—and maybe bad—had happened at the shop. I waited till the coast was clear and then I sneaked out!"

"There *is* something wrong," said Susan, feeling tearful all of a sudden. "Someone locked us in our rooms . . . I had to climb down a tree to get out!"

Arthur's eyebrows shot up his forehead. Instead of asking her to explain, he gestured for her to get on his bike. "Sounds like we'd better get there fast!" he said.

Susan revealed more details as they rode along the streets of Plumford on Arthur's bicycle. Susan had never ridden a bike, so she sat on the seat while Arthur stood up and pedaled, leaning his weight on the handlebars. Scallywag was too big to fit in Arthur's saddlebag, so they took off her rope leash and she ran alongside.

They were an odd-looking pair: Arthur in long shorts and a pajama top and Susan with her ribboned braids flying out behind. The bike wobbled and wavered, sent off course by the weight of two riders instead of one, but Arthur was a capable cyclist and managed to keep his bike from falling over.

"*Burglars*?" said Arthur as they left the road and free-wheeled down a narrow, unlit path close to his school. Wet nettles and weeds brushed against their legs.

Susan clung to the crossbar tightly. "That's who I thought they must be. What do you think they've come to steal? Mr. Hardbattle's books?"

Arthur made a face, turning the handlebars sharply to avoid a fallen branch. "Mr. Hardbattle's books can't be worth *that* much," he said. "And he isn't rich. The cash register's practically empty, and he doesn't have any signet rings or gold medallions or things like that. He hasn't even got a TV!"

Susan struggled to stay on the seat as they went over a bump in the path. A loud, crackling rumble followed a flash in the sky and made her squeal.

"It's just a thunderstorm. You'll be okay," said Arthur, pedaling faster.

Arthur's spurt of speed and his knowledge of short-cuts saved them from getting totally drenched. They were fairly damp but not dripping when they arrived outside Hardbattle Books. They dismounted clumsily as another lightning flash lit up the sky. A crash of thunder swiftly followed.

"Electricity in clouds," whispered Arthur. "Nothing

to be scared of, Suze." He crept toward the shop and put his finger to his lips. "Shh!" he said over his shoulder.

Susan reattached Scallywag's leash, and Scallywag sank to the ground, worn out from having run several miles across town. Her tongue lolled from her mouth and her sides heaved. She was so tired that the thunderstorm failed to trouble her.

Arthur examined the facade of Hardbattle Books. None of the windows had been broken and the lock on the door had not been tampered with. At first glance the interior of the shop seemed dark, but when Arthur peered through the window, he saw glimmers of deep gold light at the very back of the shop.

"Someone's there!" he whispered to Susan. "But it beats me how they got in. There isn't any sign of a break-in as far as I can see."

Susan tugged Arthur's pajama sleeve. "Whose car is that?" she asked.

Next to the curb, in the space in front of Mr. Hardbattle's van, was a battered old Land Rover. As Susan and Arthur stared at it, bewildered, they heard the creak of a bicycle, which sounded as if it needed oiling, and saw a man in a hunting cap pedaling quickly in their direction. Arthur pulled Susan away from the portion of sidewalk lit up by a streetlamp. They gaped at the cyclist from the shadows as he pressed his brakes and came to a stop. Alighting from his bike, the man retrieved a briefcase from a basket, looked around him to check that no one was watching, and walked straight up to the bookshop's door. There, he knocked in a sequence: once, three times, twice, and four times more. He turned up the collar of his raincoat and cast furtive glances over his shoulder as he waited to be let in. The door opened a crack and there was a murmur of voices. When the man was ushered into the shop, they heard the bell jingle-jangle. The door was closed firmly behind him.

"That was just plain odd!" said Arthur, not completely convinced that what he had just witnessed was the typical behavior of a burglar. "Who do you think that man was, Suze?"

"I don't know, but I thought he looked shifty," Susan whispered in reply. "Not the sort of man that Mr. Hardbattle would be friends with. I wish we could see what was happening inside the shop!"

"The way Mr. Shifty rapped on the door was strange," commented Arthur. "It was almost as if he was giving a secret knock! Even if we copied it, I'm not sure we'd be let in . . ." He hesitated while he thought about what they should do next. "Perhaps we should try around the back," said Arthur. "If the burglars didn't get in the building from the street, they must have broken a window or jimmied the door at the back of the house. There's a path somewhere that leads to a gate in Mr. Hardbattle's yard. Come on, Suze! Let's try to find it!"

They had started to sneak along the row of houses in search of a path that linked all of the backyards when the sound of another vehicle approaching made them stop in their tracks.

This time it was a van the size of a small truck. Its driver parked in front of the Land Rover, and three stocky men got out. They hunched their shoulders against the wet weather and, hands in their pockets, walked up to the door. One of them lifted his fist to deliver the secret knock.

"Change of plan!" whispered Arthur to Susan, turning on his heel and tiptoeing back toward the bookshop. He paused by his bike and removed the pump. "I've got an idea!"

Chapter Twenty

Shady Dealings

Arthur dropped to his hands and knees when he passed in front of the shop so that his head did not show above the windowsill. Taking care to keep to the shadows, Susan crawled behind him, and a panting Scallywag brought up the rear. When they were a stone's throw from the three men, Arthur called his stalking party to a halt, signaling by raising his hand. He and Susan crouched together, not even daring to whisper, waiting for the door of the bookshop to open.

The men did not appreciate being made to hang around outside in the rain. They buttoned up their jackets and grumbled about getting wet. When the door creaked ajar they squished into the doorway, eager to get dry, but an unseen person drove them back.

"Password first!" the person said.

"We got ourselves a stickler 'ere!" complained one of the men, turning to his two pals. "What's the flamin' password, lads? Anyone remember?"

Both men shrugged, then one of them had a flash of inspiration. "Some geezer's name, wasn't it? A Mafia Mr. Big, it sounded like . . . Poppa Peddle or someone . . ."

"Popocatépetl," said the man behind the door. Judging their effort to be close enough, he allowed the three men to enter.

Arthur readied himself as the men trooped over the threshold, waiting for the moment to make his move.

When the door was a split second away from clicking shut, Arthur sprang into action. Leaping forward, with one arm outstretched, he lodged his bicycle pump in the gap between the door and the doorjamb. His aim was true, and the pump did its job, keeping the door of the bookshop open. Arthur waited to see if anyone noticed that the door had not closed properly, but he did not hear any utterances of annoyance, and the door remained ajar.

Arthur was so pleased that his plan had worked and so keen to discover what was happening within the shop that he did not give a second's thought to the bell above the door. Susan whispered a warning in his ear just in time.

They concluded that their entry would have to coincide with a thunderclap, which, with luck, would cover the clamorous jingle-jangle of the bell. A flash of lightning gave them their cue, and the instant they heard the first crackle of thunder, Arthur and Susan nudged the door open and sneaked inside the shop. Before closing the door behind him, Arthur retrieved his bicycle pump, then he ran to join Susan and Scallywag, who had taken refuge behind a tall bookcase. They huddled there in the dark, their hearts thumping wildly.

When Susan and Arthur were satisfied that their entrance had not been detected, they left their hiding place behind the bookcase and crept through the maze of books toward the hum of voices. As they ventured deeper into the shop, their surroundings grew lighter so that they could see the outlines of books on the shelves and very nearly read their spines. Somewhere, in a hidden recess of the shop, a source of light was brightening the gloom.

"Over there!" whispered Arthur to Susan, pointing with his bicycle pump. "Candles and a whole load of people! Look!"

Both children peered around a bookcase and saw a gathering of twelve or more people standing in pools of light thrown by the wavering flames of six thick candles.

"Are *all* these people burglars?" Susan asked. She had expected to be afraid but found that she was more puzzled than scared. "Geez, Arthur! Aren't there a lot of them?"

The "burglars" were milling around a table display of some kind. There were the three broad-shouldered men, Mr. Shifty (who had taken off his hunting cap but still sported his bicycle clips), and a woman in a green paisley headscarf and rubber boots. When Arthur spotted Mrs.

Voysey-Brown and Jimmy among the throng, he started to think that Susan had been mistaken and that the people in the shop were not burglars at all. But then he saw someone flaunt a wad of cash and hand a thick stack of bills to Jimmy. A sale seemed to be going on. It was not unlike a rummage sale, the kind held in the playground at Arthur's school on weekends. Were the three houseguests selling Mr. Hardbattle's books and pocketing the proceeds? Arthur trembled with outrage, alerting Scallywag that something was wrong. A growl started in the dog's throat, and instinctively Susan tightened her grip on Scallywag's leash to prevent her from rushing into the small crowd of people.

A well-to-do voice raised itself above the commotion: "These rugs are exuding a strong smell of garlic! Or is it these opera evening gloves? The wretched smell seems to be floating right underneath my nose!" The woman in the headscarf replaced the soft leather gloves on the table and, in her prissy voice, continued to complain. "Must we view these artifacts in such poor light? Surely, we could switch on the electric lights and do away with these candles!"

"And have the cops sniffing round 'cause a shop's open after hours?" said one of the heavyset men beside her. "'Ave some sense, love! Blimey!"

"They aren't buying books, Arthur!" Susan said as more money changed hands and somebody walked out with an umbrella stand and a porcelain vase. Arthur and Susan watched, bemused.

"It's expensive junk, that's what it is!" declared Arthur. "Where can it have come from? I've never seen any of it before."

Every so often, Mr. Claggitt made an appearance, tramping downstairs in his hiking boots, his arms laden with stuff.

"Where's he getting it all from?" murmured Arthur, daring to lean around the bookcase to get a closer look.

Susan remembered the banging noises she had heard in her room prior to her tree-climbing escapade. At the time, she had thought the sounds had originated from the roof, but it seemed more likely now that they had come from the attic instead. She shared her new theory with Arthur.

But if Mr. Hardbattle had all this valuable stuff in his attic, why didn't he sell it to help him keep his business afloat? pondered Arthur, feeling more confused by the minute.

Before he could try to make sense of it all, Arthur became distracted by an argument over a piece of jewelry.

"Five thousand pounds?" Mr. Shifty snorted. "My good woman, I wouldn't give you five *hundred*!" He scrutinized a bow-shaped brooch through an eyeglass, shook his head, and handed it back to Mrs. Voysey-Brown.

Extremely unimpressed to be offered a tenth of her asking price, Mrs. Voysey-Brown resorted to calling Mr.

Shifty names, including a crooked old goat, a swindler, and a rip-off artist. "You know very well," she said, "that this diamond brooch is worth a mint. You can't expect me to believe that a *lady* would wear a *fake*. And when I say 'lady,' I mean the wife of a *lord*!" Mrs. Voysey-Brown looked down her nose at Mr. Shifty. "These gems are genuine, and you can't convince me otherwise, you foul, insipid man!"

Before Mrs. Voysey-Brown could close her fingers over it, Arthur got a good look at the brooch and realized that it was the very same one he had found in the gutter outside the shop the day he had cleaned Mr. Hardbattle's van. He frowned. Something was bothering him. How had Mr. Claggitt managed to get into the attic? Despite searching for ages, Mr. Hardbattle had not been able to find the key to the padlock. Could it be that the houseguests had put all the antiques in the attic themselves and used the padlock to stop anyone else from finding their haul? Where had the three of them been in the hours before Arthur found the brooch? Touring estates, they had said.

Arthur gasped. He fished inside his pocket and found the newspaper article he had ripped from the *Plumford Gazette*. Tilting it toward the light, he read the whole thing. It mentioned an outbreak of shoplifting and various burglaries in the town, but the article concentrated on the plundering of estates on May thirty-first.

Among the items stolen were statues, a silver teapot, vases, figurines, paintings, oriental rugs, and a diamond brooch identified as missing by Lady Smythe-Hughes. In one fell swoop the mystery had been solved!

"Hey, Suze!" said Arthur, shoving the article under her nose. "All that stuff is stolen! And these people—Mr. Shifty and the rest—they must be dealers . . . shady ones who aren't concerned about buying stolen goods!"

There was a loud bump and a discordant series of *clangs* and *tings*, which sounded as if somebody had dropped a set of silverware on the floor. Moments later, a flash of lightning lit up the shop and Arthur and Susan ducked behind their bookcase, but not before they glimpsed Mr. Claggitt emerging from the stairwell, his arms full of silverware and his boots caked in yellow mud.

"Had a little accident," they heard Mr. Claggitt say. "I'm no stranger to those, of course. Fallen into a fair number of crevices in my time, but I've never fallen down a staircase."

Arthur and Susan froze when they heard Mr. Claggitt's words and saw the vibrant color of his boots. They both realized immediately that the second-to-last stair had turned to custard, which meant that in the next few minutes the magic would go haywire.

Torn between wanting to see the magic misbehave and getting out of the shop to a place where their safety could be assured, Arthur and Susan waited to see what would happen.

"How much for this?" The woman in the headscarf had the nerve to remove a picture from the wall, which belonged to Mr. Hardbattle. As she thrust the painting of Lake Tahoe at Mrs. Voysey-Brown, a flock of ducks circled the lake and flew straight out of the painting. They flew in a *V* formation all around the shop, emitting loud quacks with every flap of their wings.

"Where'd they come from?" One of the beefy men shielded his head with a silver tea tray as the flock of ducks flew past. "Ruddy 'ell! They'll wake the neighbors! Hilary, don't you usually carry a shotgun in your trunk?"

"Yes, I do," the woman in the headscarf said. "I've got my twelve-gauge in my Land Rover, but I couldn't possibly shoot these ducks! Duck-shooting season doesn't start till September!"

The man put down the tea tray and called to his friends, "Come on, fellas! We should go! In five minutes, the cops are gonna be crawling all over this joint!" Buttoning his jacket over a small clock and a marble bust, the man set off at a jog toward the door.

At the mention of the police, everyone seemed to agree that they had spent enough and that they had no room left in their vehicles or in their briefcases for anything else. Purses were put away and wallets were snapped shut. Unnerved by the ducks, which they seemed to regard as some sort of booby trap, all of the dealers gathered their purchases and fled.

"We ought to scram too," said Arthur to Susan. He knew from Mr. Hardbattle's instructions that it was not wise to stick around when the magic lost control, and besides, they had seen everything they needed to see. As they turned to leave the shop, Susan accidentally stepped on Scallywag's paw.

The dog's yelp of pain was shrill, and in seconds Susan and Arthur had been discovered and surrounded.

"Well, well, well . . . what have we here?" said Mr. Claggitt, holding a candle up so its golden light fell on their horror-stricken faces.

"I could've sworn I put that pooch in the shed," muttered Jimmy, "and how did Susie get out of her room?"

Mrs. Voysey-Brown eyed Jimmy coldly. She looked the most displeased to have been spied on. "Susan can't have been in her room when you locked it, you fool!" she snapped.

Mortified that they had been caught, Arthur and Susan were also disturbed by the change they could detect in the air. The magic's energy was building, and it was unlikely to be long before the magic let rip.

Standing close together, they weighed their chances of slipping past the three grown-ups and reaching the door to the street.

"We should at least try," whispered Susan.

Arthur nodded. "Yeah. Ready? On the count of three . . ."

But suddenly a noise like a popping cork caused Arthur and Susan to glance at each other, and their uneasiness turned to fear when a few seconds later the floor of the bookshop began to vibrate. After a similar interval, the bookcases started to tilt and books fell to the floor, sending up clouds of choking dust. If Mrs. Voysey-Brown had been auditioning for a horror film, the scream she gave would have earned her the part. Everyone else doubled up, coughing, but when the air had cleared a little, Susan and Arthur seized their chance to escape.

They darted past the three grown-ups, intending to race as fast as they could through the shop until they reached the way out. If their route had been straight and their path unobstructed, they might have achieved their aim, but the shop was a labyrinth and Arthur and Susan had to keep changing direction to weave in and out of the alcoves. Their task was not made easier by having to swerve to avoid falling books or scramble over mounds of them.

Without Susan's flashlight, they would have been very lucky to stumble on the exit, but even with its beam they kept hitting dead ends. Every time they had to turn around and go back, they grew more panicky, conscious that their pursuers were right on their tail.

The turning point came when the books joined in the chase. Finding themselves at the mercy of Mrs. Voysey-Brown (who could run like a gazelle when she felt like it), Arthur and Susan thought they were done for. However, their view changed when a heap of books nearby sprang to life and formed a staircase that the children eagerly scurried up. (The lower part collapsed when Mrs. Voysey-Brown tried to do the same.)

As the chase progressed, Arthur and Susan were saved over and over again by the books. In addition to staircases, the magic conjured up bridges, slides, and, on one occasion, a moving walkway.

All this exertion meant, however, that the magic tired itself out. Before half an hour was up, the floorboards stopped vibrating and the books lay still. Silently, the ducks glided back into their painting, landing on Lake Tahoe with a waggle of their tails.

Youth was on their side, but Arthur and Susan did not turn out to be the fittest in the shop. Drawing on his impressive reserves of stamina, it was Mr. Claggitt who emerged from the wreckage, triumphant, with a child in each hand and Scallywag hanging off his trouser leg. Years of clinging to rock faces with his fingertips had made Mr. Claggitt's grip incredibly strong and, although they tried their hardest, neither Arthur nor Susan were able to free themselves.

A candle was found and relit, and a couple of chairs

were recovered from underneath a pile of books. Mrs. Voysey-Brown and Jimmy sat down on the chairs, while Mr. Claggitt brought Arthur, Susan, and Scallywag to sit on an overturned bookcase. Everyone looked exhausted and the worse for wear.

"We know you're behind all the burglaries in the papers!" burst out Arthur, aiming a kick at Mr. Claggitt's shins.

Mrs. Voysey-Brown smiled. "Is that so?"

"It's wrong to steal," said Susan. "I think it might be against the law."

"So, what you gonna do, pipsqueaks?" Jimmy said, smirking at them. "Hand us over to the cops?"

"Maybe we will!" said Arthur boldly, sticking out his chin.

Clenching the collar of Arthur's pajama top, Mr. Claggitt gave him a shake.

"No, you won't, sonny boy," he said, "and I'll tell you why. You and little Susie here are in this up to your necks—"

Before Mr. Claggitt could expand on why Susan and Arthur would be unwise to involve the police, there was a noise on the stairs and Miss Quint appeared at the top in her robe and slippers. She looked angry and also a little smug.

"I had a hunch it was *you*!" she said, pointing a finger at Jimmy. "You're the sort of prankster who would lock us in our rooms. Thought it was hilarious, I'll bet! Well, as you can see . . . I'm not easily beaten. You'll have to try harder than that to get the better of Beatrice Quint!"

Having decided that Jimmy was the culprit who had locked her in, Miss Quint proceeded to tell them how she had engineered her escape. Not possessing the sort of shoulders that could knock down a door, she had settled on attempting to pick the lock. After hours of trying, she had finally found the winning combination of nail file and bobby pin.

When she finished blathering on about how resourceful she had been, it dawned on Miss Quint that Arthur should have been at home in bed and that the shop looked as if a herd of wildebeest had rampaged through it.

"The magic's gone crazy again," said Arthur, seeing the look of surprise on her face.

Slowly, Miss Quint began to accept that she had probably made a mistake. Too proud to ask the others to explain what had happened, she tried to hide her embarrassment by babbling at top speed. "I was about to insist that you let Mr. Hardbattle out of the bathroom, but I heard him snoring as I came past the door. It would be kinder to let him sleep, I think, all things considered. So *that's* why you locked us in our rooms! You wanted to keep us safe while the magic caused trouble. Well, why didn't you say?"

"Actually—" began Arthur, but Miss Quint would not

listen. She figured she had solved the riddle of why five people were gathered downstairs in the middle of the night.

"It's sweet of you to tidy up the mess," she interrupted, eager to make amends for her blunder accusing Jimmy of playing a practical joke. "It's kind . . . very kind, but Arthur and Susan should be in bed. The clean-up can wait until tomorrow, don't you agree?"

Arthur could not believe his ears. He wondered if it was sleepiness rather than stupidity that caused Miss Quint to misinterpret what was going on.

"But, Miss Quint—" began Arthur.

"There's something we have to tell you!" said Susan.

Miss Quint wrinkled her nose with displeasure and hinted that they should be quiet.

"Whatever you children have to say, I'm sure it can wait until morning," she said. "Arthur, did you arrive on your bike? Well, what are you waiting for? Off you go!"

Chapter Twenty-One

After the Storm

By morning, the sky had been wiped clean, the rain clouds had moved on, and the thunderstorm's bequest to the new day was a cool, fresh breeze. Puddles shone, grass gleamed, and birdsong pierced the air.

Outdoors, all was right with the world, but inside the bookshop was a different story. Books and furniture were strewn everywhere, and Susan was having an awful time trying to make Miss Quint see reason.

Both had risen early. Miss Quint wanted to get up at first light so that the bookshop could be restored to a half-decent state by the time it was due to open, and Susan, who had barely slept a wink, wanted to tell Miss Quint as soon as possible that Jimmy, Mr. Claggitt, and Mrs. Voysey-Brown were a bunch of thieves.

As soon as she heard the jiggling of a doorknob and the creak of the broom closet door opening, Susan jumped out of bed, pulled on some shorts, and followed Miss Quint downstairs.

Miss Quint had already begun to clean up when Susan made an appearance, and she refused to pause from sweeping the floor to focus on what Susan had to say. While Miss Quint's indifference was discouraging, Susan did not let it deter her from launching into her account of what had happened during the night. She explained about her trek across town, Vijay's map, her ride on a bike, the secret knock, and the sale of stolen antiques.

When Susan finished, Miss Quint straightened up and examined the head of her broom. "This could use stiffer bristles," she observed.

"You do believe me, don't you, Miss Quint?" asked Susan, wondering if Miss Quint had heard a word she said.

Having fixed her eyes firmly on the floor during Susan's lengthy narration of events, Miss Quint looked up and gazed directly at her. "It sounds far-fetched," she said. "Could you have dreamed it?"

Susan was indignant. "Of course not!" she said.

"You expect me to believe that the people staying here—my guests—are a band of scheming crooks?" asked Miss Quint. "Jimmy's just a normal kid who likes to play the fool, and you can't think a respected mountaineer like Mr. Claggitt would be involved in anything underhanded! As for Mrs. Voysey-Brown . . . have you ever heard of a film star leading a life of crime?"

"But it's true!" insisted Susan.

"True, she says!" muttered Miss Quint, shaking her head in disbelief. She propped her broom against a bookcase and knelt down on the floor to gather some books.

Susan did not offer to help immediately because Miss Quint had frustrated her, but standing by and watching while someone else worked made Susan feel increasingly embarrassed, and after a couple of minutes she offered to lend a hand.

It was only when they happened upon some antiques among the debris that Miss Quint began to believe Susan might be telling the truth. They collected a brass doorknocker, a picture of fruit in a bowl, a silver tea tray, and an ornamental lion. Miss Quint locked them all in the closet under the stairs and apologized to Susan for doubting her.

"It's quite *incredible*, but it does make sense," Miss Quint conceded, weighing the evidence in her mind. Crime had never been a major problem in Plumford. It was only after she had wished for the book characters to be real that the incidents of burglary and shoplifting soared, and on the day that antiques had been stolen from the estates, Jimmy, Mr. Claggitt, and Mrs. Voysey-Brown had admitted to driving into the country in Mr. Hardbattle's van.

Miss Quint praised Susan's courage and ingenuity

before scolding her. Climbing down a tree in the dark Miss Quint described as "reckless," and roaming the streets of Plumford on her own she summed up as "foolhardy." Finally, she made Susan promise that she would never go off by herself at such a late hour again.

They wrestled with a bookcase and managed to stand it upright.

"What should we tell Mr. Hardbattle?" asked Susan as she started to fill the empty shelves.

"I'll tell him that it was me who locked him in," said Miss Quint, "and that I did it for his own safety because the magic was about to go wild."

Susan picked up another stack of books from the floor. "Shouldn't we mention that he's got some burglars living under his roof?"

"No, we certainly shouldn't!" said Miss Quint. She noticed Susan looked troubled about keeping this information from Mr. Hardbattle, and thought of a way to calm her. "I'll tell you what," said Miss Quint, squeezing Susan's arm and speaking in a gentle voice. "While Mr. Hardbattle's opening up, you and I will run upstairs and speak to those three scoundrels. We'll make them see that what they've done is wrong and tell them to give back all the things they've stolen. There won't be any need to bother Mr. Hardbattle once this mess has been sorted out. He's got enough on his plate, poor man, with arranging the move for the magic."

The plan met with Susan's approval, and they carried on with their wearisome task. But they had to stop their tidying temporarily when, at seven thirty sharp, the phone rang.

Miss Quint snatched up the receiver. It was Arthur. Having had a restless night like Susan, he had woken up at six and waited until a civilized hour before calling the shop.

"So, Suze has told you everything?" said Arthur.

"She has," replied Miss Quint. "Though I'll admit I was skeptical at first. It seems beyond belief that our guests are involved in the burglary business!"

"Yes, it does," said Arthur curtly, "but they are."

Miss Quint heard creaks through the ceiling and, panicking, almost dropped the phone. Worrying that Mr. Hardbattle had woken up and might come downstairs and overhear their conversation, she insisted that they end their call immediately. Arthur agreed to meet Miss Quint and Susan later on that morning at a café in town where they would be able to talk freely.

At ten o'clock, Arthur, Susan, and Miss Quint convened at the Blue Wisteria Tea Rooms. They found a table in the darkest, most secluded corner.

"The question is, what are we going to do?" said Arthur, perusing the menu while he waited for an answer.

No one spoke, but Miss Quint made a high sound in

her throat. She took a paper napkin and dabbed away tears, which were welling in her eyes.

"Oh, Miss Quint!" said Susan, overcome with sympathy.

Arthur looked up from the menu and was surprised to see Miss Quint in such a wretched state. He was just about to ask what had caused her to get so upset when he saw a waitress approaching with a notepad in her hand. He thrust the menu at Miss Quint, and she hid her tear-streaked face behind it.

Arthur ordered for the three of them, and when the waitress was out of earshot, he whipped the menu from Miss Quint's hands.

"What on earth's the matter?" he asked.

"You'd think, wouldn't you," Miss Quint said, her voice cracking slightly, "that when people have been accused of stealing, they'd try to deny it or be ashamed of what they'd done! Not our bunch of miscreants! They confessed to the thieving just like that!" Miss Quint snapped her fingers, then her bottom lip trembled and more tears flowed. "And were they repentant?" she said. "Not a bit of it! They boasted about how clever they were and wouldn't hear of ending their crime spree, let alone returning what they'd already taken."

Arthur took a deep breath. "Then we'll have to go to the police."

"We can't!" said Susan. "We're part of the gang!

We've handled stolen goods! And we haven't just handled them—we've eaten them!"

"What *are* you talking about?" asked Arthur.

"The ice-cream cones!" said Susan, gripping the edge of the table earnestly. "We each had one on that day we went to Plentiful Sands."

Arthur was appalled. "You mean those ice-cream cones were *stolen*?"

"*And* the beach ball *and* the deck chair *and* the sun hats *and* the bucket and shovel," Miss Quint revealed. "Jimmy pilfered all of them from people on the beach."

Arthur's mouth sagged open in shock. He had remembered the shopping trip Jimmy, Mr. Claggitt, and Mrs. Voysey-Brown had made when they first arrived. On that occasion they had come back with a scarf and two gold watches. At the time their purchases had not aroused Arthur's suspicions, but once he learned of their criminal tendencies, he realized the items had probably been stolen. However, he had forgotten all about the trip to the beach and was dismayed to think that he had gobbled down somebody else's ice cream.

"It seems it was Jimmy who led the others astray," said Miss Quint. "He told Susan and me that he'd been thieving since he was a kid, and that he only took the job as a bellhop so that he could steal from the hotel's wealthy guests!"

Arthur urged Miss Quint to change the subject quickly when he spotted the waitress coming toward them, carrying a tray. They smiled politely when the woman placed their order in front of them. Arthur had asked for two lemonades, a pot of tea, and a plate of pastries.

"What *I* don't understand is why they did it," said Arthur. "Mr. Claggitt's so obsessed with mountains; I wouldn't have thought he is the money-grubbing type."

"He's the most enthusiastic burglar of them all!" said Miss Quint.

"He likes scaling walls," explained Susan as she reached for a cream tart with a raspberry on top.

Miss Quint wholeheartedly agreed. "Mr. Claggitt told us that his grappling hook has seen more action in the past few days than it did when he went up Mount Everest!"

"What are they planning to do with the money?" asked Arthur.

"They're using it to finance their new life," said Miss Quint, pouring herself a cup of strong tea. "Free room and board at Mr. Hardbattle's house is like living in squalor, according to them."

"They're leaving Plumford," said Susan, "and going abroad!" To an untraveled person like Susan, the idea of journeying to another country was almost as exciting as going to the moon. "Isn't that so daring, Arthur? Abroad is very different from here, you know. They speak in languages you can't understand and the food is inedible, so Miss Quint said—"

"They have their hearts set on Switzerland," cut in Miss Quint. She sounded resentful.

"Why Switzerland?" asked Arthur, helping himself to a little cake.

"It meets their needs," Miss Quint snapped, bitterness drawing her lips into a thin line. "Mrs. Voysey-Brown's above the rest of us, being an actress in films. She's got expensive tastes. She's used to fine dining and glitzy resorts, and those kinds of places are right up Jimmy's alley because of the rich clientele they attract. Switzerland's full of fancy hotels and, more important, it's got the Eiger."

"What's that?" Arthur asked.

"It's a mountain," Susan told him. "Mr. Claggitt said it's very big and its north face is a real stinker to climb."

Arthur could not get his head around the fact that the three book characters had raised enough cash to leave the country. "Won't it cost a lot to get to Switzerland and pay hotel bills and climb the Eiger? Do they have that kind of money?" he asked.

"They're a few thousand short, apparently," Miss Quint informed him.

"If only we could go to the police and get them arrested!" said Arthur.

"If we hand them over to the police, we'll be taken into custody too, as accessories," Miss Quint told him briskly. "And anyway, the police would realize they're not British citizens—or any kind of citizens—and then I'd have to explain where they came from . . ."

"The police would find out about the magic!" said Arthur, his heart sinking rapidly. "They'd raid Mr. Hardbattle's shop!"

"You see?" said Miss Quint. "Our hands are tied."

Arthur groaned and fell back limply in his chair. "Things couldn't possibly be worse!" he complained.

"Oh yes, they could!" objected Miss Quint. "Yours wasn't the only telephone call we had this morning."

Arthur smacked his forehead in despair. "Who else called?"

"Mrs. Carruthers," said Susan. "Her voice sounded funny, so I didn't know it was her at first. I asked her how her bees were, but she didn't have time for small talk. She said she needed to speak to Mr. Hardbattle urgently. He was in the bathroom. It took me forever to find him. He had creamy white soap all over his chin. When I told him who was on the phone and what she'd said, he ran downstairs without rinsing his face or anything!"

Fearing that Pam Carruthers had been the bearer of unwelcome news, Arthur asked Susan what she had said.

"I couldn't hear," Susan replied, "but Mr. Hardbattle

kept saying, 'Oh no!' and 'Oh, how awful' over and over again."

Arthur looked to Miss Quint for an explanation.

"A tree fell down last night," she told Arthur solemnly. "The tree got struck by lightning in the storm. It landed on that dear little cottage and reduced the place to rubble."

"He's acting like he's given up!" said Arthur as he and Susan stared across the shop at Mr. Hardbattle. The old man sat behind his desk, dazed and sorrowful, his shoulders hunched. In front of him sat a cup of cold tea that Miss Quint had made for him but that he had not touched.

The news that the cottage had been badly damaged was a blow to them all, but while the others vowed not to let it defeat them, Mr. Hardbattle sunk into a deep depression. Arthur, Miss Quint, and Susan tried to rouse him out of his stuporlike state, reminding him that there were still eight days left before the rent was due, but Mr. Hardbattle would not be cheered up. He had made up his mind that their undertaking to move the magic was hopeless, and he resigned himself to losing his business and his home.

Seeing Mr. Hardbattle so down in the dumps upset

Arthur, and he wished he could throw himself into the task of finding another home for the magic. However, Arthur was smart enough to realize that the three burgling houseguests was a more pressing problem at the moment.

In the Blue Wisteria Tea Rooms, Arthur, Susan, and Miss Quint had decided that they would have to put a stop to the thefts themselves. With some detective work, they aimed to discover how Jimmy and his gang were planning to add to their haul—and to stop them from doing so. In the space of a few days, the three artful thieves had amassed a small fortune, but they needed even more money to cover the cost of their adventure abroad. They would have to pay for forged passports, luggage, and plane tickets, and once they left England they would still need a nest egg large enough to fund their new lives.

"One more big job—that's what they said," revealed Susan when she, Arthur, and Miss Quint met up in the park to walk Scallywag on Friday afternoon. Susan was their eavesdropping champion. She was adept at finding hiding places to hear conversations without anyone knowing she was there. "And they plan to pull it off on Saturday."

"Saturday? You don't mean tomorrow?" said Miss Quint.

"The day of the carnival," said Arthur. "Of course! While the whole town is watching the parade, it should be simple for Jimmy's gang to steal loads of stuff! What kind of thing are they planning, Suze?"

Susan bit her lip. "I didn't hear that part."

The gang's preferred meeting place was Mrs. Voysey-Brown's room. It was the largest bedroom in the house. Before Mrs. Voysey-Brown had moved into it, Miss Quint had commandeered it for herself, and before that, the room had been the chosen sleeping quarters of Mr. Hardbattle (who didn't like to kick out a relation of Arthur's and said he would sleep in the bathroom instead).

That evening after supper, Susan managed to sneak inside the room and find a suitable hiding place. She chose the wardrobe and crouched down in a corner, concealing herself behind a long winter coat. Leaving the wardrobe door ajar, Susan was able to listen to the gang's plans when they held one of their hush-hush meetings half an hour later.

"The jewelry shop on Twopenny Lane!" she said to Miss Quint after gulping down a large glass of water (it had been stifling in the wardrobe and she had been in there for over an hour).

"Okay," said Miss Quint, stern-faced and businesslike.

"I'll telephone Arthur, and then we should go to bed, Susan. It's crucial that we get a good night's sleep. We'll have to be at our best tomorrow if we're going to foil their plans!"

Chapter Twenty-Two

Brass Bands and Banners

When Arthur rode his bike through Plumford on Carnival Day, he saw that city workers had been busy overnight. At the edge of the sidewalk, barriers had been put in place to keep the public from crossing the street once the carnival parade got under way, and zigzagging from streetlamp to streetlamp were several hundred feet of flag streamers. The triangles of yellow, red, white, and blue flapped lazily in the breeze as Arthur pedaled his bicycle beneath them.

It was eight o'clock in the morning and the weather was as glorious as the carnival organizers had hoped it would be. The sky was lapis lazuli blue and the sun was far too bright to look at. As Arthur whizzed along on his bike, he passed plenty of early risers like himself who were all busy with some job or other to help prepare for the Plumford Carnival. Trash collectors and road sweepers made the streets look spick-and-span; a frowning pair with clipboards checked the timetable of events, and ladies from Plumford's Flower Arranging Society swarmed around a booth in front of the library that had been erected to provide a sheltered seat for the parade judges. The judges' job was to award a prize to the most impressive float. Last year's head judge was the town's bank manager, but this year the Plumford Carnival Committee set their sights a little higher. It was something of a coup when Lady Felicity Smythe-Hughes, the wife of a poultry tycoon, agreed to preside over the panel of judges.

When they learned that an aristocrat was to officiate, the ladies of Plumford's Flower Arranging Society resolved to decorate the booth with expensive blooms, which they thought was the sort of lavish gesture a person of nobility merited.

There were barricades everywhere and most of the roads in the center of town were closed off to traffic, but luckily no one was too concerned with one young boy on a bike.

When Arthur reached Hardbattle Books, Miss Quint, Susan, and Scallywag were waiting for him on the sidewalk outside. Miss Quint had packed a knapsack with three sandwiches and two large bottles of lemonade to satisfy their appetites while they kept the jewelry shop under observation. Miss Quint's choice of attire was usually stylish and a little eccentric, but today she dressed down. Her outfit of a pair of wide-legged pants, a sleeveless top, and sunglasses had been carefully selected to help her to blend in with the crowd. Around her neck she wore Mr. Hardbattle's old binoculars, which he used to watch herons on vacation on the Norfolk Broads. Miss Quint had no interest in birds. She intended to use the binoculars to look out for thieves.

Susan had changed into something new: a pair of capri pants and a T-shirt with sequins sewn onto its front. She had also unraveled her braids so that her hair fell loosely down her back. For the first time since she arrived in Plumford, she did not look peculiar. Arthur thought she could easily pass for a girl in his class or one of his sisters' friends.

"All set?" asked Miss Quint.

"Did you remember the things?" pressed Susan.

Arthur dismounted from his bike. "Yes," he answered. "I've got my kazoo and the ball of string."

"Excellent," Miss Quint said, patting each child's shoulder. "Let's go, team!"

The jewelry shop was on Twopenny Lane, not far from the library and the intersection with Swan Street, which were both on the parade route. It took them twenty minutes to walk there, and once they arrived, they looked closely at the shop. It was owned by a woman named Geraldine Jennings. Arthur and Susan gaped at all the treasures in the window, pointing out trays of gold necklaces and rings set with enormous gems, while Miss Quint got out her tape measure and noted the width of the doorway. She also counted the number of steps leading up to it (three) and saw that a concrete slab outside the shop was liable to tip if its top left-hand corner was stepped on.

After they carried out their inspection, they crossed the road and sat down on a bench positioned in an alcove not far from Jennings the Jeweler's. Miss Quint reached in her bag and drew out two comics, which she handed to Arthur and Susan. Next, she produced a newspaper for herself. Behind their periodicals, they went over their plan.

"Are you clear about what you have to do when the gang gets here?" hissed Miss Quint.

"I'm going to slip inside the shop unnoticed," said Susan, "before the thieves get out of Mr. Hardbattle's van."

"With my kazoo," reminded Arthur, handing it to her behind his open comic book.

"What will you be doing, Arthur?" Miss Quint prompted.

"I'll be unwinding my ball of string," Arthur said, "and positioning myself on one side of the doorway. You'll be on the other side, won't you, Miss Quint?"

"I will," confirmed Miss Quint. "A-plus so far. Well done!"

Susan lowered her comic and grinned. "I will wait

until they've grabbed all the jewelry they want, and then when they're ready to leave, I'll blow on the kazoo."

"At which point," said Arthur, turning to Miss Quint, "we raise the string above the doorstep and hold on tightly . . ."

"And the whole darned lot of them tumble down the steps," finished Miss Quint with an air of supreme satisfaction.

"Then I grab the jewels and take off on my bike," said Arthur, "only returning when the coast is clear."

"That's right," said Miss Quint. "And when we hand them back to Mrs. Jennings the jeweler, she offers us a huge reward!"

Miss Quint's final comment made them all laugh, and they felt confident enough to revel in how simple—yet ingenious—their plan was.

"And if any of them hop over our string, they'll land on that loose concrete slab and fall flat on their face," said Miss Quint delightedly. "Our plan is foolproof. I don't see how it could go wrong!"

The morning wore on. Underneath the bench, Scallywag rested her head on her paws and went to sleep. Susan, Miss Quint, and Arthur swapped their reading material and got up occasionally to stretch their legs. The shops on Twopenny Lane opened their doors and the volume of pedestrian traffic increased. From their seat on the bench, they could see the top of the road where crowds were beginning to gather to watch the parade, which was due to start at eleven o'clock. Arthur saw his father walk past with his youngest sister, Tilly, in tow. He was hidden behind Miss Quint's newspaper at the time and so his father and sister did not see him, but he watched them walk the length of the sidewalk to Swan Street and claim their place in the front row, directly behind the barriers.

"I assume the gang won't get here until the parade starts," said Miss Quint.

"That makes sense," said Arthur.

They waited for another half an hour. Jimmy's gang did not show up.

At the top of Twopenny Lane, the crowds continued to swell until there was no room left on the sidewalks. In the distance, Miss Quint, Susan, and Arthur could hear a brass band striking up a tune. Fainter still were the whine of bagpipes and the steady pounding of drums. The parade had started.

"It would've been fun to see all the floats," said Arthur with a pang of regret.

"I should have been on one!" said Miss Quint, sounding disappointed as well. "The Women's Institute has the honor of leading the whole procession this year. They're dressing as Hawaiian hula girls, and the float's all decked out like a tropical island, with palm trees and coconuts and everything."

Two children walked past at that moment, both licking ice-cream cones topped with raspberry sauce.

"They look delicious! May I have one of those?" asked Susan, gazing earnestly at Miss Quint.

Agreeing to Susan's request, Miss Quint opened her purse and placed some money in her hand. "Oh, very well, dear! Could you get us all ice-cream cones? There's a shop around the corner, behind the library, that sells them. It's called Clements. Off you go!"

"But, Miss Quint . . . ," protested Arthur.

Susan picked up Scallywag's lead and said, "Scally! Let's go for a walk!" before setting off down the street with the dog trotting beside her.

Arthur turned to Miss Quint, frowning. "What if the thieves turn up?" he said. He thought that an ice-cream cone would be nice, but he viewed Miss Quint's decision as a poor one.

"We'd be very unlucky for them to come in the next three minutes!" scoffed Miss Quint. "Stop worrying, Arthur! Susan won't be long."

They waited patiently at first, but after Susan had been gone for more than five minutes, they both began to feel anxious. They decided Arthur should go to the ice-cream shop to see why Susan had been delayed, but before he could take more than a few paces, Scallywag came running, trailing her leash along the ground.

Arthur's stomach gave a lurch. He guessed immediately

that something had happened to Susan. Without checking with Miss Quint, he flew off down the street, almost colliding with a lady and her shopping cart as he turned the corner onto Oldbrook Road.

"Susan! Susan! Where are you?" he yelled. His eyes darted from one side of the street to the other, and his heart did gymnastics in his chest. Hearing the squeal of tires, he raced ahead and was just in time to see the rear of a vehicle vanishing around a corner. Arthur stamped his foot with frustration and felt something soft and gooey under his shoe. He lifted up his foot and saw that three ice-cream cones had been dropped onto the sidewalk. The cones were crushed and their creamy scoops were a partially melted mess. He could see the mark his shoe had made on them. A second footprint was visible too. It was much larger than Arthur's and had chunky treads like the kind commonly found on sturdy footwear. Arthur realized with a jolt of horror that it was the print of a hiking boot.

Arthur started to run back the way he had come, knowing that he would need his bicycle to have any chance of rescuing Susan. Now that he had seen the bootprint, he was convinced that the vehicle that had sped out of sight was Mr. Hardbattle's van and he had no doubt that Susan was bundled into it.

Arthur raced past Clements and the rear of the library. When he turned onto Twopenny Lane, he had to dodge through a cluster of gossiping shoppers to get to Miss Quint. She had hitched her bag onto her shoulder and was holding Scallywag on her leash, agitation on her face.

Not waiting until he got closer, Arthur shouted out the news: "She's gone, Miss Quint! They've taken her!"

When Arthur heard the far-off whine of police sirens, he thought for a moment that he was imagining them. There was a buzzing noise as well. Everyone around him seemed to be talking at once.

"Yes, isn't it awful?" said a woman, responding to Arthur's announcement. "Kidnapped in broad daylight, right under the noses of all the local bigwigs. They found a ransom note pinned to the library bulletin board. A hundred thousand dollars, they've asked for!"

"What?" said Arthur, baffled by what the woman had said. He was amazed that the news of Susan's kidnapping traveled so fast, and such a high ransom seemed incredible. How could the gang think he and Miss Quint could possibly raise that much money?

"Of course, if they'd known how much her husband was worth, they might have asked for a million," the woman babbled excitedly.

"A million?" said Arthur, confused. "Whose husband? What has that got to do with Susan?"

The woman gave Arthur a scornful look. "She's not named *Susan*," she said. "Lady Smythe-Hughes's first name is Felicity!"

Chapter Twenty-Three

In Hot Pursuit

"Those devious old scoundrels!" spluttered Miss Quint when she and Arthur started to piece together what had happened. "They never had any intention of robbing the jewelry shop. It was all a ruse to throw us off the scent."

Arthur was so angry and his hands were shaking so badly that he could not manage to unlock his bike. "I'll bet they knew Susan was listening in on their plans," he said. "They fed her a load of lies when she was hiding in that wardrobe. They're probably laughing their heads off at us!"

Miss Quint tried to help Arthur by holding his bicycle steady while he knelt beside the front wheel and wrestled with the lock.

"They must have thought Christmas came early when they found out the chief judge of the parade belonged to the nobility!" she ranted, gripping the handlebars tightly. "If Jimmy and those rotten cronies of his get their hands on that ransom money, they'll be in the Swiss Alps before you can say 'cuckoo clock.'"

"There!" Arthur announced with relief as he twisted a key and his lock snapped open. "Now I can go after them!"

"I wonder why they needed to take Susan," reflected Miss Quint. "Maybe she saw them in the process of shoving Lady Smythe-Hughes into their van. They must have smuggled old Fancy Pants out of the library's rear entrance."

Arthur leaped onto the seat of his bike and placed his foot on the pedal, ready to speed away.

"You haven't really got a chance of catching them, you know," Miss Quint felt obliged to point out. She strained her neck and looked toward Swan Street, where people in the crowds were jostling to get a good view of the parade. The procession still seemed to be going on despite the kidnapping of one of its judges. "It's a shame we can't find ourselves a better mode of transportation," she commented.

Suddenly, Miss Quint twisted Arthur's handlebars, forcing his front wheel to face the crowds at the top of Twopenny Lane. "I've got it, Arthur!" she cried, running up the slope toward the sounds of tubas and trumpets belting out a military march. "Follow me if you want to save Susan!"

Somehow they fought their way through the crowds of people, who were waving flags and cheering as the first of the floats rolled past. Miss Quint was thankful she had chosen to wear pants as she performed a scissor jump over the barriers and into the road.

Arthur happened to find his father and sister in the throng and thrust his bicycle at them with only the briefest of explanations. Then he followed Miss Quint, vaulting over the barrier and into the path of the town's brass band.

He dashed after Miss Quint, who had caught up with the leading float and was running alongside it. The float was a monstrous truck with a platform mounted on its trailer. Just as Miss Quint had said, it was carrying the members of the Women's Institute. Made to resemble an island paradise in the Pacific, the float had been covered with sand and planted with artificial palm trees fashioned from cardboard, chicken wire, felt, and crêpe paper. In the center of the float was a papier-mâché volcano, and around it, dressed in grass skirts and garlands of tissue-paper flowers, were the ladies of the Women's Institute.

Like someone with a death wish, Miss Quint hurled herself in front of the truck and waved her hands to halt it, causing the crowd to gasp in fear. The driver was forced to come to a stop, and once he stepped on the brakes, Miss Quint hammered on the door of the cab until he opened it to ask her what the devil she thought she was doing.

"Out!" said Miss Quint, grabbing the startled truck

driver by his shirt lapels as he leaned toward her to tell her that she was unhinged. He fell unceremoniously out of the cab and, without wasting a second, Miss Quint picked up Scallywag and sprang into the driver's seat. Arthur raced around to the passenger door, which Miss Quint duly opened for him, and climbed in next to her.

The driver tried to jump in front of his vehicle, but Miss Quint was not as compassionate as he had been and almost mowed him down.

"Idiot!" said Miss Quint as she rolled down the window and shouted to the ladies on the truck platform to hold on. Then she put the truck into gear and roared off up the street.

So many roads were cordoned off that Miss Quint had a good idea of the route Jimmy and his gang would have to take to get out of Plumford. Shooting past bemused spectators who had lined the streets to see the parade, Arthur glanced in the side mirror and saw the hula dancers (most of whom were of retirement age) clinging to the palm trees, their mouths hanging open in shock.

"I think we'll go down here," said Miss Quint, grappling with the oversized steering wheel and guiding the truck through a row of traffic barricades, crushing them under the truck's massive wheels.

"Oops, I think we just lost Mrs. Tidwell," said Miss Quint, glancing in her mirror and biting her lip guiltily.

Arthur double-checked that he had put his seat belt on.

The narrow streets of Plumford's shopping district were not designed for seven-ton trucks to hurtle down them at forty miles an hour. Miss Quint attracted a lot of attention as she scuffed curbs, whacked the roofs of bus stops, and dented the odd trash can or two. The spectacle of twenty or more terrified members of the Women's Institute, wearing Hawaiian costumes and holding on to handcrafted palm trees, drew even more amazed stares from everyone they passed.

Arthur heard the sound of sirens gradually getting louder. He was torn between telling Miss Quint to floor it so that they could outrun the police and asking her to slow down so that he did not have to hold on to the door handle for dear life.

At one point, they heard thumps on the roof of the cab and, in their mirrors, Arthur and Miss Quint saw some of the more sprightly members of the Women's Institute hurling coconuts at them.

"I think we should go a bit slower," he said. "Our passengers are getting upset."

"Nonsense!" insisted Miss Quint, pressing the horn to let an old man at a crosswalk know that she was approaching fast. "If they've got the energy to throw armfuls of coconuts, they'll have the strength to hang on for hours yet!"

Eventually, having blown through the heart of Plumford, they chanced upon Mr. Hardbattle's van. Miss Quint let out a war cry when she saw it and pressed the accelerator to the floor. In her excitement she lost focus, and the seven-ton truck weaved all over the road. There were screams from the ladies of the Women's Institute, and a line of people waiting by a hot-dog stand found themselves buried in a heap of sand.

Miss Quint changed gears and steamed toward the van, and for the next five minutes the two vehicles played a game of cat and mouse.

It seemed as if the gang of kidnappers had gotten away when the van turned down a narrow alley that the truck could not get through without bringing down the buildings on either side. However, it was in this alley that the gang's luck ran out. Swerving to avoid a cat that had darted into its path, the van plowed into some trash cans and its engine stalled. Miss Quint and Arthur heard a throbbing, whining noise as the van's engine struggled to restart.

"It won't fire up!" said Arthur.

"We've got 'em!" Miss Quint cried and switched off the truck's engine.

Fearing that the stop was only temporary and that Miss Quint would start up the truck again and continue the nightmarish journey, the ladies of the Women's Institute who had managed to remain on board deserted the truck hastily. Most of them scurried into a nearby café for a much-needed cup of tea, but one or two preferred to dash to the pub next door for a glass of something stronger.

Once the truck's engine died, Scallywag emerged from the floorboard, where she had spent the entire journey hiding beside Arthur's feet. When Miss Quint and Arthur jumped down from the cab, Scallywag leaped after them and together they ran up the alley, determined to bring the gang to justice.

The van's front doors opened before they got to it and Jimmy and his accomplices attempted to flee. Scallywag tailed Mrs. Voysey-Brown and, barking crazily, she pinned the woman against a wall. Arthur, who had started to learn football, performed a well-timed tackle and brought Jimmy to the ground. Then he sat on him so he could not get away. It was left to Miss Quint to take on Mr. Claggitt but, enlivened by the thrill of driving the truck, she was not daunted one bit. Charging at him with a plastic soda bottle in her hand, she battered his broad back with it, then opened its top and sprayed him with its contents. Mr. Claggitt coughed and spluttered and rubbed his stinging eyes, and, while he was occupied with that, Miss Quint scooped up the keys to the van, which he had dropped on the cobblestones.

When Miss Quint opened the rear doors of the van, Susan was the first to tumble out, shading her eyes against the dazzling sunlight. Before Arthur and Miss Quint could throw their arms around her, Susan held out a hand to the van's other passenger, a slim blonde dressed in a pink silk suit, a pearl choker, and a fancy hat.

"Thank you, treasure," said Lady Smythe-Hughes, taking Susan's hand. She stepped down from the back of the van with the utmost grace, as if such a skill had been taught to her at finishing school.

"Are you hurt, Your Ladyship?" inquired Miss Quint. She wasn't sure whether to curtsy, not having met a lady before.

"Oh, no, we're quite all right," said Lady Smythe-Hughes. "We're made of stern stuff, aren't we, Susan?"

For a member of the aristocracy, Lady Smythe-Hughes did not seem at all stuck-up. She insisted they call her Felicity, and when Scallywag ran over to her and was so eager to say hello that she put her paws on Lady Smythe-Hughes's skirt, she laughed and gave the dog a friendly pat.

Despite Lady Smythe-Hughes's down-to-earth ways, Arthur was embarrassed to be in her presence with smudges of dirt on his clothes, which he got when he rolled on the ground catching Jimmy. Leaving Scallywag to guard the gang, Arthur hurriedly brushed himself down, then approached Lady Smythe-Hughes and Susan with a beaming grin.

"You're safe now," he told them.

"Thanks to you!" said Lady Smythe-Hughes. She reached out to shake Arthur's hand and made the same grateful gesture to Miss Quint.

As the sounds of police sirens drew closer, Miss Quint took Arthur aside to discuss what should be done next. They decided Arthur should stay with Susan and Lady Smythe-Hughes to answer any questions the police might have, while Miss Quint rounded up Jimmy's gang and took them away. As much as they deserved to be punished for the double kidnapping, it was better all around if they avoided being caught.

While Arthur and Susan talked to Lady Smythe-Hughes, Miss Quint slipped away and ordered the gang into the back of Mr. Hardbattle's van. Then she opened the hood and peeked inside to figure out why the engine had stalled. Diagnosing an overheated engine, which Mr. Hardbattle had warned her might happen, she cooled it down using water from a bottle kept underneath the driver's seat. Once this was done, the engine started up on the first try and Miss Quint drove up the alley, turning the corner with a squeal of tires.

She was only just in time. Seconds later, a string of police cars screeched to a halt in front of the truck, their blue lights flashing and flickering. The police were almost beaten to the scene by members of the local press, who swarmed around Lady Smythe-Hughes with their cameras, notepads, and microphones.

"Smile, Suze!" said Arthur as a newspaper photographer took their picture. "I think this might make the front page!"

Chapter Twenty-four

Trunk's find

Arthur and Susan basked in all the media attention, spelling out their names to journalists and hearing the click of cameras every which way they turned. After a few minutes, the police broke up the crowd and Susan and Arthur were whisked away in a police car, to be questioned at the local station about the whole kidnapping affair. The police were desperate to find out the identities of the kidnappers, but Arthur and Susan played dumb, providing vague descriptions that had the officer in charge of facial sketches scratching his head. When Arthur was asked who had been with him in the truck, he was even more evasive and insisted that he could not think of her name.

"Come on, young man!" prompted a chief inspector. "You were sitting next to the woman! You must have known her name!"

"It's on the tip of my tongue," Arthur said unhelpfully.

Arthur heard the police officers talking and knew

Miss Quint was in serious trouble, having broken several laws in her efforts to catch up with Mr. Hardbattle's van. She had hijacked a truck, exceeded the speed limit of thirty miles an hour, and driven like a lunatic (or, as the police preferred to put it, "without due care and attention"). Neither Arthur nor Susan gave Miss Quint up but, because there had been several hundred witnesses (including twenty-seven irate hula dancers), Miss Quint's name was soon discovered by the police.

Miss Quint knew the police would come for her. She parked the van outside Hardbattle Books, leaving Jimmy, Mr. Claggitt, and Mrs. Voysey-Brown with their hands tied behind their backs, locked inside. Then Miss Quint changed out of her sleeveless top and pants and into a sensible blouse and skirt and a pair of pumps, which she felt was a more appropriate outfit to wear for an interrogation. She was also organized enough to pack a bag with a change of underwear should she be kept in a cell overnight. When Officer Chubb showed up in his police car, Miss Quint was ready and waiting for him.

The lecture she got was fierce and lengthy. Barely allowing her a chance to speak, a grumpy detective sergeant made Miss Quint admit that she had acted recklessly and foolishly, and that she had endangered the lives of some of Plumford's finest townswomen, not to mention Lionel Sayer, the driver of the truck, and a Mr. Wilfred Tottle, who had barely survived crossing the road.

Eventually, Miss Quint's severe reprimand came to an end when the station's chief detective entered the room. He said that, although she had broken quite a lot of laws, she had more than made up for her misdemeanors by rescuing Lady Smythe-Hughes and a child not fully identified but claiming to be called Susan. Lady Smythe-Hughes, so the chief detective said, was as pleased as punch with Miss Quint and her young helpers and asked that they receive the highest praise for displaying such courage and quick thinking.

The result was that Miss Quint got off scot-free.

Arthur, Susan, and Miss Quint were driven in a police car back to Hardbattle Books, and at the end of the journey, Officer Chubb asked all three for their autographs. Arthur and Susan were happy to scribble their signatures in his notebook, but Miss Quint turned down Officer Chubb's request with the words "Don't be ridiculous!"

"Get used to it. We're famous now," said Arthur, handing the officer his notebook and pen.

"Better open up," said Officer Chubb, gesturing to the doorway of the bookshop, where the sign had been turned so that it said CLOSED. "I think you'll find you've got a customer waiting."

They looked to where the officer was pointing and saw a hunched old man standing patiently beside the door. He was wearing his hat and raincoat despite the sunny weather and had a suitcase at his feet.

"It's Mr. Hardbattle!" Miss Quint cried. "What is he thinking? The crazy old coot! Why would he close the shop on a Saturday?"

Arthur flung open the door of the police car and rushed to Mr. Hardbattle's side. "Have you got your energy back?" he asked the old man. "Are you going on another expedition around the country to find the You Know What a new home?"

Gazing at Arthur with dull, lifeless eyes, Mr. Hardbattle patted Arthur's shoulder. "It's time to face facts," he uttered in a feeble voice. "My bookselling days are behind me. I've been on the phone with an old folks' home in Ivychurch. They said that, if I didn't mind sharing a room, I could move in right away."

The others piled out of the car and joined Arthur and Mr. Hardbattle on the sidewalk. Officer Chubb gave a cheerful wave as he drove away, but nobody waved back. They were far too busy digesting Mr. Hardbattle's shocking announcement. Their elation at foiling the kidnapping plot was replaced with a feeling of dismay.

Mr. Hardbattle picked up his suitcase with a weary grunt. "There's just one thing, Arthur, before I catch my bus: could I depend on you to look after old Scallywag? They don't allow dogs at Sunset Lodge."

"But, Mr. Hardbattle, you *can't*—" began Arthur.

"You're worried about your aunt and uncles, I know," Mr. Hardbattle said. "They're welcome to stay until the lease runs out, but then they'll have to move on, I'm afraid. The same goes for you and your niece, Miss Quint," he said, giving them all a watery smile. "I'm glad that I waited until you got back. Didn't want to leave without saying good-bye." He handed the shop keys to Miss Quint and lifted his hat in farewell.

There was a moment of dreadful silence, during which Scallywag whimpered and Arthur, Susan, and Miss Quint each tried to think of what they might say to change Mr. Hardbattle's mind.

"But there's still a week to go!" said Arthur as Mr. Hardbattle turned to leave. "All sorts of things might happen by then. We could find a new place for the magic tomorrow! You can't quit! Not yet!"

"I'll miss you!" said Susan, close to tears.

"Well, I won't!" said Miss Quint, the harshness of her words making Susan and Arthur gape. "Nor will Trunk, I doubt," continued Miss Quint heartlessly. "And as for Scallywag—she'll forget you in a blink! She's bound to prefer a nice, *young* master. I'm really looking forward to driving your van. I might even take it up to Scotland on vacation. Five hundred miles all in one trip shouldn't put too much of a strain on the engine, and once we're in Scotland, I think it would enjoy zooming up and down all those *enormous* hills . . ."

She hesitated, worried that she might have gone too far. Miss Quint knew she was taking a huge gamble by pretending that Mr. Hardbattle's imminent departure did not bother her.

Mr. Hardbattle failed to take a single step in the direction of the bus stop. He wavered, as if he were a fern whose fronds had been caught in a gentle breeze.

Sensing that his nerve was weakening, Miss Quint prepared to deliver her killer blow. "It's a shame you can't wait an hour or two," she said. "I'd made up my mind to come clean at last! There are a few things I should have told you. You see . . . I didn't follow your instructions to the letter. Still, if you're sure you have to go *right this minute*, you'd better. So long!"

Mr. Hardbattle put down his suitcase. A glimmer of his old spirit flickered in his eyes. "You've called my bluff!" he said to Miss Quint, not seeming too displeased about it. "The wiles of women are a wonder to behold!"

Miss Quint seized Mr. Hardbattle's elbow with one hand and unlocked the door of the bookshop with the other. The bell jingle-jangled as she led him inside. Trunk, who had been sitting on his shelf, feeling lonely, clambered to his feet and did a little jig.

"So, you didn't mean all those things you said?" said Susan to Miss Quint. "Phew! I'm glad about that!"

Once they had all trooped into the shop, Miss Quint sent Susan upstairs to put a kettle on the stove. In the meantime, she and Arthur revealed to Mr. Hardbattle all that had happened in the week he had not been in

Plumford. To their surprise, he took it all in stride. When he found out about the lies he'd been told, he was hurt and a little angry, but he quickly decided to forgive them. His mood had improved considerably since Miss Quint persuaded him to stay.

"Good gracious me!" Mr. Hardbattle murmured as he stroked a bookend that had jumped into his lap. "What a week! All those wishes! A tea party, a winged girl, and stolen goods, you say?" He was not outraged so much as astounded. Grateful to both Miss Quint and Arthur for helping to lift his spirits, he gazed at them with affection.

Susan arrived with a tray of teacups and a plate of pink wafer cookies, which Miss Quint did not like and, for that reason, were the only ones left in the tin.

"Ah, here's the winged wonder!" Mr. Hardbattle said, eyeing Susan with interest as she lifted the teapot and prepared to pour.

Revitalized by their refreshments, they began to discuss what should be done about the three kidnapping burglars locked inside the van. Mr. Hardbattle argued in favor of letting them out, but the others were less willing to give them their freedom, knowing how cunning they could be.

"What we really need to do is return them to their books!" said Mr. Hardbattle, putting his teacup aside and rising from his chair. "If we all have a good look, I'm sure they'll turn up!"

Arthur and Miss Quint, who had searched every inch of the bookshop more than once—without success—did not share his optimism. Nevertheless, they humored the old man and joined the hunt.

Searching on his knees under the desk that held the cash register, Arthur paused to say hello to the origami sheep before straightening up and going through the objects on top of the desk. When he heard a soft thumping noise above his head, he looked up and saw that Trunk had gone berserk again. The elephant was charging up and down his shelf, coiling and unfurling his trunk. He had behaved this way before, when Arthur was searching for the missing books on his own and again when Miss Quint did the same.

"Trunk!" called Arthur. "What's the matter with you?"

As soon as the elephant realized he had someone's attention, he stood stock-still and extended his trunk, almost as if he were trying to point something out. Arthur followed the direction of the elephant's trunk and his eyes settled on the fireplace.

"You want us to light a fire? Is that it?" asked Arthur, bewildered. "But it's the beginning of June! The temperature's warm enough, don't you think?"

Arthur turned to another area of the shop in which to search. He did not see Trunk watching him sadly with his black felt eyes or notice the great shuddering sigh the elephant gave. No one witnessed what happened next, apart from the black cat bookends and one of the ducks from the painting that was flying past Trunk's shelf at the time and almost crashed into the hatstand in confusion.

It was a sight never before seen in Hardbattle Books. Trunk shuffled forward to the edge of his shelf, where he had spent every single day since his little girl had left him behind, and let himself fall.

He landed with a thump on his bean-filled backside and sat still for a moment, in shock. Then he got to his feet and walked across the wooden floor, past the origami sheep, which bleated with surprise, and the wastepaper basket, which toppled over in alarm, emptying its trash all over the floor. Trunk continued across the room and came to a stop in front of the fireplace. His ears crinkled when it occurred to him how dirty he was going to get, but with a do-or-die kind of shrug, he scrambled into the fireplace. Instantly, he sank up to his bottom in ash. Reminding himself that he could be sponged clean (it said so on his label), Trunk ignored his predicament and looked up the chimney. He knew what he was searching for and spotted it in less than a minute: a little cubbyhole that had something tucked inside.

Trunk waded through the pit of ash and jumped onto the hearth. Then he studied the fireplace tools and selected one. Grasping the poker between his soft front feet, he plunged back into the fireplace, and gave the things in the cubbyhole a good, hard prod. *FLUMP* . . .

FLUMP . . . FLUMP went the books as they landed in the ash heap, covering Trunk from head to toe in pale gray powder. He flapped his large ears and blinked.

The sound of the books falling in the fireplace alerted the others to the elephant's discovery. Once they got over the shock of seeing Trunk in a place other than his shelf, they reached in and seized the books.

"Well, I never!" Mr. Hardbattle said, blowing ash from the book he held so he could read the title. Miss Quint and Susan did the same with theirs. Ashamed that he did not realize what Trunk had been trying to communicate, Arthur lifted Trunk and told him he was a superstar.

"These are the books we've been looking for!" confirmed Miss Quint, flicking through the soot-covered book in her hands, *Tinseltown Ticket*. "But how did Trunk know where they were?"

"He must have seen the culprit put them there!" suggested Arthur.

Mr. Hardbattle frowned. "Aren't we expecting to find one more? Perhaps I should feel around." He stooped to pick up the poker, but Arthur stopped him.

"No!" he said quickly. "That's all of them! I mean . . . Trunk's the sort of elephant to do a thorough job. If there was another book up there, I'm sure he would have found it."

Arthur felt himself blushing. He tried to avoid Mr. Hardbattle's searching gaze.

"Um . . . ," said Arthur. "What should we do now?"

"I think it's high time we let those scoundrels out of my van," Mr. Hardbattle said. "Don't you?"

Chapter Twenty-five

Brought to Book

Their hands now untied, the three gang members crawled out of the back of the van with scowls on their faces and stood in sullen silence. Peeved that their plan to kidnap Lady Smythe-Hughes had failed, they were also annoyed about being imprisoned in the van for hours on end. While Mr. Hardbattle locked the van doors, Miss Quint and Scallywag made sure the wily trio did not make a run for it.

"Into the bookshop, if you please," Mr. Hardbattle said, leading the gang over the threshold. Miss Quint and Scallywag brought up the rear.

Standing next to each other behind a table, they looked like the accused in a courtroom. From their perch on Mr. Hardbattle's desk, Arthur and Susan watched the three criminals, feeling only faintly afraid. The gang looked disheveled. All of them were sweating after their long stint in the van. Mrs. Voysey-Brown's mascara had melted in the heat and there were black smudges all around her eyes. However, she was not as damp as Jimmy, whose bellhop suit was mostly polyester, or Mr. Claggitt, whose hair was sticking up in spikes, having had an entire bottle of soda sprayed over it.

"Nice nephew, you are!" Jimmy growled at Arthur, raising his arm to shake his fist. His sleeve was torn and muddied. "I could get the cops to arrest you for assault!"

"That fib has been confessed to," Mr. Hardbattle said. "You're not Arthur's uncle. I'm aware of who you really are. No more lies, please, and no more threatening language, either! It surprises me that you'd want to involve the police. I think they'd be more interested in your gang than in young Arthur here."

"If we go down, we'll take you with us!" vowed Mr. Claggitt angrily. "One mountaineer goes over the edge; all the rest follow. That's how it is. We're like a climbing party attached to the same rope!"

"What he means," said Mrs. Voysey-Brown, casting her eyes to the ceiling in a long-suffering way, "is that we'll tell the police you helped us."

"They wouldn't believe you!" said Arthur.

"You seriously think they'd take your word over ours?" Mr. Hardbattle said, getting angry. "The testimony of well-brought-up children, a respected member of the Women's Institute, and a gentleman who works in a bookshop?"

"You're the owner," murmured Miss Quint. "Do yourself justice."

"That *we* would be considered more unreliable than a rough bunch of freeloading layabouts?" Mr. Hardbattle shook his head.

Though warned that if they were not careful they'd find themselves in a police cell, Jimmy, Mr. Claggitt, and Mrs. Voysey-Brown continued to be sulky and insolent. Only when Mr. Hardbattle drew their attention to the three books Trunk had discovered in the chimney—*Tinseltown Ticket*, *Rockfall!*, and *Champagne for Geraldine*—did their attitudes improve.

"We're sorry, ain't we, mates? We were wrong to do what we did!" said Jimmy, falling over himself to apologize. "Let us make it up to you, eh? Tell you what, sir . . . how's about we give you a hand in the shop? I'll shelve these books for you, okay?"

He moved to pick up the books, but Miss Quint was too quick for him. She snatched up a newspaper, rolled it into a tube, and rapped Jimmy on his knuckles.

"I'll thank you to leave those books where they are!" Miss Quint told him sternly.

In an attempt to improve relations between the two camps, Mr. Claggitt spoke up next. "You're a reasonable chap, Hardbattle, I can see that," he said, giving the old man a nod. "Can't we let bygones be bygones? We've broken the law, I won't deny that, but thanks to your good self and your fine team of helpers, we've seen the error of our ways. We won't be tempted back into a life of crime, so keep your head, sir, I beg you, and don't do anything hasty." When Mr. Claggitt had finished his speech, he smiled in a weak, fake way that made Arthur feel sick.

The word "sorry" was not in Mrs. Voysey-Brown's vocabulary. Instead of taking a cue from her colleagues to appear repentant, she placed the blame squarely on their shoulders, insisting that she had been a pawn in the whole affair.

"This wretched scheme was Jimmy's idea," she grumbled in her husky voice, "and Claggitt urged him on. I wanted nothing to do with it! It's those two you should punish, not me!"

Mrs. Voysey-Brown's flagrant attack on her two companions started a free-for-all during which the three gang members turned on one another.

"What nonsense!" exclaimed Mr. Claggitt, his eyebrows shooting toward his hairline. "How could you tell such bold-faced lies? You're as much to blame as we are."

"I'm not as greedy, though," retorted Mrs. Voysey-Brown, distancing herself from the burly mountaineer. "I would have been content with a suite at the Savoy, but *you* had to set your sights on *Switzerland*!"

"Deny me the Eiger, would you?" Mr. Claggitt roared. "You're a heartless woman, Dolores! It's been awful this past week without a summit to conquer!"

"Shut your pieholes, the both of you!" Jimmy said, losing his temper. "If I hadn't been so quick to realize Miss Quint wasn't kidding about us being sprung from books, you wouldn't still be here at all, you thankless clods!"

When their differences of opinion looked like they were developing into a brawl, Miss Quint stepped in and told them to pipe down and pull themselves together. She glanced at Mr. Hardbattle, and then at Arthur and Susan, and finally at the three books.

"Let's do it, shall we?" Miss Quint said.

While her friends flicked through each book to find a suitable page so they could begin the unwishing, Susan sat down quietly on a chair by the hearth. She held Trunk in her lap and patted his plump body to get rid of the ash that still coated his velour hide. She had no idea why, but the recent drama and confessions gave her a sinking feeling in her stomach. Susan did not understand what Arthur and the others were about to do. All she knew was that she did not want to play any part in it. Sensing her anxiety, Scallywag did what she could to alleviate Susan's feelings of distress and licked her ankles.

Overjoyed to be on the verge of getting rid of the three troublemakers, Miss Quint and Arthur forgot to think of an errand on which to send Susan so she would leave the room. As a result, Susan was there, watching, when the last three party guests were unwished.

Having traded insults and fallen out with each other,

none of the gang members seemed upset about being sent back to their books. Their dream of living in the lap of luxury in Switzerland was gone and, having almost been caught by the police, it no longer seemed such a terrible thing to be returned to their stories.

Before the unwishing got under way, the thieves were made to hand over the money they had made from selling the stolen goods. Arthur unpinned the diamond brooch on Mrs. Voysey-Brown. He also asked them to write down the names and addresses of all the dealers to whom they had sold things. Miss Quint said she would arrange for that information to be left with the money and the unsold antiques (currently in the closet under the stairs) on the doorstep of the Plumford police station.

Mr. Claggitt and Mrs. Voysey-Brown were dealt with first. The magic disposed of them swiftly, snuffing them out like feeble flames. When it came to Jimmy's turn, Mr. Hardbattle chose to impart some words of wisdom before the deed was done.

"It's clear that you possess brains, young man," Mr. Hardbattle said, eyeing Jimmy earnestly. "It's a great pity, however, that you could not think of better ways to make use of them. I trust you will endeavor to do so in the future."

"Don't count on it!" Jimmy said, flashing his cocky grin.

Mr. Hardbattle sighed.

Glancing down at *Champagne for Geraldine*, Arthur found Jimmy's name in the text. He put his finger on it and started to say the words that would send Jimmy home. At the critical moment, the arrogant sneer on Jimmy's face faded and, for a brief second, he looked somber.

When the bookshop had been emptied of the three undesirables, there were several minutes of celebration. Miss Quint seized Mr. Hardbattle's hand and waltzed him around the shop; Arthur whooped for joy and Scallywag chased her tail. Over by the fireplace, Susan gave Trunk a kiss, which caused the plump little elephant to turn a backward somersault. Susan was pleased that the robbers had been sent packing, but she did not feel as ecstatic as the others. The method of the gang's removal had shocked her, and she suddenly felt an urge to be by herself. Deciding to take a walk in the park, she got up from her seat and replaced Trunk gently on the cushion of the chair. Before she could reach the door, however, it opened and the bell above it jangled as a customer entered the shop.

All the joy in Arthur's heart evaporated when he saw that the customer was Mr. Beaglehole. Scallywag was similarly horrified, and Arthur's reflexes had to be quick to grab hold of her collar before she launched herself at the man.

"I've come about my book!" Mr. Beaglehole said in his usual abrasive manner. He marched up to Mr.

Hardbattle's desk and planted his fat, pink hands on it. Then he began to examine the pile of books he found there.

It was a hot summer's day and Mr. Beaglehole was wearing shorts; the sight of his bulging, fleshy calves was too much for Scallywag to bear. Arthur kept his hold on her as she bared her teeth and scrabbled at the floor, straining to get close enough to give him a nip.

"The name's Beaglehole," said Arthur's teacher, his eyes settling on Mr. Hardbattle, whom he decided was the person in charge. "I ordered the darn thing days ago. What kind of place are you running here, anyway?"

When Mr. Beaglehole revealed who he was, Mr. Hardbattle's back stiffened and he carefully adjusted his glasses.

"I am the owner of this bookshop," Mr. Hardbattle said. He removed his hand from Miss Quint's waist and dipped his head politely, thanking her for their impromptu dance. Then he walked behind his desk.

"Is that your teacher?" whispered Miss Quint, stooping to speak to Arthur.

He nodded, unable to stop a look of intense dislike from creeping onto his face.

Miss Quint glared too, and so did Susan. Even Trunk made an effort to fill his eyes with loathing, but as they were very small and made from felt, it was quite a challenge to get the emotion across.

Mr. Hardbattle turned to rummage through some books in a box behind him. He drew out a slim blue volume with a triumphant "Aha!"

"That mine?" Mr. Beaglehole asked.

"Yes, by good fortune, it seems that your book has arrived," Mr. Hardbattle told him. He glanced at the book's title and a nervous tic jiggled his eye. "*The Future Is Nuclear*, hmm?" he said. "I hope very much that that *won't* be the case. There are preferable, less toxic alternatives."

"Yeah? What would you know about it?" Mr. Beaglehole said.

"Bits and pieces," Mr. Hardbattle answered.

Mr. Beaglehole made a disparaging noise. "Well, I happen to teach that boy over there geography, so I think we can both assume that I'm more of an expert than you!"

Mr. Beaglehole may have majored in geography, but he was woefully uninformed about the subject of magic. He did not know, for example, that if a bookshop filled with magic is exposed to a glut of negative energy emitted by several people and directed at one focal point at the same time, it can cause plants to tremble in their pots and stairs to turn to custard.

In the bookshop, there was a kind of a lull. The only sound was the blaring, monotonous voice of Mr. Beaglehole, making one complaint after another. Arthur glanced around. The air seemed to be pulsing. It felt like a storm was brewing.

"Twenty-five ninety-nine?" raged Mr. Beaglehole. "For that teeny-weeny paperback?" He snatched the book from Mr. Hardbattle—and that was the moment the storm broke.

Books flew off the shelves, flapping their board covers as if they were wings, and dropped like rocks onto Mr. Beaglehole's head.

"Ouch! Yow! Ooh!" cried Mr. Beaglehole, too surprised to comprehend what was going on. He tossed *The Future Is Nuclear* onto the desk and folded his arms over his head to protect it. "Goodenough, is that you?" he bellowed. "Stop throwing these books at once!"

Arthur could not help laughing. "It's not me, sir," he said.

Next, the staples and thumbtacks combined forces to launch an offensive on Mr. Beaglehole's toes. (He was wearing sandals, which made his feet vulnerable to attack.) Breaking out of their colored-pencil corral, the origami sheep joined in the onslaught, tickling his ankles with their paper hooves as the staples and thumbtacks did their worst.

Mr. Beaglehole lifted his knees in a kind of dance, wailing with pain.

"Watch out!" warned Miss Quint. "The rubber bands want their share of the glory!"

Mr. Hardbattle ducked behind his desk as the entire box of rubber bands lined up on the rug and pinged themselves at the teacher's bare legs. That assault proved to be the last straw and, dodging the black cat bookends attempting to trip him, Mr. Beaglehole stumbled out of the doorway and ran off down the street.

Chapter Twenty-Six

New Pastures

"You were awesome!" cried Arthur, applauding the magic. He had enjoyed the spectacle of his bullying teacher reduced to a cowering wreck.

Mr. Hardbattle frowned and shook his head. "Don't show such appreciation, Arthur. That sort of behavior shouldn't to be encouraged."

Reluctantly, Arthur stopped clapping. He tidied up the shop instead, helping the others to pick up the books that had bombarded Mr. Beaglehole. After that was done, he crouched on the floor to collect all the staples, thumbtacks, and rubber bands. He sorted them into piles and replaced them in their containers.

"Well done, everyone!" Arthur whispered when he thought Mr. Hardbattle was out of earshot.

Arthur jumped when he felt a tap on the shoulder. "Now, Arthur!" Mr. Hardbattle scolded. "That fellow needed to be brought down a peg or two, I agree, but you must accept that the magic crossed a line. It's totally out of control."

Proving once more how thorough he was, Mr. Hardbattle broached another subject. "Before we resume our search for somewhere else to put my magic," he said to Arthur, "I think there's another matter that we should attend to, don't you?"

Arthur felt a horrible prickling sensation creep up his spine. The uncomfortable feeling had almost reached the nape of his neck when the shop bell jingle-jangled and his dad peered around the door.

"Arthur, there you are!" said his dad with relief. "I wasn't sure if this was the place. I've brought your bicycle, just as you asked. What were you thinking earlier, charging off in that great big truck? Wait till your mother hears what you did!"

Trying not to sound too conceited, Arthur informed him that he had been on a rescue mission to save Lady Smythe-Hughes. "You must have heard she'd been kidnapped," said Arthur. "You'll see: my picture will be in the paper—and my friend's will, too." He beckoned to Susan so that he could introduce her.

"Good heavens!" Arthur's father said. "What a heroic thing to do!" He held out a hand to Susan. "Pleased to meet you, dear."

"And this is Mr. Hardbattle and this is Miss Quint,"

said Arthur, completing the introductions. "Oh! Where's Tilly?" he asked his father.

"Right here," his father said, tugging on a small hand. Tilly's arm and sleeve were visible, but the rest of her remained out of sight, loitering just beyond the doorway. "She's the reason we didn't get here sooner," Arthur's dad explained. "Your sister wanted to see the whole parade. She's been babbling all day but, bless her, she's suddenly decided to be shy!"

It was Susan who persuaded Tilly to come into the shop by telling the little girl there was magic inside. Wrinkling her nose and declaring that the shop smelled like poo, Tilly stepped through the doorway and began to look around.

On the cushion of the chair where Susan had left him, Trunk sat bolt upright. His ears unfolded and raised themselves high. Keeping his black felt eyes trained on Tilly, he pushed himself off the seat cushion and landed on his bottom on the floor. Once he had jumped up, he approached the girl in fits and starts, until he shook off his hesitance and ran to her with his front feet outstretched.

"Look, Daddy!" Tilly said, cupping her hands around her knees and bending over to look at him. "A walking hippopotamus!"

Trunk did not appear to mind that he had been misidentified. He took the last few inches in one bound and jumped into her arms.

"He's all squishy-squashy!" said Tilly delightedly, hugging the elephant to her chest.

Everyone in the bookshop stared. Arthur, Mr. Hardbattle, Susan, and Miss Quint could not believe their eyes. Before today, Trunk never strayed from his shelf, and now here he was, in the embrace of a little girl. Not having come across a soft toy that could move of its own accord, Arthur's father was more mystified than anyone.

"But that's not . . . ," began Arthur. He knew that Trunk had been left behind in the bookshop, and since that day had been waiting for his little girl to return and claim him, but Arthur was sure that Tilly was not that little girl. "Mr. Hardbattle," he whispered, "Trunk's made a mistake. I think I'd better tell him—"

"Don't you dare," Mr. Hardbattle whispered back. He gave Arthur a look before addressing Arthur's dad. "My elephant seems to have taken to your daughter, sir. I wonder if she'd like to keep him?"

Arthur gasped. "Mr. Hardbattle! But . . . you can't . . . what about the other girl?"

"A word, Arthur," Mr. Hardbattle said. He steered Arthur across the shop to a more secluded area. "Listen," he said to Arthur after reaching a suitably quiet corner, "Trunk has been sitting on that shelf above my desk, mooning over his owner, for the past ten years. She's never going to walk back through that door—at least, not as the little girl Trunk remembers."

"Oh," said Arthur, swallowing. "I see."

When their little talk was over, they rejoined the others. Miss Quint had been explaining to Arthur's dad about the magic in the shop and, although he voiced disbelief at first, he was starting to realize that Miss Quint must be telling the truth.

"There's magic all around me now? No kidding!" he said.

His aged knees protesting as he did so, Mr. Hardbattle crouched down to speak to Arthur's five-year-old sister. "Why don't you choose a book, my dear, and read the little fellow a story? I'm sure he would like that."

Tilly nodded and ran to a rack of picture books. She selected one, sat down and crossed her legs, then settled the elephant in her lap.

Although no one could have guessed it from the euphoric angle of his tusks, Trunk knew that Tilly Goodenough was not his owner. A few hours ago, this knowledge would have bothered him, but since leaving his shelf he felt like a different elephant. It was as if he had leaped from the past into the present when he jumped those few feet onto the floor.

The little girl who was reading to him had brown eyes instead of blue, but otherwise she was very much like his little girl. She had the same rosy cheeks and clear-cut voice and the identical way of squeezing him gently around his middle. Trunk had come to feel at home in the bookshop, but what he wanted most of all was to be loved and cuddled and read stories to. If this little girl was Arthur's sister, then there was a good chance that she was a nice, caring child and a fair possibility that he was destined to be a very happy elephant.

"Time to go, Tilly!" said her father. "The animals have to be fed, and I'm cooking supper tonight. Arthur, you'll be home by six, won't you?"

Tilly closed the picture book and scooped up Trunk. As she and her father left the shop, the elephant peeped over Tilly's arms and waved his trunk at them all to say farewell.

A tear slid down Mr. Hardbattle's cheek.

"I'm a sentimental old fool, that's what I am," he said, dabbing his eyes with his handkerchief.

Susan stood at the door and waved at Trunk and his new little girl until they were out of sight. "I'm so glad he's found a new home," she said. "He looked awfully happy, didn't he?"

"He did," agreed Mr. Hardbattle. "Everyone has a place where they feel they should be. Mine is this bookshop, and yours . . ."

Susan wondered why Mr. Hardbattle had stopped midsentence. He had been about to tell her where she belonged. Puzzled and bewildered, she thought about asking him to continue what he had been going to say. Then she saw that Mr. Hardbattle was staring intently at Arthur, and that Arthur had his eyes fixed on the floor.

"I'll come out with it," Mr. Hardbattle said. "I think you know where this young lady's book is, Arthur."

"I . . . ," Arthur began and got no further.

Mr. Hardbattle nodded. "I thought so," he said. "I think you'd better get it, don't you?"

Arthur's eyes flicked up guiltily and met Mr. Hardbattle's unflinching gaze. He knew there was no denying it. Mr. Hardbattle was far too smart, and lying was not Arthur's strong point. Without a word, even to Miss Quint, who was staring at him open-mouthed, Arthur went outside, got on his bike, and rode home.

The book was under his mattress, where he had shoved it a week ago, realizing that he did not want Susan to be unwished. He had told himself he was just *borrowing* the book, and he hoped Mr. Hardbattle would not consider his furtive deed stealing. As he cycled back to the bookshop with *High Jinks* in his saddlebag, Arthur thought of a hundred reasons to convince Mr. Hardbattle that Susan should stay in Plumford and not be returned to her book.

When he reentered Hardbattle Books, Arthur discovered that Miss Quint had been thinking the same thing. She and Mr. Hardbattle were having an argument.

"She could live with me. I could adopt her," said Miss Quint, holding on tightly to Susan's hand.

Mr. Hardbattle's mouth contracted. Clearly he did not agree. "That wouldn't work! Susan isn't a real child. There's no certificate recording her birth. You'd get into hot water with the authorities—"

"Paperwork can be faked!" Miss Quint insisted stubbornly. "If Jimmy's gang can get hold of crooked dealers, I can find a forger."

"You're missing the point," Mr. Hardbattle said, frustrated that Miss Quint would not see reason. "Susan isn't like other children. She's a character from a book. She won't get any older. Don't you think people will find that odd? How will you cope in a few years' time, when she's still eleven and you're an old lady?"

Miss Quint looked ready to punch him. "I'm only forty-four!" she shrieked. "I'm in my prime! You make me sound as if I'm already retired!"

Despite listing all their reasons, neither Arthur nor Miss Quint could persuade Mr. Hardbattle that Susan should remain with them. He was sympathetic, but firm.

"This is what comes of being careless and not sticking to my instructions," he said, wagging a finger at Miss Quint. Not letting Arthur off the hook either, Mr. Hardbattle aimed his next rebuke at him. "If you hadn't hidden her book and had sent Susan back earlier—"

"I couldn't!" said Arthur, the words sticking in his throat. "I've come to like her. She's my friend."

Mr. Hardbattle was moved by Arthur's admission, but he still would not let it influence his judgment. He handed Miss Quint the copy of *High Jinks* and asked her to find the appropriate page. Miss Quint could barely see through the unshed tears in her eyes.

While Miss Quint was leafing blindly through the book and Arthur was frowning, lost in thought, Susan stood quietly between them. She had known somewhere, deep down, that she did not belong in this world, but she had desperately wanted to be a part of it, and that desire had confused her memory. She had grown very fond of Miss Quint and Arthur and dear old Scallywag, and to be parted from them would be dreadful. If she had not felt so hollow inside she might have caused a fuss, but making a scene was not in her nature and, besides, she knew it would do no good. Her fate was sealed and she would have to grin and bear it.

Arthur, however, had not finished protesting. "This isn't fair!" he railed. "It's cruel, that's what it is! Susan's happy here with us. If you send her back to the book, what kind of a life will she have? She'll have to stand by those dumb old railings, waiting for a turn on those stupid swings today and every day afterward . . . FOREVER!" Arthur's throat felt tight and hurt so much that he could not utter another word.

When they had said good-bye to Trunk, they knew he

had a wonderful future ahead of him. Susan's departure was not like that at all.

After five whole minutes of looking, Miss Quint came across the right page and felt her heart plummet.

"Found it," she told Mr. Hardbattle.

Susan put her arms around Arthur and hugged him. Then she stood on tiptoe to kiss Miss Quint and bent down to say good-bye to Scallywag. Finally, after straightening her shoulders, she nodded at Mr. Hardbattle to show that she was ready to leave.

At the moment of unwishing, Arthur turned away. He missed seeing Susan grow fainter and fainter, until she was a mere ghost and eventually disappeared.

Miss Quint startled. She felt a tingling in her fingers and, wiping away her tears, she looked down at the copy of *High Jinks* in her hand. The book was growing. Its spine was stretching and its pages were multiplying. It got larger and larger and heavier and heavier until it doubled in size.

"Ooh!" she exclaimed. "Well, I never! Arthur, look!"

Despondently, Arthur lifted his head.

On the front cover, which had been plain green, the face of a girl was slowly forming. She had a lively smile and long brown hair and was wearing a T-shirt with sequins on it.

Another change was taking place on the cover of the

book. Little by little, the title was fading and new words appeared in its place. Arthur cried out when he realized what it said. The book had renamed itself *The Adventures of Susan*.

Arthur felt a sudden wave of happiness wash over him. "How did that happen?" he asked Miss Quint.

She was as astounded as Arthur, but between them, it did not take long to figure out.

"Remember *A Tale of Derring-do*?" Miss Quint said. "When we sent the knight back without his sword? It altered the whole story."

"Susan changed a lot while she was with us," said Arthur, thinking of the strange, clueless girl she had been and the plucky, fun friend she had turned into.

"Yes!" said Miss Quint, remembering only too well the dreary child without a name whom she had tried to get rid of. "And think of all the thrilling things we've done together! When we sent Susan back, the book hardly recognized her. It couldn't make such an interesting girl stand by the swings for all eternity!"

"It had to give her more exciting things to do," said Arthur, smiling at the picture of Susan on the book's front cover. "Good old Suze! I bet she's having a whale of a time. I can't wait to read what she's up to!"

"May I?" Mr. Hardbattle said, taking the book from Miss Quint's hands. He had not enjoyed making Miss Quint and Arthur do something that caused them so much grief, and he was as pleased about the outcome as they were. "How about that!" he said, passing the book to Arthur. "Something to put on your bookshelf, I think."

Arthur was required to say a double thank-you because at that moment the paperboy arrived with the evening edition of the *Plumford Gazette*. On its front page, just below the headline COURAGEOUS KIDS OUTWIT CROOKS, there was a photograph of Susan, Lady Smythe-Hughes, and himself. Mr. Hardbattle insisted Arthur keep it as a souvenir.

"There's this as well," said the paperboy, crouching on the floor to pick up an envelope someone had dropped through the mail slot and onto the doormat. It had a gold coat of arms on the front and was addressed to Arthur, Susan, and Miss Quint. The envelope was passed to Arthur, and he turned it over, broke the wax seal on the back, and opened it up.

"It's an invitation!" he said, glancing at Miss Quint and grinning. "Lady Smythe-Hughes has asked us to tea!"

"When?" said Miss Quint, clapping a hand to her mouth.

"This coming Tuesday, at four o'clock."

Miss Quint gave a squeak of excitement and rushed to the telephone to make an appointment at the hairdresser's.

When Tuesday came, Miss Quint and Arthur were picked up from Hardbattle Books by a chauffeur-driven Mercedes. They sat on the red leather seats, making faces at each other and pressing the intercom button to talk to the driver, whose name was Phil. When they neared Thiselton House, the home of Lord and Lady Smythe-Hughes, Miss Quint grew fidgety and kept asking Arthur if her hair could use one more brush or if her lipstick needed touching up. She had bought a new hat for the occasion and readjusted its angle until Arthur pleaded with her to leave it alone. Arthur loosened the knot of the tie his mother made him wear. He felt as if he were being strangled.

The driveway was so long that Arthur mistook it for a road. It passed through fields, woods, and miles of rhododendrons. Finally, the driveway came to an end, sweeping in a grand curve in front of a large, pearl gray mansion with more windows than Arthur could count. They did not have to ring the doorbell to announce that they had arrived. A butler was already waiting for them with a door held open. As they walked down a hall with a marble floor, they saw three or four people (who they learned were only a small fraction of the staff) and were taken to a huge, high-ceilinged drawing room where tea had been laid out on a linen tablecloth. Opposite the drawing room was the library, and Arthur took the opportunity to peek inside.

"Look! They like books!" he said. "Perhaps Lord and Lady Smythe-Hughes would like to visit Mr. Hardbattle's shop and buy up some of his!"

"It's an idea," said Miss Quint, crossing the hall to join him. "Mr. Hardbattle needs to find money from somewhere. He said if he had the funds he'd take me on as assistant manager, but we're no nearer finding a place for the magic, and there are only three days left!"

Lady Smythe-Hughes arrived soon afterward and they all assembled in the drawing room for tea, which was beautifully displayed on delicate plates with a rose and chrysanthemum design. Lady Smythe-Hughes was pleased to see them but disappointed to hear that Susan had not been able to come. They exchanged pleasantries at first, but they soon progressed to the juicier topic of the kidnap. Lady Smythe-Hughes explained that the gang had swooped on her when she left the judging booth to use the restroom at the library.

Miss Quint almost choked on her smoked salmon sandwich to hear a woman of such good breeding mention the toilet.

"Oh, I nearly forgot!" said Arthur, reaching into his blazer pocket. "I think this might belong to you." He brought out the bow-shaped diamond brooch and offered it to Lady Smythe-Hughes, who pounced on it in delight.

"Arthur! You darling boy!" she said. "I lost this when we were burglarized! Where did you find it?"

Arthur thought carefully before he gave her an answer. "In the road," he said at last. "The robbers must have dropped it there."

"I'm so terribly grateful for what you did," gushed Lady Smythe-Hughes. "If there's a favor I could do for you in return, you only have to ask!"

After they had eaten their fill of exquisite sandwiches and cakes, Lady Smythe-Hughes volunteered to show them her fine collection of antique perfume bottles. They walked into the hall, and there they met her husband, Lord Smythe-Hughes, who was taking off a pair of muddy green rubber boots.

Lady Smythe-Hughes introduced her husband to Arthur and Miss Quint. He had heard of their role in his wife's rescue and said he was honored to make their acquaintance. Lady Smythe-Hughes explained that they had just had tea and that she was taking her guests to view her perfume bottle collection.

Seeing the unimpressed look on Arthur's face and guessing that Arthur felt the same way about perfume bottles as he did, Lord Smythe-Hughes clapped Arthur on the shoulder and made a suggestion: "Like to take a walk around my poultry farm, young man?"

"I heard someone say you were a paltry millionaire," said Arthur, waiting while Lord Smythe-Hughes put on his boots again.

"*Poultry* millionaire!" corrected Lord Smythe-Hughes, finding Arthur's error amusing.

While Miss Quint and Lady Smythe-Hughes disappeared to the East Wing to coo over odd-shaped pieces of glass, Arthur strolled around several acres at the rear of the house, which was dedicated to Lord Smythe-Hughes's poultry business. It was a free-range poultry farm; the birds wandered wherever they pleased, popping into their huts at nighttime or to lay an egg. There were huts and sheds dotted all over the plot, plus a lake the size of a football field, with an island for ducks and geese.

In one rather overgrown corner, Arthur and Lord Smythe-Hughes passed a tall, cylindrical tower with battlements at the top. The building was old, with only a handful of windows, and its bricks were overrun with ivy. Chickens wandered in and out through its open doorway, and Arthur heard clucking coming from inside.

"That's the funniest chicken house I've ever seen!" he said, peering through the entrance and seeing nests scattered around, brown speckled eggs in one or two of them. As Arthur turned to leave, his hand snagged a cobweb. He paused and took another, more deliberate look inside.

"It's not really supposed to be a chicken house," said Lord Smythe-Hughes. He explained that the building was a folly, an ornamental building erected on a whim. Lord Smythe-Hughes said that he hated to tear it down since it was part of the history of the estate, but he had no real use for it.

"Could somebody live here?" asked Arthur.

"Good heavens, no!" Lord Smythe-Hughes chuckled. "Who'd want to live in a rundown tower without heat or water, right in the middle of a chicken compound?"

Arthur said nothing but grinned to himself.

As they continued their walk, Lord Smythe-Hughes pointed out dozens of different breeds of chickens and ducks, some rather rare, but Arthur found it difficult to concentrate. He was itching for the tour to be over so he could go back to the house and tell Miss Quint what he had seen.

Eventually, they reached the rear of Thiselton House, and Arthur ran up the steps and dashed inside. But before he could locate Miss Quint, he bumped into Lady Smythe-Hughes, who was tending to a magnificent flower arrangement in the hall.

"Hello, Arthur!" she said, smiling. "Did you enjoy your walk among all those feathered creatures? They're my husband's pride and joy!"

"Yes," said Arthur, swiftly moving on to the thing at the forefront of his mind. "Lady Smythe-Hughes, could I ask you something? It's about that *favor* . . ."